Summer of Silence

By the same author

The Janus Face

PART ONE

One

'DO YOU HAPPEN to know a good doctor?'

Joanna Cameron was in the staff room for the afternoon break. Most of the other teachers had already left to go back to their classes and only Mrs Jenkins – Irene, remained. Joanna thought that being local, she was probably the best person to ask. Almost immediately she wished that she hadn't.

Irene wittered on, giving surgery times and recommendations. 'There's only Dr Patterson in the village. If you want someone else you'll have to go into Eastport. There are two doctors there, Doctor Nyles and Doctor Frederick. Doctor Nyles is new. Doctor Frederick was practicing when I was a child, but if you want my opinion . . . you're not ill, are you?' she concluded.

'Oh no.' To Joanna's annoyance she blushed. Aware of the tension in her voice she added, 'James and I thought it was time we registered with a doctor, that's all.'

They took their tea cups to the sink and swilled them round, leaving them on the draining board to dry. Through the staff room window the distant surge of two hundred voices reached them like ocean spray from the playground.

By unspoken agreement, Mrs Jenkins went first as befitted her seniority, drying her hands on the towel that she took home each week to launder. Surreptitiously Joanna wiped her hands down the sides of her skirt. In silence they left the stale tobacco fug of the staff room for the clogging chalkiness of the corridor.

'If there's anything else you need help with. . . .' Irene stopped outside her classroom door, confident in her role as mentor. Joanna nodded her thanks and walked on down the corridor. The pervading sense of her inferiority caught her out once again. She had been at the school for nine months while Irene was part of the furniture. She comforted herself with the knowledge that Irene's formal teaching qualifications (if any), were probably minimal, for when discussions about training arose the older woman pointedly changed the subject. Years of experience, however, had promoted her to the charge of form Five A, probably the best of the bunch at Robert Hooke Secondary Modern, a school not noted for its academic prowess. Joanna, newly arrived from teacher training college and in her probationary year, had Five C, the no hopers. Next year, with luck, she had been hoping for something more challenging, perhaps form Four A, but now this . . . this little problem had arisen.

She hadn't said anything to James yet but she had just missed her second period. The knowledge filled her mind. Faced with the thought of it an answering tightness constricted her stomach, part excitement at the knowledge that she was capable of motherhood, but mostly dismay at the immediate consequences for herself and James.

It would be their first wedding anniversary in two weeks. When James got his new job with the Water Board, it had seemed incredibly good luck that Joanna should find a teaching post only two miles away. Time to tie the knot. Everything seemed to be going their way. With two wages they had felt confident about taking out a mortgage on a dinky little dream cottage and now. . . . Joanna had no idea what James would think. Of course they planned to have children, but not yet. Definitely not yet.

Continuing back along the corridor she braced herself for the last lesson of the week. Social Studies they called it, a vain attempt to give class Five C some sense of who they were and where they fitted into the scheme of things. In less than a month most of them would be out there in the world. What happened then was the ultimate test.

Reviewing her first academic year, Joanna experienced a

rather surprising feeling of pleasure. Somewhere at the back of her mind she felt that she hadn't done such a bad job, and as for the pupils, she would miss them – well, some of them anyway. She opened the classroom door just moments before the bell sounded, giving herself about thirty seconds before they arrived.

Last September, faced with thirty blank faces, she had decided to use the Social Studies lesson as a means of introducing Five C to the concept of statistics. Over the first weeks each child drew up a fairly detailed profile of themselves which they were able to compare with the rest of the class in terms of age, height, percentage of boys to girls, eye and hair colour, position in the family and so on. There was also a fun section on their own interests, favourite foods, best wireless and television programmes, favourite film stars and singers, sports and hobbies. If they went away with nothing else they would at least have this documentary record of who they had been at fifteen.

Some of the class had worked really hard, including graphs, bar and pie charts, newspaper cuttings and drawings. For Joanna it had been invaluable in helping to get to know the children in her care.

As they trouped noisily into the classroom, she took a deep breath, paused to give them time to settle down, and said, 'Right, today we're going to talk about careers.'

Surveying the mass of raw talent before her, her uncertainties resurfaced. Would she have failed them when it came to taking their place in the outside world? Only time would tell. She drew comfort from the knowledge that she had probably started fourteen years too late.

With an heroic effort, she said, 'I want you to get out your history books and read the chapter on the Industrial Revolution and then I want you to come up one at a time so that we can talk about your future.'

One by one they came, confessing to their ambitions. 'School Teacher,' a silent voice echoed in Joanna's ear – but your truancy record is second to none!

'Go in a bank.' (What as – a robber?)

'Work in the Bookies. (You can't even calculate your own dinner money!)

'Be an airline pilot.' (Some hope.)

'A cowboy.' (Go west, young man!)

'Work for me dad.' (Who else would employ you?)

The litany of forlorn hopes continued as Joanna discussed their chances, gently steering them towards something more attainable. She wondered if there was any point to it. Was this not just a cynical exercise which she was required to go through?

Listening to the potential new workforce, she thought: for ninety-nine per cent of them, the reality will be either Dixon's factory or summer jobs, then the council waiting list, marriage, babies and start the whole cycle over again. Was this what life was all about?

She sighed as the next child took her place beside the desk.

'And what about you, Maisie? Have you thought about what you want to do when you leave?'

The girl standing in front of her looked more like a twelve year old, her pinched, beaky little face devoid of expression. She gave an answering shrug and Joanna bit back a moment of frustration. There was something not right with this girl. She was like a room with no doors or windows, no way in. Yet the room wasn't empty. Look at those poems she had written, and her essays. Strange stuff. Disturbing really, but she had a way with words – on paper. Aloud she would barely put two syllables together.

Maisie Morris was also one of the few children in the class with a head for figures. If she hadn't been so strange, Joanna was sure she would have passed the eleven plus with ease. What was it? She thought about Maisie's project: the glowing account of her father the fighter pilot, her brother who had been picked to play football for England, her show pony on whom she won at all the gymkhanas, her brilliant solos at ballet school. Fantasy. All fantasy. Of the real Maisie, there was no sign. Drawing in her breath, Joanna made the effort.

'Well, there must be something you'd like to do.'

Maisie gazed away into the corner. As the silence became oppressive, she mumbled, 'S'pose I'll go in a shop.' Six words in a row – surely this must be a record?

Joanna picked her way carefully. 'Is that what you want? You could do better than that, you know.'

Did she see a flicker of recognition in the otherwise expressionless face?

Trying again, she said, 'In three weeks you'll be leaving school. Whatever you decide now will affect the rest of your life. Isn't there some sort of training you'd like to do?'

Maisie transferred her attention to the ground. Her appearance made Joanna twitchy. She longed to tidy up the girl's thick brown hair which looked as if someone had taken the sheep shears to it. With a bit of attention she could be pretty but she seemed to have no interest whatsoever in her appearance. Joanna looked pointedly at the undernourished frame in the skimpy striped dress, the hem too long, the cuff of the sleeves flapping loosely as her Wurzel Gummidge arms hung limply at her sides. Maisie made no response. She was still wearing ankle socks whereas the rest of the girls had long since moved on to stockings and bubble cuts, pencil skirts and Max Factor.

It seemed that the only thing that mattered to Maisie was the make-believe life that she lived inside her head. It partly accounted for the fact that she had no friends to speak of. Shamefully, Joanna echoed the opinions she had heard the other children voice – Maisie was weird. In spite of herself, the words *runt* and *stunted* tumbled over each other, playing roly-poly in her brain. In an effort to be professional, she tried to shut them out.

Just as Joanna had forgotten what she had asked her, Maisie said. 'Something on a farm.'

'I beg your pardon?'

'What I'd like to do.'

'To work with animals?'

Maisie looked non-committal.

Joanna thought back to the parents' evening the night before. Mrs Morris, Maisie's mother, had come by herself. This wasn't unusual. Few fathers of Robert Hooke pupils felt that their children's education had anything to do with them. Mrs Morris herself looked uncomfortable, as if she was the pupil and expected a telling-off.

Optimistically, Joanna hoped that she might get to the bottom of the mystery. Surely Maisie's mother would be able to throw some light on the family?

She chose her words carefully. 'Well now, Mrs Morris. Maisie does quite well in her lessons but she seems. . . .' She was lost for the right description so she asked, 'What is she like at home?'

'All right.'

Joanna wondered if Maisie's lack of communication was inherited from her mother. She tried again. 'She does all her homework and has a good attendance record but she seems – well, she doesn't seem to live in the real world. Could there be something worrying her, do you think?'

Doris Morris shrugged. 'Proper dopey, our Maisie.'

The mother's insensitivity irritated Joanna. Trying to keep her expression neutral, she said, 'I don't think that's true. I wonder if there isn't something else?'

Mrs Morris looked uncomfortable. The set of her mouth was reminiscent of her daughter's, a face hardened into lines and wrinkles – by disappointment? Unless things changed, one day Maisie would look the same; gaunt, worn down by experience, her youth eroded. Joanna's gloomy thoughts were interrupted as Mrs Morris said, 'It hasn't been easy for me, not since Bert died. I've had to cope on me own, what with that and having a job, and having me Dad living with me, and now me Aunty Rene – Dad's sister that is. . . .' She gave Joanna a look that challenged her to find fault.

'Oh, I'm sorry.' None of this had appeared in Maisie's project and no one else had told her.

Mrs Morris grudgingly accepted the condolences.

'How long have you been a widow?' Joanna asked.

'Going on five years.'

That would make Maisie about ten or eleven when her father died. With a surge of exhilaration Joanna felt herself to be proved right. Such a shock would no doubt account for the girl's failure when she took the eleven plus, especially if she had been fond of her father. She wondered if instead of being 'dopey' as her mother claimed, Maisie was in fact extremely bright and her defence against the humdrum routine of the classroom was to retreat into herself?

'Have you any other children – a son?' As she asked the question she thought of Maisie's description of her brother the footballer.

The mother's face seemed almost to implode. Her lips worked soundlessly as she shook her head. 'After what happened – the accident, Bert lost interest – you know. . . .' She blushed, her hollow cheeks quickly suffusing with colour.

What *had* happened? Joanna did not pursue it. Later she would ask around, find out about Mr Morris's accident and about how he had died. For a wild moment she wondered if indeed he had been a fighter pilot but looking at the poor, ill-educated and badly spoken woman in front of her she knew that it could not be true. She returned to the safer subject of Maisie's school record but in the end there was nothing much to say. The visit left more questions than it answered.

Aloud, she said to the girl standing before her, 'Well now Maisie, most jobs on a farm seem to be for boys.' Seeing the shutters begin to come down again, she quickly added, 'But I'll certainly see what I can do.'

Two

DORIS MORRIS STOOD at the scullery sink, the tap cascading water into the washing-up bowl. This was the place she spent more time than anywhere else, except of course in bed. She had never really stopped to think about it before, but she felt at home here, safe somehow. Between these four roughly-plastered walls that Bert had painted green with a left over tin he had brought home from work the year before he died, she knew exactly what her role was. This was where she prepared meals for them all, bottled fruit and salted runner beans, boiled up the Monday washing, rinsed out their odds and ends during the week, scrubbed, cleaned and cooked and was generally useful. All for Dad, and Maisie, and now of course, for Aunty Rene.

Taking a saucepan from the cupboard she half filled it with water and stood it on the draining board then, from the large container marked 'flour' she extracted half a dozen potatoes and added them to the washing-up bowl. Half past four. This was the daily routine, like making the beds each morning and emptying the chamber pots – if only they had an inside lavvy.

Fish and chips tonight, being Friday – not that they were Catholics mind, but that's what they always had. Before refilling the kettle and putting it back on the gas stove to boil she emptied the remainder of the hot water over the potatoes. Perhaps one day they would have hot running water, and electricity in the bedrooms, even a bathroom.

The catalogue of missing facilities took her back to London, to number twenty-nine Winterbourne Square, which had every luxury imaginable. For eight long months Doris worked there when she was fifteen – the same age as Maisie was now. Girls today didn't know when they were well-off, not like in her day, being shipped off into service and not a moment to call your own.

Winterbourne Square consisted of big, detached houses with black, wrought iron railings around a private garden in the centre, and with a gate that was locked at night. Here, nannies walked the babies to give them fresh air and families exercised their dogs. The houses were four stories high – five if you counted the basement, which was where Doris spent most of her time.

It all came flooding back, the dark, cavernous, overheated basement; the freezing eight by eight attic box which she shared with Audrey Clark. Wonder whatever became of her?

Those parts of the house where they worked and slept were as lacking in facilities as Doris's home was now, but the rest of it – the drawing-room, and dining-room and the master bedroom – were like palaces. She remembered the sideboards with their huge, ornately-carved mirrors which must never reflect the merest speck of dust; the silverware that glinted against the blinding whiteness of the damask tablecloths; the lace bedcovers that were such a nightmare to launder.

She wasn't sure what had stirred it all up. Perhaps it was talking about Maisie's career. Or when the teacher had asked her about other children. Embarrassing that, she hadn't known how to explain.

Like mist it curled its way into her memory. It was years now since she had thought about London, but like some time traveller she was carried back there, fifteen years old again, under-housemaid, lost and homesick in a doctor's palace in Ealing.

There was some sort of scandal. At the time she didn't know what it was, but it involved the woman who stood every evening opposite number twenty-nine, illuminated by the gas lamp. She looked a poor woman, thin, wearing what was once a smart coat but surely designed for summer evenings. She wore a hat that sported a bedraggled feather. Something about her reminded Doris of a chick that had been left out in the rain.

It was November and the gas lamp put up an uneven struggle against the thick, enveloping fog. Every evening the woman would stand there waiting. Once Doris saw a man stop and speak to her. He was not a gentleman. He wore heavy boots and a black cap. His coat was black too, but from soot rather than fabric dye. Once it might have been brown, or even camel. The woman nodded and followed him away. This seemingly innocent meeting caused the scandal.

The next evening a policeman called at number twenty-nine. He came to the back door. Only people of quality called at the front and in any case, this way it was more discreet. Cook grudgingly invited him into the kitchen where he stamped his feet, keeping to the doormat so that the drips from his cape did not dirty the stone slabs.

'Just a message for the doctor,' he said. 'Just to let him know that the little business has been cleared up.'

What business? Doris watched the policeman. He had pale blue eyes and straight, light brown hair, turning dark where the rain had seeped under the edge of his helmet. He was tall. Young. Her heart began to beat faster.

Cook relented and offered him a cup of tea. Wiping his boots on the mat he took off his cape and draped it round a chair near to the range, then placed his helmet on the scrubbed deal of the kitchen table. Doris watched him plaster back his hair with large fingers as he sat down.

'Doris, get the constable a cuppa.'

Doris hastened to oblige while Cook cut him a piece of seed cake. She chatted to him about the scandal but Doris could not understand what all the fuss was about. Above the hiss of the kettle, the crackling of pork in the oven, the roar of the fire, she missed some of the conversation, but words like: 'No better than she ought to be,' and 'Fined ten shillings,' reached her.

As she handed the constable the cup of tea he smiled at her. She felt all sort of wobbly inside.

'Doris, the sugar!'

Overcome with embarrassment, she went to the cupboard for the china bowl and teaspoon. In her haste she caught the spoon on the lip of the bowl and some of the sugar spilled on to the table and on to the floor.

'Doris!' Cook gave the constable a look which said: What are young girls coming to these days? But the constable winked at her.

'Never mind, lass, we all make mistakes.'

In that moment. Doris fell in love.

From that day, Police Constable 273, Kenneth Harris, called regularly at number twenty-nine, just to make sure that everything was all right and that the mysterious woman had not had the effrontery to return.

After a week or two Cook had his cup out ready. She would sit and chat to him about 'them upstairs', and Doris noticed that she always tied her apron strings tighter around her waist before admitting him to the sanctum of their kitchen. This was disconcerting because Cook was quite old. She did have a husband but he was away in the army. Doris had seen his photograph, wearing his dress uniform; a short, sturdy man with luxuriant black hair and a droopy moustache, sporting a tunic that seemed to act like a corset for he stood straight as a ramrod. Doris, young and romantic, could not imagine how Cook was enamoured of such a jowly, scowling man, but Cook went all soft and coy when she talked about '*My Albert*'.

With envy Doris noticed how nice Kenneth was to Cook, how he entertained her with stories of things that had happened on his beat. But it was for Doris that he saved his special smile.

One day as he was about to leave, he said to her, 'Are you going home for Christmas, love?'

'No. I've got to work.' She remembered the stab of homesickness for her sisters, for all the family traditions which that year would go on without her.

'Got any time off?'

'Saturday's my half day.'

'Righty ho. I'll meet you in the square. Two-thirty. We'll go up west. I'll take you out to tea.'

*

Doris's reverie was rudely interrupted as the back door opened and her father came in. She glanced down guiltily at her watch, wondering if she had been day-dreaming for hours. It was twenty-five to five.

'You're early.'

Her father hung his jacket on the back of the door. 'Just finished putting a primer on the garden shed. Can't do any more 'til it dries.'

Doris transferred the bowl of potatoes from the sink to the scullery table so that he could wash. Briskly rolling up his sleeves he lathered his hands beneath the running cold tap, twisting them this way and that to wash off the pink, coal tar soap which clung to the thick, still black hairs on his arms.

'Where's Rene?' he asked.

'In the front room.' At least, Doris hoped that's where she was. Aunty Rene had got proper forgetful lately. Just recently she'd started calling Doris 'Mum' as if she was her daughter. Proper daft. She kept on asking who Maisie was too, sometimes mistaking her for her sister Edna who had been dead these twenty years. Doris shook her head in wonderment.

Dad grunted as he wiped his hands on the towel which hung on the back of the larder door. Moments later he went back out into the garden to see how his beans were doing.

Doris peeled the potatoes with fierce energy. In spite of herself her thoughts drew her back to London. . . .

Doctor and Mrs Ferney allowed their staff one Saturday afternoon off a fortnight and all day Sunday once a month. Before long, these brief moments of freedom became the very centre of Doris's existence. Sometimes when it was her time off, Kenneth would be working and she suffered agonies of frustration. Using the excuse of posting a letter or visiting the tuppenny library, she would creep out to meet him on his beat. She loved to see him in his uniform, the dark serge of his tunic, the creases down his trouser legs that looked sharp enough to cut yourself on, and his fine helmet. He looked so smart and capable. Doris liked the way he told her what to do. He never seemed to have any doubts about what was right and wrong.

One evening, when the Ferneys were away staying in the country, Kenneth asked Cook's permission to take Doris out for the evening. It was wonderful. They went to the Music Hall and she'd never seen anything like it before. First there was Isabelle Lee, such a famous singer and wearing the most daring of dresses that showed her legs right up to the knee. Doris felt a long forgotten moment of eroticism, remembering how Isabelle – 'Liberty Belle' – twirled her parasol and invited the men in the audience to '*Come and kiss me happeny!*' It had seemed so risqué then. Then there was Geoffrey Savant, such a smart gentleman in his evening dress, who gave a long recitation about a soldier and a village maid which ended with the girl drowning. It quite upset Doris.

Afterwards they had a slap-up supper at a little pie shop Kenneth knew and then she walked home, bold as brass on his arm. At the corner of the square he stopped against the railings and turned her to him.

'Give us a kiss then, girl.'

She let him kiss her. He was a deal taller than her and she had to stand on tiptoes to reach his lips. They had known each other for two months now and this was the first time she had allowed him any familiarity.

'You're a splendid lass.'

Looking out of the scullery window, Doris saw her father inspecting his dahlias for earwigs. Wouldn't he have been mad if he'd seen her back then! The thought of his cold, glowering disapproval sobered her.

Again she drifted back forty years.

'I've got to go now.'

Kenneth linked his arm through hers and walked her along to number twenty-nine. They stopped just to the side of the five wide steps that led up to the front door. Through a gate in the railings a narrower flight led down to the basement. This was where Doris would go in. She hoped that Cook would not look out of the window and see her. She wouldn't half be cross.

'See you on your day off then? Same as usual?'

She nodded. Before she could turn away though, Kenneth caught hold of her arm. 'Wait a mo, I've got something for you.'

She looked at his outstretched hand in surprise. He held a slim, oblong package which he pushed towards her.

'What is it?'

'Open it and see.'

Mystified, she began to unwrap the gift, tilting it in the direction of the gas lamp for illumination. Inside the paper was a pale blue box. Still curious she struggled to open it, eventually locating a small golden knob on the side which she pushed in. The box clicked open and lifting the lid she stared at a gold watch, nestling on a white satin lining.

'I. . . .' She raised her eyes in amazement to meet Kenneth's blue ones.

'Just a little token of my respect.'

'I can't possibly take this.' She remembered disturbing gossip about girls who accepted gifts from men.

'Nonsense.' Kenneth took the box from her and extracted the watch, slipping it about her wrist. The gold band expanded and when fastened, fitted her perfectly – like Cinderella's glass slipper, she thought.

'Thank you.' She could not stop herself from leaning forward and kissing him on the cheek. It shone pink with pleasure.

'I'll try and see you before, but if not, same as usual next time?'

'See you next week.'

The following afternoon, to Doris's disappointment, Kenneth did not pop in as he often did when he patrolled the square as part of his beat.

'No sign of Kenneth,' remarked Cook.

Doris said nothing. His absence set up a fluttering in her chest as if a baby bird was trying to warn her of some danger. As she buttered pieces of fruit loaf for the nursery tea, her hands trembled. Only the thought of the watch, hidden under her mattress, warded off the sense of foreboding.

Kenneth did not come the next day either, or the next. On Wednesday, Cook went into town to view the latest stock of groceries at Mylton and Laceys, high class provision merchants. Normally she placed a weekly order with their delivery man who came to write down her requests in his duplicate book which bore the firm's name and the motto: 'Second to None'. The goods ordered arrived promptly the next day. Occasionally she went personally to view the stock.

Cook was gone quite a long time. It was raining when she came in and for several seconds she stood just inside the door, shaking out her cape and taking off her hat. She took an old copy of the *London Review* that they used for lighting the fire when Doctor Ferney had finished with it. Screwing up some pages she stuffed them into the toes of her outdoor shoes before placing them beside the range to dry.

There was something not quite right about Cook. She gave off an aura of dismay, as if she had just heard bad news. Although Doris had her back to her as she peeled potatoes at the sink, it was as if she had all round vision. She could not fail to notice the warning look that Cook gave to Mrs Herring, the housekeeper. After a few moments they went out into the passage.

Doris knew that it was something concerning herself. By now, her hands were shaking so much that as she put the saucepan to boil on the range it splashed water sending up a noisy cloud of steam. When the two women came in it was with a a new air of resolve.

'Doris, leave what you're doing and come here a minute.'

Doris wiped her shaking hands on her apron and went across to Cook. What had she done that was so awful?

'What do you know about PC Harris?'

'Um. . . .' She didn't know what she was supposed to know. Had they found out that he had kissed her, or even worse, about the watch? Did they think she'd let him have his way with her?

She was about to defend herself when Cook said: 'Did you know that he was married?'

Doris swallowed down the news as if it was senna, something so unpalatable that it threatened to make her sick.

'No M'm.'

'Well, he is. He's been off duty because his daughter has been very ill with suspected diphtheria.'

Daughter? Doris would not allow herself to think ahout it. It must be some other policeman. It must be a mistake.

'Well, he won't be calling at this door again.' Cook rolled up her sleeves as if she might personally take her rolling pin to him. 'You – you haven't done anything silly, have you?'

Doris shook her head, blushing scarlet with misery.

'That's all right then. You'd best get back to work now and put him out of your mind.'

Doris bobbed her head at Cook and fled for the sink and the familiarity of the vegetables. All the time she knew that there must be some mistake.

On Saturday afternoon she left the house to go to the library.

'Go and get yourself something to read, child, something uplifting.' Cook shook her head, 'You look like a dying duck in a thunderstorm.'

Cook, a kindly woman, chivvied her out even though it was not her afternoon off. 'Don't be longer than half an hour.'

At the library, Doris gazed listlessly at the shelves. She had no appetite for reading, or for anything else. To prove that she had done as she was told, she selected a book by Ethel M. Dell, whom Cook particularly liked, and paid her money to the assistant.

As she was scurrying along Avalon Street, her head bowed against the grim January drizzle, she heard Kenneth calling.

'Doris, wait a minute.'

She increased her pace, anxious only to get home, unable to face him with her own misery, but within a few paces he caught her up.

'Doris, it isn't what you think.'

'Then you're not married?' She could not hide the hope in her voice.

He looked away and sighed. 'It was a long time ago. I stay for the children's sake, but. . . .'

Doris stared at her feet.

Kenneth said, 'I really want to see you. I never intended you any harm. You mean more to me than. . . .'

'No! It's wrong. Here, you'd best take your watch back.' Her voice wobbled dangerously.

Kenneth stayed her hand. His touch melted her resolve. He said, 'You keep it. I hope one day you won't think badly of me.'

Doris started to weep.

'Doris!' He tried to take her in his arms but she lashed out at him.

'Let me go!' He stepped back to let her pass. The last vision she had of him was of his blue eyes almost black with pain, rain rimming his lashes, his shoulders bowed in defeat.

After that, Doris fell ill. She lived in a kind of wet cocoon, permanently tired, permanently hopeless. At one point they wondered if she had contracted diphtheria but her symptoms went on for too long. Six weeks later Doctor Ferney decided that the best thing was for her to go home. He wrote a letter to her parents explaining that living in London did not suit their daughter and that she should find employment nearer to home. She never saw Kenneth again.

It was nearly seven years before she started going out with Bert. It was quite by chance, really. By then Doris had a job in another doctor's house, as it happened. She was nursemaid to the doctor's children, Charles and Elizabeth. Another girl, Ruby, was housemaid. Doris didn't mind Ruby. She was all right really, a bit silly sometimes, but all right.

It came as a shock therefore when Ruby announced that she was going to get married and would Doris be her bridesmaid. That's when she met Bert. At the wedding. He was the bridegroom's brother and best man. After the ceremony and the photos and the sit down tea, it was expected that they would dance together, not that Doris could really dance. Bert wasn't much better. Twice he stepped on her toes and her satin slippers didn't offer much protection.

She couldn't help wondering: If she had met him anywhere else, would she even have noticed Bert, or he her, come to that? As it was, they'd sort of drifted on together for a couple of years, her going to his house for tea on Sundays and both of them bicycling over to visit her aunts on Saturdays, until one day he'd said,

'I suppose we ought to get married.'

Doris thought: I suppose we should. That was that then. Bert's brother was best man and Ruby was matron of honour, a sort of tit for tat.

Her thoughts hopped back from her wedding to the meeting at the school last night. All this talk of careers. What they meant was a good steady job. Doris bristled with satisfaction. Well, it hadn't taken her long to sort that out. Lot of nonsense it was, inviting parents to go to the school. Probably just so as the teachers could get overtime. Well, she didn't get overtime and she had been the one to find Maisie a job already.

She peered round the door into the living room to look at the clock. Ten to five. Maisie was late. She felt a moment of irritation because if the girl had only come straight home she could have gone down the surgery and got her prescription, and a note for work too to say that Doris wouldn't be in next week. Having her bunions done, she was. Her feet were that bad she couldn't put up with it any longer. That meant being off work though. Good job Maisie was about to start earning. Her brow clouded as she realized that she would still be off her feet when Maisie started the job. Oh well, never mind. The girl would have to pull herself together and get organized. Doris had had to do so at her age; besides, these days she did a hundred things at once so there was no reason why Maisie shouldn't do the same.

A cold shadow touched her as she recalled the teacher's comments. Was there something worrying Maisie? Something serious? Doris had woken up that morning and before her eyes were even open her stomach began churning like a tin bath on an ocean. It wasn't the first time she'd felt it, a sudden, unexpected wave of fear as if something awful was about to happen, only nothing ever did. Strange she hadn't had that premonition when it would have meant something, and been useful. She wasn't like Madam Fortune, seeing into the future. But the feeling was still there, fearful. threatening.

She forced her thoughts back to Maisie. Perhaps she had a young man, a secret admirer. No. Doris shook her head. The girl never went out long enough to meet anyone. Always moping around the house. That was a worry too. She'd never been right really, not since. . . .

She began to chip the potatoes with furious energy, driving out the thoughts. At that moment she heard her daughter coming down the path and with a tremor of satisfaction she thought: A good steady job will do her the world of good. Working out there where she would meet people might bring her out of herself. In fact, it's probably just what she needs.

Three

AS THE SOCIAL Studies class came to an end, Maisie packed her books into her satchel and made for the door. She was the first to reach the school gate, barging her way past several small knots of girls lingering to share last moments of gossip before the weekend claimed them. Living in the country, the school covered a wide catchment area so many students could not see their friends outside of school hours. Maisie, her head full of the future, hardly noticed them. At weekends she saw no one from Robert Hooke Secondary. Mostly she saw no one of her own age at all.

As she turned left out of the school gate her brain was fully occupied, for inside her head a series of professions presented themselves for her consideration.

Vet? That would be a good job. Then she could have cured Benjy their old dog, so that his back legs did not buckle every time he stood up which meant he had to be put to sleep. *Thank you, Miss Morris. You are a miracle worker. We are all eternally grateful.*

Air hostess? That would be a good job too. Maisie paraded before her own eyes in a navy blue uniform with a pencil skirt and a chic little hat, her hair done up in a neat chignon and her feet encased in smart black court shoes. You'd have to speak French, though. *Chic,* that was a French word. It was a pity they didn't do French in Five C, not like Five A where they took their O Levels. A pang of envy touched her. By taking their exams, the students in Five A unlocked a door to all kinds of possibilities.

She pushed her regret aside. Perhaps it wouldn't take long to learn a foreign language. Several. Mrs Cameron would know.

Maisie thought with admiration of her form teacher. Mrs Cameron was young and pretty. She was married to a good-looking man with brown curls and muscly shoulders – Maisie had seen him once when he came to pick his wife up after school, driving their new Vauxhall Cresta. She knew that his first name was James. Joanna and James. It must be lovely to be called Joanna. It must be lovely to have a car and to be married to someone like that.

Reluctantly she dragged her mind back to her qualifications, or lack of them. To be an air hostess you'd have to know First Aid as well. She put her airborne career on hold.

As she crossed the road at the junction with the High Street, nearly colliding with a bread van, the driver honked at her with a gesture of despair. Hardly bothering to notice, Maisie gave her thoughts free range. The roads and lanes that led to West Street she negotiated by instinct, not troubling to glance to left or right. Other vans, cars, bicycles criss-crossed her path like dodgem cars but by some miracle she passed unscathed between them. All that mattered were the possibilities that filled her head.

Being a film star would be great. Who should she be? Her mind wandered to the fairy tale that had preoccupied her for months, the marriage of Grace Kelly the film star to Prince Ranier of Monaco. Was there ever anything more romantic? Did princes really marry ordinary girls? Except that Princess Grace wasn't ordinary. She was American and beautiful. Her father was said to be rich. Maisie sighed. Whatever happened, princes didn't marry girls from Robert Hooke. She remembered the newsreel of the wedding with Princess Grace in a dress covered in lace: *an intoxication* the man doing the commentary had called it.

Maisie sighed. On the other hand, Prince Ranier was quite old, and certainly not handsome. Her own prince would look more like Mr Cameron – James. Denying herself the pleasure of recalling his physical appearance, she thought again of her film career. She would like to be someone young and pretty with a pony tail and black pumps and a gingham dress with a Peter Pan collar and a circular skirt. She touched her own thick, ragged hair, wondering how long it would take to grow into a pony tail.

Another image fixed itself firmly in her mind. Last Saturday she had seen *Rock Around the Clock* at the cinema. Never, ever had anyone in the village behaved like the young people in the film, abandoning themselves to the jungle beat of music, swinging their bodies about with an edge of anarchy that was exciting, dangerous. Afterwards in the privacy of her bedroom she practiced jiving but she didn't have any records to play and anyway, it was no good without a partner. The vision of herself as bobby soxer darkened. Her thoughts turned to more attainable goals.

She'd meant what she'd said about a farm. It would be good there with all the animals to look after, almost as good as being a vet.

The prospect of the weekend stretched ahead. Mum would be nagging her to go to the beach like most of the local youngsters did. '*You don't get enough fresh air, young lady.*' Maisie didn't want to. She couldn't swim very well and with the summer holidays starting it was always too crowded. Besides, her skin was that pale, pinky colour that just blistered and never went brown.

Perhaps she'd go to the library and see if they had a book about working on a farm. It might have some helpful tips. She'd have to go anyway, to change Aunty Rene's book. '*Get me something nice, our Maisie. Something with a proper story.*' Not that Aunty Rene ever read them. She left the books in funny places like the larder, but finding something that she liked was a bit of a nightmare.

Then she'd have to go shopping for Mum. Every Saturday Mum sent her to the Co-op with a list of weekly things. Mum's feet were bad these days and she couldn't carry heavy bags. And Grandad? His runner beans were in full fruit now. Tonight he would make them up into bundles wrapped in newspaper and tied with string, and send Maisie round to the greengrocers with them first thing in the morning. She hated having to go but last week she'd come back with ten shillings for the lot and Grandad had given her two bob for herself. That would just be enough to get her into the Regal again tomorrow night for the film and an ice cream. *Titanic* was on, with Clifton Webb, about a big ship sinking. It should be good.

It did not take Maisie long to walk home. She was one of the lucky ones who did not have to take the bus. Some of the class lived as much as eight miles away. She wouldn't like that. She got sick on buses. And in cars. Perhaps she would get sick in an aeroplane too so being an air hostess might not be such a good idea.

As she opened the back door, Mum was cutting potatoes into chip-sized shapes. A pan was already belching blue smoke on the gas stove and pieces of cod sizzled in the frying pan. Mum hacked at the potatoes on a badly scoured and discoloured board which had stood on the edge of the kitchen table ever since Maisie could remember. Doris sliced with fierce determination. Aunty Rene stood in the doorway watching her.

'For goodness sake, Aunty, take that cardigan off. You'll roast.' Aunty Rene peeled off her cardi to reveal another one underneath. Mum sighed with frustration, 'And the other one. Then go and lay the table.'

Maisie wondered whether to say anything about the careers talk but before she could do so, Mum said, 'Go and help her find the knives and forks.' Before she could do so, Doris added, 'Oh, and I've found you a job. Don't know why they make such a fuss about it. Mr Stephenson wants someone in his shop. I told him it'd suit you fine. There'll be overtime too. You can help in the caff-part during the summer evenings, get some tips, and when the season ends you'll still be able to serve the wet fish.'

Wet fish. Maisie was aware of something closing off inside her. Fishy Stephenson's shop! Fish. Cold and smelly. Not even live ones. It felt as if the walls were shrinking, the ceiling descending on her head. She might not know what she wanted but it certainly wasn't this.

'I hate fish!' She shuddered.

Mum pulled a disapproving face. 'Don't be so daft. Surely you can wrap up ten penn'orth of plaice!'

Before Maisie could comment, Mum continued, 'Anyway, Mr Stephenson wants someone straight away so what with me going into hospital and all, it means you'll have to leave school this week.'

'Not go back?' The thought jolted her to a standstill. Not be there on the last day when everyone would say goodbye, when the teachers would stop treating you like children and more like friends. Besides, she had to see Mrs Cameron to ask about her career and to get her autograph. A wave of misery swept through her then, looking at Mum's tight mouth, the tense narrow shoulders, something inside of Maisie seemed to perish. Swallowing down her dreams, she crossed to the kitchen drawer and took out four knives, forks and spoons. As Aunty Rene wandered back into the kitchen wearing both cardigans again, Maisie said, 'All right, Mum. When do I have to start?'

The next morning Maisie got to the doctor's surgery well before nine but to her dismay there were already several people ahead of her. Sitting on one of the chairs that lined the waiting room she felt the too-familiar anxiety begin to gnaw at her stomach. She hated coming here. Hated it. It didn't matter if she was coming for herself or as today, for her mother. The same panic seemed to take hold of her. It was a crazy feeling, an urge to run away and hide from something terrible. Taking a deep breath she tried to suppress it, focusing instead on what she was going to say. '*Please can I have a susstificate for me mum's legs? Me mum wants a sick note for while she's in hospital.*'

Although the feeling of menace was still there, somehow she managed to keep it under control. To distract herself, she fell instead to wondering what was on the other side of the surgery door. The waiting room led directly into the surgery which in turn led through into Doctor Patterson's house. When he poked his head into the waiting room to call you in, there were two doors back-to-back that you had to negotiate, so that the other people waiting wouldn't hear what you were talking about when they were closed. Inside the surgery itself there was also a door on the far side but that was normally closed too. Maisie wondered if he kept it locked. Just once, when she had come about her tonsils, it had been ajar and before Doctor Patterson closed it, she had glimpsed a long corridor with a coat stand and paintings and rooms leading off it. Thinking of home, Maisie couldn't imagine living in a great big old house like that. Only rich, important people like doctors had cars and big houses. Besides, what a lot of cleaning!

She tried to imagine Doctor Patterson having his breakfast with his wife before starting work for the morning. Sometimes he was late opening and he always said, '*Sorry about this, I was called away on an emergency.*' Maisie suspected that he had simply overslept.

Mum had often told her that Doctor Patterson had delivered her, which made him sound like the milkman. She fell to musing about the various delivery men who called at their house, the baker, the coal man, the rent man, the man who came with the accumulator that kept the wireless working – although Mum said that they were being phased out which meant buying another wireless, one that ran off the mains. These days you could even get ones with batteries that you could carry around with you. It would be great to have one of those but there wasn't much chance of that.

Mum still hadn't managed to afford a telly. This was another thing that made Maisie feel left out. At school the others talked about the programmes they had seen the night before and as she listened, she pretended to herself that she knew all about them. They sounded really good, better even than the pictures, because you could get up and make a cup of tea if you wanted to and you didn't have to have the light off. She'd love to be able to watch the programmes every evening but Mum said apart from the cost and it being bad for your eyes, Maisie wouldn't get her homework done – not that that had done her much good. Not now.

The grim reality of the fish shop threatened. How on earth was she going to bear it? She'd die if she had to talk to the customers. And imagine having to serve someone that she knew! Besides, she didn't fancy touching the fish. It was so cold and dead, staring at you like that with those glassy eyes, accusing you somehow. Supposing she dropped some? Supposing they asked for something and she didn't know what it was?

At that moment the door from the outside opened and to her amazement, Mrs Cameron came in to the waiting room. She hesitated when she saw Maisie, before saying, 'Good Morning, Maisie, not ill, are you?'

Maisie shook her head and her face went red because two of the other patients were looking at her.

She wondered what Mrs Cameron had come for. It had never occurred to her that teachers might get ill and if they did, that they would use ordinary doctors like Doctor Patterson. She studied her fingers. Mrs Cameron didn't look ill either. but she supposed she must be. Maisie hadn't the nerve to ask. Her Mum would have done. '*Under the weather are you?*' That's what she called being ill. A funny thing to say really. Everyone was under the weather, except perhaps people in planes.

Mrs Cameron sat almost opposite her and after a moment picked up a copy of *Punch* magazine from the little table in the middle of the room. Her thick black hair was cropped short and had a soft wave to it. As she flicked through the pages, she asked, 'Any more thoughts about a job?' Maisie's heart plummeted. She couldn't tell Mrs Cameron; not now, in front of all these people. Besides, she was afraid that Joanna would be annoyed. How could she explain that it wasn't her idea to work in a fish shop?

Again in response she shook her head and wished she had had the foresight to pick up a magazine as well then she could have pretended to read it. Now, it would look rude to get one when Mrs Cameron was talking to her.

Just as she was thinking with misery that she would never see her teacher again, Mrs Cameron smiled at her and said, 'I haven't forgotten about the job, you know. If I hear of anything suitable, I'll let you know.'

Four

'WELL, YOUNG LADY, I'm pleased to confirm that you are definitely pregnant.' Doctor Patterson smiled benignly over the top of his spectacles at Joanna. 'How long have you been married?'

She told him. Her smile felt wooden. Why couldn't she express what she really felt? Was it expected of all married women that they should be pleased when they had a first baby?

The doctor proceeded to weigh and measure her, then took her blood pressure.

'No problems there. Any questions?'

Joanna shook her head and he advised her on diet and rest.

'I finish teaching in three weeks,' she informed him when he drew to a halt.

'Working, are you?' He looked surprised.

'I teach at Robert Hooke. This is my first year.' She hesitated. 'We hadn't exactly been planning on having a baby so soon.'

His response was non-committal, looking at the rims of her eyes and asking about morning sickness. As he sat back, he said, 'It's never too soon. People who put it off end up finding excuses to delay it further – wait for a promotion, get a bigger house, buy a car. In my opinion if you wait for the right time, there isn't one. Just be glad that you're healthy. Drink plenty of milk, now. Early nights, regular exercise. Come back and see me in a month.'

He smiled his dismissal and Joanna felt like one of her own

students. Thankfully there was nobody else she knew in the waiting room. She hoped that Maisie wouldn't broadcast it around that she had seen her here. Perhaps she should get a doctor in Eastport after all. But then again, if she was leaving the school, it wouldn't matter. A grey dampness settled on her. She didn't want to give up teaching. Not now. Not when she felt she was getting on top of things. Without even asking she knew that it would have been pointless suggesting to Doctor Patterson that she might try to 'postpone' things. Anyway, if that was the case she should probably have come when she first suspected, but at the time she had hoped that she was mistaken and that the 'problem' would go away of its own accord.

Weighed down by some undefined gloom, she walked back home. James thought she had gone shopping. He'd been understandably surprised when she hinted that she wanted to get to the stores early. Saturday was their morning for lying in bed and indulging in some extra. . . .

'You going off me?' he had asked, when she slipped out of his snuggling embrace. Perhaps she should have stayed. Perhaps if she were to provoke him into some really violent love-making it might unseat the baby. The baby. She had a mental vision of it swathed in a woolly nappy, like the infant on the green Fairy soap bars, sitting on a little cushion somewhere inside of her, with a question-mark-quiff of hair. Get out, you little bugger! Her hand came to rest on her abdomen and she felt – betrayed.

Before they had moved here, her own doctor at home had advised her about contraception and about the safest times. There was no excuse really. She had a cap but often it was too much trouble to put it in – especially when they were both snuggled up warm and close and James was hard and urgent. Besides, she was regular as clockwork. Easy enough to work out the safe times – except that even when it wasn't safe she couldn't deny him – or herself. It was her fault as much as his. More really. She was the one who was expected to keep an eye on things.

She sighed audibly as their cottage came into view. Other fears assailed her. How would they keep up the mortgage payments with just one income? She felt a sudden surge of love for the cottage, with its stone walls and deep roof, sadly slated instead of being thatched but they had been going to change that – not now, though. Not now.

As she reached the gate she saw James in the garden. He was digging over a vegetable patch, the good red earth sticking to his spade as he drove the blade deep into the ground. What was he going to plant – brussels sprouts, winter cabbage, parsnips? All ready for the approaching cold. She tried to take comfort from the thought of being a housewife and doing all the things that her mother did, but in her heart she rebelled. Part-time housekeeping was all right but being stuck here day after day, sewing cushion covers and making jam would be enough to drive her insane.

You'll have the baby to look after, her *alter ego* observed but that too seemed more like a punishment than a gift.

James looked up as she lifted the latch. 'Get what you wanted?' He looked at her empty hands then frowned at the expression on her face. 'What is it?'

'I'm pregnant.'

His face froze. 'Pregnant?'

'Yes, you know, when a mummy and daddy plant a seed and all that.'

He shook his head impatiently. 'D'you. . . ?'

'Did I plan it? Of course I didn't.'

'I was going to say do you mind?'

She collapsed in upon herself, moving to the comfort of his arms. 'I should feel pleased,' she said. 'The doctor assumed I was, but—'

James hugged her. 'Is it money you're worried about?'

'Partly, but – I don't want to give up my job.'

He nodded sympathetically. 'Bit of a bugger, then.'

She drew back so that she could look at him. 'And you? What do you think?'

He shrugged. 'I've never seriously considered it. Not as something likely to happen in the near future. I – I'll need a little time to get used to the idea.'

She had the horrible feeling of letting him down, of imposing a burden on him. 'Let's go back to bed,' she said.

'Now?' He looked startled.

'Is there a law that says we can't?'

'No. I – I wanted to get these plants in before they dry out.'

'Suit yourself.' She flounced away from him and went indoors, knowing that she was being unreasonable.

'Damn it. Damn and bugger and shit!' She expelled her anger, feeling instantly ungrateful, remembering her cousin Joan who had had a mongol baby. She should be grateful, should be hoping for a healthy child. Cousin Joan had been pleased and look what had happened to her.

James came in in his stockinged feet. A grin played about his mouth as he looked her up and down through half closed lids. 'I can't concentrate on digging, not now you've put the idea into my head.'

Blowing the gloom away, Joanna's face relaxed as she went to him, kissing him. Hand in hand they made for the stairs.

'I'll be gentle,' he promised as he peeled off his shirt but her suddenly hungry hands made sure that he was anything but.

Five

MAISIE WAS DUE to start work at Stephenson's Fish Emporium at eight o'clock on Monday morning. On Sunday night she slept badly. All kinds of *what if*s kept going through her head, to none of which she knew the answer. When the alarm went off she was having a bad dream. She knew that it was nasty even though by the time she awoke she couldn't remember what it was about.

Reluctantly she dressed in her school skirt and blouse because, as Mum said, she wouldn't be needing them any more and she didn't want her other clothes stinking of fish all the time, did she? As she buttoned her blouse it felt like she was putting on a disguise that no longer belonged to her. These were the clothes in which she sat at her desk and wrote her essays, day-dreamed about the future. This was a school uniform, for someone who went to lessons and joined, uninvited, in the laughter at other people's jokes, nodded in agreement at opinions which she would never have the temerity to voice herself. Now these clothes were being betrayed, given a new, alien role as a shopgirl's outfit.

'I'll be up the hospital by the time you get home.' Mum gave Maisie's collar a tug to straighten it. 'Mind everything I've told you, now. I've pinned up the week's menus inside the larder door. You sure you know how to cook it all?'

Maisie nodded. Mum gave a grim nod. 'And keep an eye on Aunty Rene. The other night she got me up about four o'clock and insisted it was morning.'

Again Maisie nodded. The day and the week stretched ahead like a trek across Africa, unknown and full of danger.

Mum made a peck in the direction of her cheek. 'Come and see me on Saturday. Don't forget to bring me in a clean nightie. First visiting's on Wednesday afternoon but you'll be at work.'

'No I won't. It'll be half day.'

Mum looked pleased and pushed her towards the door. 'Come and see me then, then. Good luck with the job, now. And remember what I told you.'

Maisie nodded, resisting the sudden urge to cling to her mother like an overgrown toddler. The vision alarmed her. The toddler she saw wasn't herself but someone like her, wispy brown hair, a thin little face, shorts, a little boy's face cast in her own image. She blinked hard to dislodge the picture and pushing her hands into her pockets, set out for the High Street and work.

Mr Stephenson was already there when she arrived, as was his assistant, Mrs Harrison, who worked in the office, taking the money and the telephone orders and making out bills. Occasionally Maisie had seen her helping out on the counter when they were really busy but Mrs Harrison always did so with her nose wrinkled in distaste, as if handling the fish was beneath her.

When she saw Maisie she looked across at Mr Stephenson and raised her eyebrows in a gesture which said: 'Surely this isn't the girl you've taken on?' Maisie guessed she wasn't supposed to see the look but she couldn't help it, because Mrs Harrison was standing almost in front of her.

In response, Mr Stephenson shrugged his shoulders and turned his cod's eyes back to Maisie. He said, 'Right girl, see that bucket there and that mop? Well, get yourself some water from that tap' (he nodded towards a tap protruding from the shop wall), 'and give the floor a good swill down. It's done every evening regular but there's no harm in giving it an extra going over.'

While Maisie struggled with the galvanised bucket and tried not to splash water all over her feet, Mr Stephenson laid out an assortment of fish on white trays to go in the window. Already the smell was beginning to make her feel queasy. Fighting down the distaste, she tried not to leave footmarks in the watery sheen that drained its way across the black and white pattern of the tiles, trickling into a narrow gulley and out towards the backyard.

The shop door opened sharp at nine. Maisie learned that Monday wasn't a good day because most people had cold meat and bubble and squeak for dinner, but it was a good day to learn the ropes: how to talk to the customers; how to encourage them to try an extra bit of smoked haddock or some cod's roe or these really fresh sprats; *just right for the old man's tea.* Mr Stephenson acted out a scenario and Maisie watched dumbfounded.

Her first customer was Mrs Lomax. Maisie had never spoken to Mrs Lomax before although she knew that she lived in the big house at the top of Endell Road and was something on the Parish Council. Mr Lomax worked away from the village and Mrs Lomax did something important with the WRVS. She had a car and everything. Often Maisie saw her in her WRVS uniform but today she was dressed in a tweed skirt, a white blouse and a blazer. As she entered the shop she surveyed Mr Stephenson's display like a kestrel waiting to pounce on its prey.

'I'll take two of those.' She stabbed a gloved finger towards a tray of cold, pink flesh. Maisie followed the white digit with its neatly crocheted cuff, praying that it might deviate towards something that she recognized. The finger pointed unerringly at the second tray from the left. Maisie froze, looking helplessly around for Mr Stephenson, who was gutting herrings with gusto at the back of the shop.

Mrs Lomax gave a tut of impatience. 'Well, girl?'

With shaking fingers, Maisie picked up two of the fish and laid them on the scales. To the left was a list of all the prices. She glanced down at it in panic. What sort of fish were they?

Mrs Lomax tutted again, impatiently. 'If you don't know what you're doing, why don't you go and ask?'

Maisie scurried to the back and waited while Mr Stephenson continued with his butchery. At last he looked up. 'Well?'

'That lady wants some of that pink fish.'

'So?'

'I don't know what it is.'

Mr Stephenson sighed and put his knife aside, wiping his hands on his scale-encrusted apron.

'Mrs Lomax, good morning. A pleasure to see you on such a lovely day. This, was it? The red mullet? My wife has an excellent recipe. . . .' He took over the sales talk, wrapping the red mullet first in plain paper then in the front cover of the *Daily Herald.*

As Mrs Lomax retreated with her parcel, he said, 'For goodness sake, speak up, girl. You'll get nowhere if you carry on like that.'

The rest of the day showed little improvement and at half past five Maisie slouched her way home, smelly, tired and with aching feet. It was awful. Awful. She didn't want to go back, not ever. Tomorrow was market day which meant it would be even busier. There would be lots more people in the town, and tomorrow lunchtime she might even have to go and help out in the caff.

As she sliced up the cold lamb and mashed up yesterday's left over potatoes and cabbage and runner beans to make the bubble and squeak the stink of fish remained in her nostrils. And under her fingernails. And in her hair. She wanted to wash it all away but it wasn't bath night until Friday. For a wild moment she remembered that now Mum was away she could do more or less what she liked, but then the thought of getting the tin bath from the shed and heating up the water and sending Grandad out of the way was too much.

Meanwhile, Aunty Rene carried an assortment of cutlery to the table. Maisie noted that she was wearing a very lacy blouse meant for evening wear that showed a large pink expanse of her interlocking petticoat. She also noted that the bundle of cutlery her great aunt clutched included the carving knife, a fish slice and several table spoons. Poor Aunty Renie. She was getting proper dopey.

That night Aunty Rene had Maisie up at two and again at four. She insisted that it was time to get up and kept calling Maisie, 'Mother'.

'Go back to bed, Aunty.'

'I'm scared. I can't find our Joey anywhere.'

Maisie had never met Joey although she had heard a lot about him. Had he lived he would bave been her great uncle, but he died in the First World War. There was a picture of him in his army uniform on the mantelpiece.

Aunty Rene wheedled, 'Can't I come in with you?'

Maisie shared a room with Mum in order that Grandad and Aunty Rene could each have a room of their own. When she had gone to bed that evening Maisie thought how nice it was to be by herself, but now, in the middle of the night when she was tired and had to get up for work the next morning, she didn't argue.

'All right. But go straight to sleep, now. I've got to get up early.'

Aunty Rene scrambled gleefully into the bed. 'I will.'

'Good night, Aunty Rene.'

'Good night, Mum.'

Somehow Maisie stumbled her way through the next days. She found it exhausting, not only standing on her feet all day, but just facing the customers. The moment the shop door opened she jumped and her heart flailed like a boisterous dog's tail. Still, she was getting the hang of it. She knew the prices of all the fish, even the bass and lobsters, the crabs and mackerel that came in fresh and straight from the fishing boats each morning.

At Wednesday lunchtime, after she had scrubbed out the shop, Mr Stephenson even gave her a bag of sprats to take home, with the words, 'Don't be late in the morning.' She clutched the bag to her, a pungent reminder of her day's work. Perhaps she could cook them for Grandad's tea. As for herself, she would never eat another fish again.

That afternoon she was going to visit Mum. She hadn't heard anything from the hospital so presumably the operation had gone all right. Maisie imagined what it must be like, having a lump sliced off your foot. It must hurt. She quickly diverted herself with thoughts of the film at the Odeon with Stewart Granger. With disappointment she realized that while Mum was away, perhaps she had better stay at home. Mum never gallivanted off to the pictures. Fancy missing Stewart Granger though. If he wasn't handsome, then. . . . She diverted herself by thinking of all the other handsome film stars she would like to meet and before she knew it, she was home.

Visiting was from half past two till four, and as Mum had only had her operation the day before Maisie knew she might not be allowed to stay long. Normally only husbands went on the first day but as Mum was a widow they were making an exception for her.

Grandad picked a bunch of sweet williams and snapdragons from his garden for Maisie to take in. He talked about sending in some runner beans too but she managed to talk him out of it. 'They get their meals cooked, Grandad.'

'Don't suppose it's like home cooking, though.'

Maisie agreed that it probably wasn't. In her rush to get home she'd forgotten to get anything to take to the hospital, but then she remembered that the paper man had delivered Mum's *Woman's Weekly* that morning. There might be a new knitting pattern or something and one of those stories that she liked.

Doris was in the women's ward of Henrietta Morpath's Cottage Hospital. There were six beds in the ward, all occupied by women about her mother's age. They all stared at Maisie as she walked in, making her legs feel jerky. She guessed that Mum had been talking about her and now they were having a good look.

The floor was covered in brown linoleum and smelt of dettol and lavender, and the beds had crisp white sheets and pillow-cases and brown, swirly cotton bed covers. Maisie kept her eyes lowered until she reached Mum's bed, which was in the far corner.

Mum sat up surrounded by pillows. A sort of cage thing was over her legs to keep the covers off, Mum looked pale and colourless, her hair and skin blending in with the bed linen.

'Hello, Mum. How are you?'

Mum closed her eyes as if to summon up the energy to answer. 'My poor old foot ain't half giving me gyp.'

Maisie glanced down at the cage and to her horror Mum pulled the covers back to show her the dressing that surrounded her foot, with some sort of needle things actually stuck into her toes. A pinky grey bloodstain oozed through the bandage.

Maisie immediately felt faint. She looked round for somewhere to sit down but there didn't seem to be anywhere. Breathing deeply she distracted herself by putting the flowers on the bedside cabinet and the *Woman's Weekly* on the bed.

'Mind my foot!'

Mum grilled Maisie about the job and the cooking and making the beds and not forgetting that the dustman came on Thursdays. She reminded her about paying the rent, and going to the shops, and checking Aunty Rene's bed every morning because *sometimes she has a little accident.*

Maisie absorbed all the instructions until she was overflowing.

'When will you be home?' she asked hopefully.

'Two weeks. Then I've got to keep off it. I won't be back at work before the end of August.' She glanced at the offending limb beneath the covers before adding, 'You'll have to do all the washing. And the cleaning. And don't forget. . . .'

Maisie looked up to see a nurse coming towards them, all navy blue ironing and crisp white starch. Pointedly, the nurse removed Mum's magazine from the bed and put it into the drawer of her bedside cabinet, then gathered up the flowers with a martyrish sigh.

To Maisie she said, 'You've stayed long enough. Your mother needs to rest now, to sleep off the anaesthetic. It takes days to get it out of your system.'

Maisie nodded, trying to ignore her sense of relief. She looked at Mum to see her reaction. Normally she would have something to say about someone being bossy like that, but for now she simply lay back and closed her eyes.

'Bye, Mum.'

Doris forced one eye open. 'I'll see you at the weekend. And don't forget Aunty Rene's library book on Saturday. . . .'

It was lovely to be back outside. The hospital had a nice garden full of flowers and she lingered a little as she walked back up towards the gate. For a moment she thought it would be lovely to go for a walk and sit in the woods on that old log, where the bracken tamed chestnut in autumn and where she had once seen a woodpecker making a hole in a tree, but then she remembered the ironing, and that Aunty Rene's knickers were soaking in a pail under the sink. Shouldering her burden she closed the lid firmly on her dreams and turned for home.

Six

'Does anybody know what happened to Maisie Morris's father?'

It was the last day of term and most of the teachers were gathered in the staff room for the morning break. The air was thick with cigarette smoke which made Joanna feel queasy. The early stages of her pregnancy were a misery. She couldn't stand the smell of tea or coffee either but habit brought her down to join the other teachers every morning and afternoon.

Owen Evans, the sports master, answered her question with one of his own. 'He was consumptive, wasn't he? Had bad lungs ever since the war.'

Joanna gave him her attention. He was Welsh, thirtyish with russet brown hair, sturdily built. She knew that he fancied her and safe behind the boundary of her marriage, she could enjoy his mild flirtation. When he wasn't in the classroom, a cigarette was moulded almost permanently between his fingers. The smell of stale tobacco emanated from his hair and his tweed jacket. His teeth, although clean, had brown stains.

'I thought there might have been some sort of accident. Something his wife said. Did you ever meet him?' Joanna asked.

Owen shrugged, losing interest. She added, 'He wasn't a pilot by any chance, was he?

'A pilot?' somebody laughed. 'He used to work at the sewerage plant. Why do you ask?'

'I just wondered.'

'What class will you be taking next year?' The subject of Bert Morris was clearly closed. Owen bent his head to one side, his eyes softening with male interest as he leaned a little closer.

Joanna flushed. 'I probably won't be here – I'm. . . .'

It was the first time she had acknowledged it publicly. Owen gave her a regretful smile and she read the message in his eye – wish I'd been the lucky one. The others voiced their congratulations. Joanna bit back the urge to say, 'I don't want it. Not now, anyway.'

Her thoughts returned to her reason for asking the original question. She had been mildly surprised to find that Maisie was not at school on that first Monday after the careers talk. On Tuesday a scribbled letter had reached the headmaster announcing that: *Maisie won't be in no more. She's started work in the fish shop.*

Joanna had felt almost affronted. She remembered Maisie standing by her desk stammering out her wish to work on a farm. The girl would hate it in a shop, having to talk to customers.

Joanna sighed, blaming herself for not taking more notice. Perhaps if she could have got to the bottom of what was worrying Maisie, things might have turned out differently. Anyway, it was too late now. Her failure cast a pall that threatened the rest of the day.

From the playground the bell sounded and she joined the rest of the reluctant staff returning to their duties. The students were boisterous today, sensing that their role was about to change. By this time next week many of them would be working adults on an equal par with her.

'Can I have your autograph, Miss?'

'Of course.' Joanna stopped to oblige although her heart was not in it. 'Have you decided what you are going to do?' she asked the lad as he leaned a little too close to her, confident in his growing manhood.

He smirked. 'Me Dad's found me a job on a farm.'

On Tuesday morning, Mrs Harrison phoned in sick at the fish

shop. Mr Stephenson came out from the office looking harassed.

'You,' he said, jerking his head in Maisie's direction. 'You can add up, can't you?'

Maisie nodded doubtfully. Her times tables were perfect and she could do mental arithmetic better than anyone in Five C.

'All right. You'll have to go on the cash desk for the day. All you have to do is take the amount written on the ticket the customers give you, write it on to the till roll and give out the change. You sure you can do that?' He led her to inspect the long wooden till with its brass handle and glass window where a roll of paper moved forwards every time you opened the drawer. 'You think you can manage that?' he asked again.

Maisie nodded once more, her heart pumping like a piston in the engine of *Titanic*. She took off her white overall and gingerly sat in Mrs Harrison's seat in her school skirt and jumper.

Being market day it was busy. Somehow Mr Stephenson managed to serve all the customers as well as gut the fish and keep up a cheery monologue. Maisie hardly had time to think about what she was doing. People handed her ten shilling notes and half crowns and she wrote down their totals and handed over the change.

Everything was going well until the telephone rang. Maisie had never had cause to use a telephone. The strident ringing made her already active heart lurch dangerously. Two women were standing at the cash desk waiting to pay. Both looked pointedly at the phone so that Maisie had no choice but to pick up the receiver. A disembodied voice echoed in her already swimming ear.

'Roehampton Lodge here. The usual order for Wednesday.'

'Mmm. . . .' Maisie had no idea what the words meant. Before she could pull herself together there was a click and silence. Shakily she replaced the receiver.

At the end of the day, Mr Stephenson added up the takings. As Maisie returned to her task of swilling out the window display, he came from the office. His expression was difficult to interpret, a twitch playing about the corners of his mouth. 'Well, girl, seems as if you've done a good job. Spot on, it is.'

Maisie felt surprised, not that the money was right, but that he should expect it to be otherwise. Sometimes he and Mrs Harrison would re-count the money several times, trying to account for some discrepancy.

Mr Stephenson expanded his already broad chest with satisfaction. 'If Ethel can't come in tomorrow, do you think you can manage again?'

Maisie nodded.

'Good girl.'

All went well until Wednesday afternoon when the telephone rang again. Maisie was away from her post visiting the lavatory. As she came back it was to see Mr Stephenson emerging from the office, his lips shut solid like a mantrap.

'What's all this about the Roehampton order?'

Maisie stared at him blankly.

'They rang up on Monday. Why didn't you write it down? Why didn't you say anything?'

She remembered the call and her face grew hot.

Mr Stephenson expelled a sigh of such proportions that Maisie feared he might cave in like some deflated balloon. 'What am I going to do?' They always have twenty cod and fifteen haddocks. We haven't got anything like that left.'

Maisie stared at the ground. Everything seemed out of focus, the sound of his voice distorted. With another mammoth sigh he stomped off into the back of the shop where the refrigerators were. Maisie just caught his parting words: 'If you don't pull your socks up, girl, you'll have to go.'

Mum came home on the following Thursday. She was there when Maisie finished work, sitting in the fireside chair that they still referred to as "Dad's". There was usually a scramble for its comfort between Mum, Grandad and Aunty Rene but for now Mum had it by right of her operation.

Mum's foot was still bandaged although the offending spikes had been removed. On her right leg she wore her plaid slipper and her left leg was supported on a pillow on a stool. Maisie's initial pleasure at the thought of not having to take all the responsibility for running the home was short-lived as Mum proceeded to find fault.

'Looks like the kitchen could do with a good going over.' She pursed her lips in a too familiar way. 'Those nets need to come down, too.' Maisie was momentarily grateful that Mum could not climb the stairs but would have to sleep in the living-room, on the little camp bed that stood in readiness along the side of the wall.

Mum cut into her reverie. 'How has Aunty Rene been?'

'All right.' Maisie answered too quickly, guilt at her lack of control over her aunt making her cheeks hot.

Mum gave a grunt of satisfaction. 'Just as long as she's no worse. Have you been remembering to change the chickens' water every day?'

'Grandad has.' The change of subject took her by surprise.

'Grandad is forgetful. I told you to do it. How many eggs have you been getting?'

Maisie hadn't collected the eggs before work that morning. Now she thought about it she hadn't shut the chickens in last night. Supposing a fox had come and eaten them?

'They're laying all right,' she prevaricated, looking round for a means of escape so that she could go and check on the hens. 'I'll put the kettle on.' She fled for the scullery.

The chickens were all accounted for and she managed to smuggle the eggs in unseen. Today was liver and bacon night with mashed potatoes, runner beans and onion gravy. Maisie felt suddenly nervous at cooking for her mother. So far the food had been all right, at least Grandad and Aunty Rene hadn't complained, not even when she had burnt the sausages. Mum was a different kettle of fish, though. She shuddered at the vision of fish in a kettle – or in anything, come to that. Her thoughts flew to the Fish Emporium. Thank goodness Mrs Harrison was back, even though the money never seemed to be right at closing time.

'I hear you're a proper little clever clogs.' Mrs Harrison had not taken kindly to Maisie's accuracy. Fortunately the telephone had rung at that moment and Maisie observed Mrs Harrison's *modus operandi,* just in case she was left alone with the fearful instrument again.

As Maisie sliced some onions, she thought of all the things that Mum would find fault with. While her mother had been away, Aunty Rene had taken to sleeping regularly in the double bed with Maisie. The worst thing was that once she had wet herself, and apart from anything else, it meant washing sheets twice the size of the ones on Aunty Rene's single bed. Maisie had considered swapping places with Aunty Rene and sleeping in her room but Mum would never tolerate having to share with her aunt. As they prepared for bed that night, Maisie said, 'Aunty, you really must stay in your own bed.'

'But I can't find the light switch if I'm took short.'

'It's where it's always been, right by the door. I'll leave it on for you if you want me to.' Like an ever-present conscience, she felt Mum's disapproval: *You can't go wasting electricity like that.* This was something else she would have to face once Mum could climb the stairs. For the moment though, she was glad of anything that would keep Aunty Rene out of her room and let her sleep in peace.

Joanna awoke on Thursday morning and carefully tested her well being. She took a deep breath and rolled over. So far so good. Slowly she sat up and was relieved to find that for the second morning in a row there was no sign of the dreaded morning sickness. It was at that moment that she remembered it was her wedding anniversary.

She turned to look at James, his face burrowed into the pillow, his strong brown hands holding on to it as if it were some sort of comfort blanket. His eyelids, delicate against the weathered brown of his face, flickered rapidly and he took a deep breath. He's dreaming, she thought, and held on to the tenderness that claimed her.

At that moment the alarm went off, the tinkly vibration jerking him into wakefulness. She smiled at him. 'Time to get up. Happy Anniversary.'

He showed a moment of disorientation, then his grin surfaced and he stretched long and hard. 'Happy Anniversary, Mrs Cameron.'

Reaching over he pulled open the drawer in the bedside table and extracted an envelope and a tiny box. The pleasure of anticipation immersed Joanna as she in turn reached for her card and gift. She had considered all kinds of presents but in the end settled for a long playing record of Charlie Parker. Even though the complex musical patterns were not really to her taste, she knew that James would love it.

She opened the card first, aware that he wasn't really much of a one for sentiment. *To My Wife on Our Anniversary.* Inside, the verse had a slightly jokey quality but she knew that it hid his deeper feelings. At her side, he gave a grunt of satisfaction as he in turn opened her card.

Aware that the time was getting on, she did not delay the pleasure of opening her present any longer. The lid to the box clicked open revealing an eternity ring in alternating chips of diamond and sapphire.

She looked at him to express her pleasure, taking it from the box and slipping it on to her finger, touchingly pleased that he had actually remembered her ring size. 'Thanks. It's lovely.'

He grinned, the twitch of his lips playing down the effort to which he had gone. Moments later he expressed his own delight as he began to read the notes on the back of the record sleeve. 'This is great! I haven't got most of these tracks.'

Charlie Parker celebrated their breakfast with them – only cereal, toast and butter because the time really was now racing ahead. As he wiped crumbs from the corner of his mouth, James said, 'I wanted to take you to the Birdcage for a meal tonight but they are closed on Thursdays. I tried a couple of the hotels but they're fully booked so – perhaps we could just go for a drink?'

She nodded just as he added, 'Hell, I'd forgotten you're not drinking these days.'

'It doesn't matter. We can sit and talk.'

Getting up from the table he bent and kissed the top of her head. 'See you later then, Mrs Cameron.'

She raised her face to be kissed properly, greedy for every show of his affection.

'Mmm. What are you trying to do, get me the sack?' He glanced at the clock and moved away. 'See you tonight.'

Joanna lingered at the table, moving her left hand in an undulating motion to catch the full benefit of the ring. This was a good beginning, a good omen for their future.

Now that school had broken up the rest of the day stretched ahead, uncharted. Ideas popped in and out of her head, some practical like ironing and taking down the curtains, others more indulgent like reading a book or taking a wander round the shops. For a wild moment she wondered about buying knitting wool and starting something for the baby but to do that was to make it too real, to let it intrude too soon into their lives. She hadn't even written to tell her mother yet. She felt mean because the news would mean a lot to her, be some compensation after her husband had died a few months before. Joanna tuned in to her own sense of loss. She missed her dad too. He would have made a wonderful grandfather. Later her mother would phone to wish her a happy anniversary. She could tell her then, but no, not today. Not on her wedding anniversary. This was her day and James's.

Making up her mind she decided that she would make a cake, nothing too clever but later she would ice it and stick their wedding cake decorations on it. Just for fun.

Fun. The word took on an ephemeral quality. This feeling of wellbeing, of anticipation could surely never last. In the distance she heard the drone of a tractor and the words drifted into her brain: *Make hay while the sun shines.*

The schools having now broken up it was busier than ever at Fishy Stephensons. The High Street thronged with holiday-makers, Mums and Dads and lots of kids – the children restless in their stripy bathing costumes, the cross over straps leaving white highways along the angry burning of their shoulders, toes rubbed sore by wet sand in their plimsolls. They came in droves, crab red, calomine patched, whining, scolding, sulking, finding fault. Who would have thought they had come to enjoy themselves?

Apart from her day shift in the wet fish department, Mr Stephenson also had Maisie working most evenings in the caff. If anything, this was even worse. People didn't form an orderly queue like they did in the shop. They wandered in in twos and fours and sat anywhere, studied the menus on the tables and then expected to give their orders straight away. In the kitchen there was often a backlog and Maisie dreaded worse than anything the moment when a customer demanded: 'How much longer, miss?'

The caff was busy in bursts, mostly dependent on the cinema opposite. When the first performance finished at about seven, families would pour in, the children tired, over-excited, the parents tetchy, longing for some peace. The next flurry was when the cinema closed around ten, closely followed by throwing out time in the pubs at ten thirty. This was even worse, mostly blokes, some really scary ones with drainpipe trousers and crepe-soled shoes that they called brothel creepers – what was a brothel anyway?

'Give us a coffee, doll.' A solitary youth slid into the seat by the window. He looked Maisie up and down in a way that made her feel hot and uncomfortable. Mr Stephenson didn't like the customers coming in just for drinks, especially not at busy times. She bit her lip, writing the single word on her order pad. Phrases drifted through her mind but she couldn't actually say anything.

'Is that all?' Mrs Bedford behind the counter gave her a disapproving look as she poured hot water from the urn on to the brown powder in a thick white cup. 'Tell him next time to go down that new coffee bar.'

Maisie nodded. She had seen the coffee bar, the Caballero, from the outside. In fact it was difficult to see inside because it was so dark. Not only were the walls some deep, jungle green, but succulent tree-like plants with huge, smooth leaves crowded the window. Risking a peep through the door she had caught a glimpse of round, black-topped tables with wine bottles standing on them holding candles that dripped grease in a molten pattern down the sides. She wondered why they didn't have proper lights.

The lad looked at the coffee and compressed his lips with distaste. 'What's this? Call this coffee?'

Maisie didn't answer. As she went to turn away, he said, 'What time do you finish? Why don't you come down the Caballero with me?'

Maisie pretended not to hear. No one had invited her out before, ever. She didn't know what she was supposed to say and in any case, the idea of going to the coffee bar was as alien as stepping into a Hindu temple, or even the Catholic church that stood on the corner of Conway Street. Those were places for other people, the chosen ones, those who were in the know.

Keeping her eyes averted she was relieved to see a couple coming through the door so that she could give them her attention. At the same time she felt that she had stepped into space, having nothing to support her, for it was only as she turned away that she recognized the couple coming through the door as Mrs Cameron and her husband. They were both talking at the same time and laughing. Mrs Cameron looked really pretty in a straight cut cotton dress which just failed to disguise the gently emerging curve of her stomach.

Maisie's entire body threatened to betray her. James and Joanna had taken a seat, also by the window and were discussing the menu. Maisie looked round hopefully to see if Mrs Bedford behind the counter might come out and serve them, but she didn't. James Cameron put the menu back on the table and looked around. He could not fail to catch Maisie's eye even though she concentrated all her energies on clearing table number five.

'Miss?'

Her face a scarlet mess, she scuttled over. James stretched back in the chair, too long and lanky for its confines. 'Right. Plaice and chips for me and – what are you having, darling?'

For the first time, Mrs Cameron looked up. Her eyes widened

as she recognized Maisie. 'Well, fancy seeing you. How are you getting on?'

Maisie was saved the agony of answering because Joanna turned to James and said, 'This is Maisie, one of my ex-pupils.'

'Maisie.' James Cameron nodded at her and she thought she would die of embarrassment. Close to, he was even better-looking than she had imagined – crisp, light brown curly hair, a lean, rather posh face, vivid blue eyes, the sort of grin that made her hot all over.

Joanna came to her rescue. 'I think I'll have some rock salmon.' To her husband, she added, 'I haven't had that for years.'

As Maisie scribbled the order she tried to force her mouth to ask, 'Bread and Butter?' and, 'Would you like anything to drink?' but nothing came out. Just as they were walking away, James called out, 'And two teas, sweetheart.'

Sweetheart! She scuttled to the counter and wordlessly handed over the order slip. Meanwhile, other couples drifted in and she was in such a tizzy she began to get everything confused. Worst of all was that James and Joanna would see, hear the other customers saying, *Hey, I didn't order this!* and *Have you forgotten us altogether?*

At the table in the window, James and Joanna had eyes only for each other. The lad with the duck's arse haircut had left. In the pub, James had downed two pints of Guinness and Joanna could almost see him unwinding before her eyes. He'd had a hard day. It was very hot and there was a problem with a pumping station that had required him to crawl down a long tunnel to inspect the damage. He had come home hot, tired and dirty and Joanna had suggested that they didn't bother to go out, but he had insisted. 'I said I'd take you out. Don't ever let it be said that James Cameron doesn't keep his promises.'

As James grew more relaxed, Joanna managed to bring the discussion round to the future. Her words came out tentatively, as if they had only just occurred to her. 'Do you think we're going to be able to manage on your money?' She posed it as a possibility, something to consider and over which they had some control, not a harsh yes or no which might curtail everything that they had planned.

James shrugged as if it was no great problem. His shirt sleeves were rolled up above his elbows and the blond hairs on his arms made her want to reach out to smooth them.

'We might have to tighten our belts,' he started, then grinned at her. 'Although probably not, in your case.' To her pleasure, he reached across and rested his hand against her stomach.

'You don't mind about the baby?'

'Of course not.' He was thoughtful for a moment, then he said, 'If you want to go back to work so much, perhaps we could get a nanny.'

She shook her head, her mind filled with the vision of a starched matron, all fuss and orders. 'We couldn't afford it. Anyway, I don't think I'd like someone else telling me what to do with my own child.'

He raised his eyebrows. 'Your child? Don't I have a part in this?' He grinned at her anxious expression, adding, 'Well, it's an option. Let's just wait until the time comes.'

In the café they ate their supper in silence, full of wellbeing. The pumping station apart, it had been a good day. Joanna's cake had been a success and they had polished most of it off with a cup of tea before they came out.

As they finished eating, Joanna turned to watch Maisie carrying an order across the room. She looked overwhelmed by anxiety and Joanna's failure confronted her again.

'See that girl,' she said to James. 'There's something wrong there.'

'How do you mean?'

'I'm not sure, but there's something not right. You wouldn't think so to look at her but she's a bright little thing. She doesn't talk though. I think it might have something to do with her father dying when she was eleven.'

James looked back at his wife. 'Come on, Mrs Cameron. I know you. You can't be responsible for everyone. Anyway, it's time we went home. I'm ready for my bed.'

At the prospect of sleeping with him, the seductive warmth of his body, Joanna put everything else from her inind, but when Maisie came over to take their money, James gave her an extra shilling, just to make Joanna feel better.

Seven

FOR THE FIRST few days after coming out of hospital, Doris contented herself with reading her *Woman's Weekly* and doing a bit of knitting. Of course she was glad to be home, but she couldn't help having a few guilty regrets. The pain apart, being in hospital had been like a holiday, what with having your meals cooked and everything, and no shopping or cleaning or Aunty Rene to worry about.

The prospect of taking up the yoke again settled upon her like widow's weeds, but she consoled herself with the thought that as long as she couldn't walk, she had no choice but to delay the moment.

Still, she couldn't just shirk her duties. Having some three-ply in the cupboard, she started on some socks for Grandad. He wouldn't wear anything except hand-knitted ones in pure wool and then only in grey, which was a pity because Doris would at least have liked to have tried navy blue for a change.

In the past she had had plenty of experience of knitting socks, not only for her father, but for Bert to wear to work, for Maisie to wear to school, and for. . . . She quickly stopped her thoughts from going down that particular path. What was the use? Long ago she had learned one lesson and it paid never to forget it – what's past is past. No good grieving. No good missing someone once they were gone, no matter how unfair their passing, no matter who they were.

In the quiet gloom of the front room with its mustard

coloured wallpaper and dark mushroom paint, and with nothing much to see out of the window except next door's dustbins, there were few distractions. True, occasionally Aunty Rene might wander in for a chat, usually about something that didn't make much sense and which left Doris twitching to get out of the chair and check up on her domain. In even rarer moments Dad poked his head around the door and asked, 'All right?', not bothering to wait for an answer. With only this for entertainment, Doris couldn't entirely stop her thoughts from leading her where she didn't necessarily want them to go.

As the four, fine steel needles clicked mechanically, she had a worry about Maisie. The girl really was working too many hours. She had trouble getting up in the mornings and never seemed to remember to hang the washing out before she went to work. Except for Saturdays, when she finished at one o'clock, she always got home too late to get anything from the shops, and as for sweeping or polishing. . . .

Part of Doris felt an uneasy guilt because the girl was being pushed too hard, but that other part of her, raised with hard work as a sort of clarion call, reasoned that young girls these days had things too easy. When she had been Maisie's age she had worked twelve hours a day, every day, and with no one to do the washing-up like Aunty Rene did now and then, and no one to peel the spuds like Grandad did at this time of the year, because he liked scraping the skin off his new crop and inhaling the aroma of mint boiling in the pan, or sometimes the earthy scent of beetroot simmering away.

'Nice bit of butter and I could eat these spuds by themselves,' he often remarked but Doris knew otherwise. Just try giving him spuds with nothing else and see how he'd carry on!

For once, she broke her own rule and fell to wondering what it would be like if Bert was still alive. There would probably be plenty of arguments, with Bert and Dad both wanting to do things their way. And what would Bert have thought about Maisie now that she was working? She felt the too familiar regret as she replayed the past. Between the unmentionable thing happening and Bert's death, he had taken little interest in anything and certainly not in Maisie – or in Doris come to that. She couldn't help wondering: if he had lived, would he have got over it? Doris had only just finished her monthlies. If he had taken a leaf out of her book and put it all behind him, then they might have had a second chance . . . another baby . . . another son? The fluttering ache surged into pain and she admonished herself. Don't be so silly now, Doris Morris.

Speaking her name, even inside her head, reminded her how ridiculous it sounded. Perhaps she should have hung on, waited for another man with a different surname. The name alone should have warned her. Her thoughts took a step further. Supposing, just supposing Kenneth's wife had died and he had come looking for her, only to learn that she was wed to someone else? She was saved from the awfulness of the prospect because at that moment she realized that she had dropped a stitch, several rows back, and right on the turning of the heel. Drat. Now she'd have to unpick it and her eyes weren't what they used to be.

She put the knitting aside and prepared to have a little doze. All this sleeping! What was the world coming to when she could fall asleep at the drop of a hat – or even the drop of a stitch? The joke amused her. Leaning back, she thought: surely it can't still be the anaesthetic?

As she closed her eyes she prepared the way to a happy dream by wondering what would happen if she wrote to the police station where Kenneth had worked. Uncomfortably she realized that by now he might even be retired, after all, he was a fair bit older than her. Worse, like Bert he might be dead. She refused to countenance the idea. Here, inside her head he would always be very much alive. Anyway, what was she going to say? *Here I am, a widow of forty-eight with sallow skin and gaps in my teeth and the same hairstyle I had all those years ago. How about it?* Some hope.

Doris loved the feeling of drifting into sleep, of giving in to the powerful need that more often than not she had to fight because there was always too much to do. As she succumbed to her dream world, a strange metamorphosis took place. From nowhere, Bert the police constable appeared, her Bert but wearing Kenneth's uniform. '*Are you coming out then, lass?*' He called her lass in the way that Kenneth had done and looked at her in that way which made her feel hot and willing and hungry for something she had never known in real life. '*Come along then, lass, let's go somewhere quiet.*'

She wanted to. How she wanted to. There was an exquisite melting feeling 'down below' and she wanted it assuaged but somehow, her dream-self seemed unable to say 'yes'. Other things kept intruding only she wasn't sure what they were, then with brutal clarity, someone was saying to her, 'It's baby Kenny, he's dying of diphtheria.'

Doris jolted awake, raw and immediate pain absorbing her. Her breath came in ragged gasps and she bit her knuckles to suppress the desire to scream. Like a blind person she struggled to feel the way back to the world of widowhood and her operation and her responsibilities.

She wanted to cry. More, to howl. She wanted to rail against the unfairness of it all. Only the pain from her pinched knuckle drew her back from hysteria, that and the sudden opening of the door as Aunty Rene poked her head into the room.

'All right then, our Doris?'

'Of course I am!' Doris snapped at her, forcing the lid firmly back on her emotions. In control now, she ignored the trembling in her heart. Her voice softened as she said, 'I tell you what though, Aunty. I couldn't half do with a cup of tea – only don't leave the gas on, will you?'

Of all the days at the fish shop, Maisie hated Fridays the most. Although the majority of the population were not Catholics, most of the hotels and guest houses served fish on a Friday as a matter of course, just to be on the safe side. As a result, each Friday the Fish Emporium was frenetically busy.

At about eleven o'clock the people in the queue heard the siren go; the same siren that once warned of imminent enemy planes but now summoned the fire brigade to a call out. Several customers wandered back outside to see in which direction the engine would go and within seconds the High Street was at a standstill as the red tender clanged its way through the traffic.

'Wonder what that is?' Mr Stephenson had just put on a pan of crabs to boil. Maisie kept religiously to the front shop. She couldn't bear the thought of their horrible death. Once she'd sat down in the bath when the water was too hot and she still remembered the shock of pain that had taken her breath away. Poor crabs. Poor shrimps and lobsters.

Outside she was aware of a commotion as somebody barged their way through the crowds, hustling into the shop ahead of several protesting customers. It was Mr Letheridge who lived two doors down from their house. He looked wildly around before he found the person he wanted.

'Maisie Morris? You'd better come home. Now. There's been some sort of explosion at your house!'

Explosion? Maisie looked at Mr Stephenson for confirmation. Surely there must be some mistake? Her boss nodded towards the door. 'Better go on then.'

Mr Letheridge looked at Mr Stephenson and shook his head solemnly. 'What a mess.'

Maisie left the shop in a daze. She wanted to ask what had happened but couldn't find the words.

As they rounded the corner into West Street she was confronted with chaos. Halfway down the road, at about the place where their house stood, a fire engine was parked outside. Next to it was an ambulance and across the road, a police car. The entrance to the house was barricaded by sightseers.

'Here she is.' Mr Letheridge wheezed as he pushed Maisie into the care of a policeman.

'Come along, young lady. This your house?'

Maisie nodded, gazing in disbelief at the mess.

'What's your name and address?'

Maisie mumbled in response.

'Speak up.' She stumbled through the information again.

'Right. You'd best come with me.'

Maisie now had an unobstructed view. She couldn't believe what she saw. It was just like the newsreels of when the bombs had dropped. Number twenty-nine looked as if it had scored a direct hit. The front was demolished and upstairs, in what was the room she shared with Mum, the double bed tilted crazily over the edge of the floor, threatening to drop into the garden below.

Where was Mum? She looked at the policeman hoping for an explanation. He did not meet her eyes.

'Come along now, love. We'll sort it all out when we get to the station.'

Dead. The word stabbed into Maisie, tearing open that old wound with a vicious, ripping twist. It took all her willpower to deny the pain. She didn't look at the police lady. She couldn't.

The last time, it had been her dad, Mum announcing it as if it was something she had washed her hands of. 'Your father's gone. I don't think he even really tried. The doctor says it was the consumption but I think he'd lost the will to live.' Without exactly saying so, Mum's words laid the blame firmly at Maisie's door, reminding her that because of what she had done in the past, the *terrible thing,* that she had sentenced Dad to die. That's what they had hinted at, the time before, when the *terrible thing* had happened. 'I'm afraid he's passed on. We did everything we could, but in the circumstances. . . .'

Dead. Gone. Passed on. Gone to sleep. With Jesus. Passed over. Gone to a better place. Maisie recited the euphemisms to herself like a liturgy, as if their very rhythm might wash away the meaning. Meanwhile, someone was gently tugging at her sleeve.

'Come along then. We won't ask you to identify the bodies. Your neighbour has agreed to do that, but we do need to ask you some questions.'

Afterwards Maisie couldn't remember what they were. Things to do with where she was at the time of the explosion and how had they seemed when she left home – Mum and Grandad and Aunty Rene. In that moment she realized that she should have been more attentive. There must have been something that she should have done. Or not done?

'Try not to take it to heart.' To her surprise, Doctor Patterson came into the room, just like last time. He smiled at her with a sort of benign yet sad expression. In spite of his attempts at kindness she wondered if he was making the same connection, about Dad, about the time before.

To the policewoman he said, 'They've moved them to the morgue. The experts have gone round to the house, but I don't think there's much doubt.' Maisie clutched at his last words. Was there some doubt? Some mistake? Perhaps they weren't dead. Not all of them. Not Grandad. Not Mum. In that moment she knew that it was her fault. She should have warned them about Aunty Rene. Maisie had been in charge. It was her responsibility to tell Mum that Aunty Rene was getting worse, that she couldn't find the light switch – or remember to switch off the gas? A gas explosion they said. Aunty Rene?

'Come along.' The policewoman tugged at her sleeve again, indicating that she should get up. 'Mr Letheridge has very kindly agreed that you can spend the night with him and his wife.'

Maisie began to shiver. The thought of returning to their road, of staying in the house next to the ruins of her life began to drag her under. She tried to say something but no words came out. Inside her head a voice reminded her: 'Well it's your fault. What else can you expect? This is your punishment, to stay next door and to know.' Defeated, Maisie followed the officer outside.

Joanna heard about the explosion the following morning when she went to buy a paper. From habit each week she bought the *Clarion* in the hope that it might offer something to interest her. In her darker moments she looked to it to provide something more potent, perhaps hope.

The elation of the evening before had evaporated overnight. As the alarm went off she awoke to a feeling of oppression which deepened as the bedroom door clicked shut behind James, with his parting words, 'We've got an emergency on at the moment so don't start worrying if I'm really late.'

Now that she was no longer at work the sense of living in an alien place grew daily stronger. Although she had been on friendly terms with the other teachers at Robert Hooke Secondary, there were none of them with whom she wanted to spend time outside of work. Besides, once away from school, she had wanted only to share her spare moments with James. Now it was different. From eight in the morning until six each evening he was away from home. Tonight it would be even longer. There were only so many things that she could do to keep herself amused. It was no good. She wasn't cut out to be a housewife. With a sense of failure she admitted to herself that she longed for company, for stimulation, even for a good cause to occupy her time. Each week she scanned the pages of the *Clarion* but reports about the WI, news of gardening clubs and amateur theatricals all left her cold.

'Terrible, wasn't it, what happened yesterday?' Her gloomy preoccupation was interrupted by the proprietor of the newsagent and tobacconists.

'What was that?' Joanna didn't enjoy their conversations. Grubby, overweight, his stale smell wafted like a rain cloud, emptying its unwelcome outpourings under her nose. Only lethargy prevented her from walking to the other end of the street and a more welcoming shop. The pewter eyes in Bob Morgan's grey face were hard, malicious, prying.

'Haven't you heard? About that explosion down in West Street? Three people killed.'

'That's terrible.' She tried to hand over a shilling but he would not be put off so easily.

'I'm not really surprised. That old woman they got living there is proper daft. Runs in the family if you ask me, daft old woman, daft girl and the mother not up to much.'

'Well, I've got to go.' Joanna pointedly picked up the *Clarion* and pushed the money across the counter but Bob Morgan was in full flow.

'Down at the fish shop I was when it happened. We all heard it. Someone came to fetch the girl. Ran like a lunatic up the road she did. Phil Harris was actually delivering letters in the street when it happened. Nothing anyone could do. They took the girl to the police station. Don't know what will happen to her. No other relatives that I know of.'

'What girl?' Joanna was aware of her increased heart rate.

'That Morris girl.'

'Maisie?'

'Maisie, Daisy, I don't know what you—'

Joanna didn't wait to hear any more. Pocketing her money and leaving the paper on the counter, she dashed from the shop. Outside she hesitated, light and dark undulating as she considered the implications. Making up her mind she turned left and headed for the police station.

At the desk she stopped to get her breath back, acknowledging that those few extra pounds were already beginning to tell. What would it be like in a few more months? As the desk sergeant came to the counter she tried to compose herself.

'I've come about yesterday's explosion.'

'You know something about it?'

The policeman, taller than her by at least a foot, was big, bulbous. He looked exceedingly unfit. Joanna couldn't keep her eyes away from the belt of his tunic which left a deep indentation where once his waist might have been. She thought that anyone trying to make a getaway shouldn't have much trouble in eluding capture.

Aloud, she said, 'I'm more concerned about Maisie, Maisie Morris. She was my pupil at Robert Hooke Secondary. I – I don't think she has any other family.' Even as she spoke Joanna had the nasty feeling that she was entering a rat's cage, easy to get into but almost impossible to get out of. What was she going to say? Or do? She hadn't thought this through. Meanwhile, the big man was transferring her to a policewoman who was familiar with the details.

'What exactly was it you wanted?' The woman seemed unimpressed by her stumbled explanation.

'I just wondered what was going to happen to Maisie, if I could help in any way.' The policewoman looked as if she could easily have been cast as a gaoler in a B movie. She thrust out her lower lip as if it helped her to concentrate.

'A neighbour took her in last night.'

It sounded like the end of the conversation. Joanna hesitated. She almost acquiesced, let herself believe that as long as someone was picking up the pieces then her worries were assuaged. Instead, she said, 'What about the future?'

The woman hunched her shoulders in a 'who knows' gesture. 'How old is she? Nearly sixteen? Too old for adoption. I expect they'll think of something. A live-in job would probably be best.'

Joanna didn't know who 'they' were but she had a troubled vision of the beadle in *Oliver Twist*. She heard herself say, 'She could come and stay with me. For the time being.'

Again the policewoman shrugged, leaving Maisie's future to the fates. She said, 'She's at twenty-five West Street if you want to find her.' As Joanna turned away, she added, 'If you do take her in, make sure to leave her address so that we know where to find her.'

'It will only be for a few days, just until they decide what to do with her.' Joanna looked to James for his response. She knew that he was tired, not wanting to think about anything that required a decision. She felt that she was asking him an enormous favour. What she couldn't explain was how much it mattered to her.

His brow furrowed and his lips pulled back in a closed grimace. She held her breath, waiting for him to speak.

'Does that mean she'll have to have the baby's room?'

'It isn't the baby's room. Not yet. You haven't even begun to decorate it.'

He shrugged. 'I was thinking of starting on it this weekend.'

Sensing her disbelief, he added, 'But of course I don't mind. The poor kid must go somewhere I suppose. Are you sure there aren't any relatives?'

'None. I've made enquiries.'

'Then so be it.'

Joanna felt absurdly grateful to him, especially as she had already visited the neighbours and agreed to relieve them of their responsibility. Maisie hadn't been there when she called. Mrs Letheridge had taken her to the florist to choose a wreath – a bit premature seeing that there would be all the business of death certificates and autopsies and probably a coroner's inquest. Three funerals. How would the girl cope? Joanna determined to talk to her at length about what had happened, not from a religious standpoint but as something inevitable, on the lines that death comes to us all. It was important that Maisie didn't feel in any way to blame.

At tea time Maisie arrived empty handed. It seemed that the front of the house had been boarded up and no one had had the foresight to allow her to collect at least a change of clothes.

She looked numbed, as if her eyes had settled upon some deep, inner vision and were no longer able to focus on the world outside.

'Come along in.' Joanna's heart went out to her. First her Dad and now this, this triple tragedy.

Maisie came cautiously inside, looking around as if she expected an ambush. She didn't say anything and Joanna ushered her to the sofa then went to make tea.

'Sugar?'

A single nod of the head. Perhaps the shock had rendered her totally speechless.

Joanna took a deep breath. 'Maisie, I'm really sorry about what's happened. I want you to know that you can stay here as long as you need to.' When there was no response, she added, 'About the funeral. There'll have to be an inquest first, to find out what happened. You might have to go and tell what you know.'

A series of expressions flitted across the girl's face, an internal struggle that seemed to overwhelm her. Finally, she whispered, 'It wasn't me.'

Joanna reached out to touch her arm. 'Of course it wasn't. Nobody thinks that it was. Besides, you were at work.' She waited but Maisie continued to gaze in upon herself.

As Joanna handed her the cup of tea Maisie gripped the saucer until it started to shake, splashing tea on to her lap. She seemed oblivious. As Joanna took the cup from her, she mumbled, 'It was Aunty Rene.'

Joanna frowned. Maisie continued to tremble, apparently immersed in a one-sided argument. 'I bet she turned the gas on.'

'Had she done it before?'

Maisie jerked her head around and stared in alarm as if she

had been unaware that she had spoken out loud. Her face coloured. Lowering her head so that her words were directed towards her chest, she said, 'She's been funny for ages.'

'Do you want to talk about it?'

A shrug.

'You might feel better if you do.'

'What about the chickens?' The girl looked suddenly panic-stricken.

'I don't know.'

'Can they come here?' Her normally impassive face was imploring.

Joanna was silent. What could she say? James wouldn't welcome a flock of birds scratching up his newly planted seedlings. Aloud, she said, 'If they are all right, we'll ask the neighbours to feed them.'

Maisie was worryingly biddable. Joanna made her scrambled eggs which she ate in silence, then plonked her in front of the television which she fixed with a dog-like stare as if she was expected to guard it. At bedtime she downed a cup of cocoa, spent about five minutes in the bathroom and came out wearing an old pair of Joanna's pyjamas that she had had when first she went to college. All the time Joanna felt that she was in the presence of a small, wild animal that wanted only to dash back to its burrow.

'James and I are in the room across the hall.' As she spoke, Joanna realized how intrusive it would be having someone sleeping so close. No energetic love making, no Saturday morning lie-ins. She said, 'If you want to, you can leave your door ajar. And keep the light on. Is there anything else you'd like?'

Maisie shook her head.

'Well, good night, then. You know where to find me if you want me.'

Downstairs, James had switched off the television and put on one of his jazz LPs. Joanna bit back the urge to ask him to turn it down.

'I hope she isn't going to just sit there every night,' he observed.

'She's in a state of shock.' Joanna rushed to her defence, but even as she spoke, she had a vision of Maisie there, between them on the sofa, an ever-present intruder into their comfortable privacy. She fought down the thought as unworthy. One day soon, they would make alternative arrangements.

Maisie stood with her toes embedded in the pile of the bedroom carpet, savouring the pleasure of its yielding softness beneath her feet. It was good here. Amazing. What with the telly and a proper bathroom and everything. Wouldn't Mum have liked it?

The thought of her mother brought the tidal wave of shock at what had happened, pressing against the dam of her chest. The dam held. She swallowed down any grief, wandering around the room, picking up ornaments and toiletries on the dressing table.

The bed looked wonderful. New. The mattress was flat and square, not old and lumpy like the ones at home. Home. In place of the familiar cottage she had known all her life, in her mind's eye she saw the shattered walls, the iron bedstead about to make a suicidal leap for the garden.

It wasn't my fault. Maisie repeated the words over and again as she turned back the pink cotton sheet and slid between the covers. *It wasn't my fault. Not this time.* She tried to be fair, to go over again everything that had happened recently to see if she was to blame, but she couldn't have known, could she? The trouble was, she had said the wrong thing. When Mum had asked about Aunty Rene, she hadn't told the truth. In future, it would be better to say nothing then she couldn't be blamed.

She wondered what would happen to grandad's onions. He had been going to lift them that weekend and lay them out to dry on some old sheets of corrugated iron that came from the bomb site at the bottom of the road. Perhaps the policemen would take them home.

As she curled up small, twisting a strand of hair between her fingers, a terrible, guilty confession squeezed its way into her mind. *I like it here, better than at home.*

Eight

FOR MAISIE, THE next few weeks were crammed with new experiences. At night, unable to sleep, she lay in the lighted bedroom with the door ajar and tried to escape from her darker thoughts by cataloguing the luxuries around her.

For a start, in the Camerons' cottage there was the telly. Every evening she watched it from seven o'clock until James said, 'Shouldn't you be getting to bed?' Joanna always added, 'You have got to get up in the morning.' Although she would rather stay and watch the programme to the very end, Maisie did as they suggested, for after all, they were only being thoughtful.

Then there was the bathroom, a separate room where you could have hot water whenever you wanted it and lie in the white porcelain bath with no one coming in. Matching dressing gowns hung behind the bathroom door – *bath robes* James and Joanna called them. At West Street, only Grandad had a dressing gown. Maisie didn't know where it had come from but it was made of a scratchy, woollen plaid and had twisted binding around the collar and a belt like a curtain loop. Grandad only wore it on bath nights, to save having to get dressed again. When Mum had gone into hospital she had had to take a cardigan.

Her mind drifted to the grey wall-to-wall carpets that covered the kitchen floor, with strange black and red designs all over it, so new and modern. James and Joanna didn't call it the kitchen though, but the lounge. There was such a lot to get used to. In the lounge, apart from the telly, there was Mr Cameron's radiogram and all his records, weird music that she had never heard before and couldn't begin to make a tune out of although she reasoned that if he liked it then it must be good.

Her mind ranged over the cottage: a telephone, an electric stove, hot water in the scullery – no, that was the kitchen. Really, it was all smashing.

Her brain still frenetically active, Maisie's thoughts wandered to the daily routine of riding in James's car, sitting next to him in the front seat and being taken right into work, with everybody seeing her getting out outside of the fish shop.

'You might as well drop her off,' Joanna had said. 'After all, you start at the same time.'

James had opened his mouth to say something, then thought better of it. Maisie didn't pursue it. All that mattered was that every morning he drove her to work. With an unfamiliar trickle of pleasure, she thought: Perhaps the people watching will think he's my husband! Of course, in the real world, such a thing would be impossible, but inside her head she could be whoever she liked.

Having only her old school uniform which she had been wearing on that fateful Friday, Joanna gave her a skirt and blouse to wear to work. The skirt was made of a huge circle of material with flowers on it and a belt at the waist, while the blouse had puffy sleeves trimmed with lace – and all to wear to work! It was almost like being a film star. Joanna had given her other things too, a dress in crisp blue polka dot cotton with a lace collar, a pink jumper which had a tiny hole under the arm, and a straight skirt with a pleat at the back because, as Joanna said, with her bulge she would never get into it.

In the darkness, Maisie flushed at the reference to her ex-teacher's condition and what must have gone on to bring it about. She wondered what it must be like to have a man like James in love with you and doing 'that' to you every night. Or was it every night? She tried to hear above the throb of her pulse but there was no sound from across the corridor.

She fell to wondering how people ever got round to such an

activity. It was all right in the films, with beautiful women and handsome men, with magic in the air, provocation, raw passion, but if you transferred that to ordinary people, like her mum and dad, how did they manage to be blind to each other's physical shortcomings? With James and Joanna it was different because they were both good looking, but even they succumbed to ordinary things like catching colds and burping. It was all a mystery.

As if to register their confusion, her thoughts turned to the events of the past few weeks. On the black side there had been the inquest, having to stand up in front of all those people like she was in the dock or something. They had asked her lots of questions but she hadn't been able to say anything. Nothing. In the end, the man in the suit said, 'You had better stand down.' A wave of murmured sympathy enveloped the court: *Poor thing. Such a pity. What a shame.*

She rolled over and crumpled the sheet to her chest sticking her thumb into her mouth, something she hadn't done since infants' school but somehow it was becoming a habit again.

She didn't want to think about what had happened next, but in spite of herself, the funerals began to play themselves out before her eyes like a newsreel. Unlike Joanna's television there wasn't a knob she could twist to turn it off.

The three ceremonies had been held together followed by burials at St Matthew's. Mum and Grandad hadn't been church-goers but past family history had dictated where the ceremony should take place, for already Grandma and Dad had taken their places among the neat humps in the churchyard. *He* was there too, isolated in a corner along with all the other children, four rows along and three graves in, with an angel sitting on top of him and a carved inscription – *Gone to Heaven.* She ought to know, she had been dragged there often enough by Mum. 'Come along, young lady, it's time to go and see your brother.' Time to go through the weekly routine of paying penance, of being found guilty once more. No chance to admit that she didn't want to go there, to show her true colours by admitting that she was someone heartless and secretly unrepentant, wanting to put it all behind her and get on with life. No chance of that now, not after the accident.

Maisie could see it all, the regular layout of the mossy paths in the cemetery – still green in contrast to the rest of the yellowing, thirsty grass – etching their way in a grid between rows of white marble tombstones. Three newly-excavated mounds stood like rotten teeth awaiting extraction. It had been complicated by the fact that Grandad had a plot reserved next to Grandma and Mum had to be laid to rest with Dad, whereas Aunty Rene had a place to herself across the pathway. Thank goodness Joanna had come with her to show her what to do.

Maisie struggled to force her thoughts away. She wouldn't think about that day. Not ever. Firmly she pushed the memories into that casket of experiences that lurked somewhere in the labyrinth of her brain. Securely she locked the lid and for good measure, added a notice reading *Do Not Enter.*

With a sigh she turned on to her other side, nestling into the pillow. Here at least she was safe.

She thought about the vicar coming to the house and trying to be nice to her. She wasn't daft. The vicar didn't really care about what had happened. It was just his job to pretend that he did. In any case, Joanna didn't like him. She made that much plain when she opened the door. She wasn't rude or anything but Maisie knew that she didn't believe in the Bible and all that lark. Anyway, it was no good him going on like that about God's will. Maisie'd found out about that long ago. If it was really true, then . . . quickly she marshalled her thoughts away from that too familiar and dangerous mineshaft. *Do Not Enter.*

At work it was different now though, all the customers saying how sorry they were and everything. Faced with all this attention she was too overwhelmed to say anything. She ought to, really. '*Come on, our Maisie, say thank you, nicely. Don't be so rude.*' Mum's voice was a whisper away. In the fish shop on her first day back at work, she overheard Mrs Harrison, cashing in on the notoriety the accident had caused and appointing herself as Maisie's spokesman.

'Such a shame. Her whole family wiped out. Just like that. Of course you can't expect anything else from the girl. Struck dumb she is. It's the grief.'

Faced with the freedom not to have to speak, Maisie silently revelled in the attention. She had never felt so important.

She rolled on to her back gazing at the smooth uniformity of the ceiling, finding no bumps or cracks to make into funny pictures. In a strange way, everything had been smashing really, until the day that was when the policeman came to say that they were going to clear the house, and did she want to go round and take anything that was hers, and anything of her Mum's that she would like to keep. The, rest, apparently, was going to the Salvation Army.

Once again, James took her in the car. Joanna had wanted to come with her too but she kept being sick again so she couldn't. Guiltily, Maisie felt the slightest bit pleased because she could have James to herself, not that she ever said anything to him, but often he would talk away as if she was a grown up, one of his friends, telling her amusing things that had happened at work – just like he told Joanna. As they drew up outside, he said, 'I'll wait for you here. Give me a call when you're ready and I'll help you carry out whatever you want.'

Taking a deep breath, Maisie turned away from the car and opened the garden gate. Everything looked the same as it had always done, until she looked up the garden path, and there was the house, all forlorn and boarded up. The police lady was there to meet her, her face pink and damp, cocooned as she was in her uniform. She came down the path carrying a key to the padlock that held the door shut. Like a gaoler she unlocked the door and pushed it open, and hustled Maisie inside with the words, 'Take your time. You can have whatever you want.' Even as she spoke she craned her neck to see past Maisie into the gloom. It dawned on Maisie that perhaps when she gone, the woman too would take whatever she wanted.

As she entered the hallway, Maisie's past began to draw her down, tugging at her like the undercurrent of the turning tide. She took a deep breath to calm herself. The house had its own, peculiar smell, still fighting for domination above the more recent odours – the singed paintwork, the scorched moquette of the fireside chair, the rotting remains from the exploding tins of corned beef, a spilled can of distemper. Maisie froze, afraid that if she ventured any further she would be sucked under by the memories.

Apart from the dust (Mum wouldn't like that), and the extra light streaming in from upstairs where the roof had partly gone, the hallway looked exactly the same as it always had done, what with the brown and yellow pattern on the hall runner, the diamonds on the wallpaper going on up the stairs – above the wainscot that was – the bottom half had been painted brown by Dad before he died. Maisie frowned. Dad had done a lot of decorating in that last year. She could almost see him, brush in hand, stopping frequently, his chest heaving like a leaking bellows, broken only by long, remorseless bursts of coughing. Had he known that he was dying? Was that what they meant about setting your house in order? The idea did not tie in with Mum's words, that he had given up and lost the will to live.

Quickly Maisie opened the sitting room door to get away from the ghosts, but she was confronted with another familiarity. Amazingly in here the explosion had hardly disturbed anything. The wooden clock was still on the mantelpiece (stopped now of course because no one had wound it up), guarded on each side by the china dogs that had been Grandma Stark's and now, presumably were hers although she didn't know what she was going to do with them. They would look out of place in her room at Mrs Cameron's – Joanna's.

She wandered around picking things up and putting them down again, at a loss as to what she was supposed to do. In the alcove to the left of the fireplace was a bookshelf on which stood twelve volumes of *The Wonderland of Knowledge* that Dad had got by saving up coupons in his newspaper. Many a winter evening she had taken down a volume and turned the pages, packed with pictures and diagrams. A whole life was between those covers. They told you everything you wanted to know, about everything.

Maisie hadn't really thought about Dad for ages. Certainly not since before the explosion but now she realized how much of him was still present in the house. She wondered: were Mum and Grandad and Aunty Rene up there with him now? She glanced towards the ceiling. Were they all watching her? '*You be careful with those dogs, our Maisie. Your Grannie's, they were.*' Perhaps Grannie was there too. Wouldn't they have a lot to talk about!

Stepping back towards the door, she visualized the family reunion. The sudden gloom began to stifle her. If that was true then he'd be there too, wouldn't he? She couldn't form his name. No one had called him by name for the past ten years. She turned her eyes to the alcove opposite, the one with the books, and with a shock realized that his picture had fallen off the wall. Did he still look the same as he did in the picture, or did you carry on growing up when you were in Heaven? If that was the case, he'd be big now, nearly twelve. She clutched at the front of her blouse to contain her thoughts. Wouldn't Mum be glad to see him? And Dad? What would he tell them, about that day? The lid on the casket of her emotions tried to push itself open. *Not my fault. It wasn't my fault!*

She scurried through into the kitchen, leaving her ghosts behind her and sat for a while in Dad's chair, trying to immerse herself in it so that when she left she would carry something of it away, like an invisible skin. At first it did not occur to her that she might be entitled to any of the bigger items and when it did, she questioned where would she put them? Gradually the darkness in her mind receded.

In the scullery she looked around at all the familiar things; the gas stove still amazingly intact, the deep, white, pitted sink where Mum had washed and peeled and scrubbed. Opening the cupboard door she found that most of the crockery had survived the impact. For ages she stared at the pattern on the tea set, blue blobs edging the round white plates and saucers, crazed by immersion into too-hot water, the bread and butter plate with its garish red and yellow parrots that Mum – in an uncharacteristic moment of rashness – had bought in the hardware store one Saturday. Embarrassed, she took the plate out and wandered back with it to the bottom of the stairs. Some chestnut fencing had been stretched across the bottom of the staircase to stop anyone from going up but two old brown suitcases stood against the wall. When she opened them, it seemed that the clothes from her bedroom had been packed for her. Her hand located something solid inside the second case – her Rupert the Bear. She pulled him out and for a moment, cuddled him as one had done when she was little. Back then she had told him all her secrets, secure in the knowledge that he wouldn't tell anyone else. He had been the one she had turned to when *the terrible thing* had happened. Having him back was a comfort and yet remembering her new persona, she scolded herself. You can't talk to a teddy bear. Not at your age. Resolutely she pushed him back inside the suitcase and slipped the plate in on top of him.

Her head still brimming with electric jolts of remembrance, she went to the front door and opened it, standing awkwardly in front of the policewoman who in turn called James to come and help her.

'Is this all you're taking?' He glanced through the door into the sitting room. 'What about the ornaments? Wouldn't you like to keep something as a souvenir?'

Maisie shook her head. How could she explain? They were old-fashioned. She had done with this life. Back there was only loneliness. Guilt. Pain. In future she wanted a life like the Camerons, modern and full of hope.

'How much longer is she going to stay?'

James was home early from work, for once arriving before Maisie got back from the fish shop. It was Friday evening and the weekend stretched ahead, marred by the knowledge that unless the girl could be persuaded to go to the cinema or the library or out for a walk they would not have a moment of privacy.

In response, Joanna shrugged. It was a real dilemma. Although she shared his feelings, she felt angry with James for mentioning it. Inwardly she blamed herself for her act of charity. Maisie seemed to be so at home that she might stay forever.

Without replying, she put the kettle on to make some coffee. In some ways Maisie was the perfect lodger. Without being asked she washed the dishes and hoovered everywhere except their bedroom. She didn't drop towels in the bathroom or leave her clothes lying on the floor. She didn't make a noise at night or bring strangers home. Religiously she paid Joanna thirty shillings every Saturday for her keep, bringing in a soggy parcel of fish as a bonus. Yes, she was a perfect lodger – that was if you wanted a lodger, which they didn't.

'I'll speak to her.' Her chest tightened at the prospect. What was she to say? 'Look Maisie, we don't want you here any more'? Perhaps she could have a word with the welfare people. They might have some suggestions. Perhaps there was a hostel or something where she could go.

When Maisie walked in five minutes later, hanging her coat neatly behind the door, James pointedly left the room.

Maisie turned and held out a flat square package. It was obvious that it was a record. 'For me?' She took it and slipped it from the bag. The centre of the black disk announced the work and the artiste: *Mr Wonderful*, sung by Peggy Lee.

'Why, thank you, Maisie.' Joanna felt a moment of amusement, guessing that this was dedicated to James rather than herself. She couldn't fail to notice the adoration on the girl's face. Walking to the radiogram, she lifted the lid and placed it on the turntable, flicking a knob. Moments later the melodic introduction filled the air.

Maisie's face turned a becoming red as the song extolled the magic of the singer's man.

As the record clicked to a halt, Joanna hovered uncomfortably. This unsolicited gift made her task the more difficult. She asked, 'Had a good day at work?'

Maisie nodded, lining her shoes up neatly next to the hall stand. Joanna fished frantically for something else to say. 'How is the job going then? Do you still like it?'

The answering shrug implied that it was all right.

Drawing in a breath, Joanna said, 'Have you thought about what you're going to do? In the future? I wondered if you'd thought about going away – you know, doing some training or something.'

She was met with a blank stare. Clearly the subtlety of her hint wasn't working. Again she drew in her breath. 'It's not that we don't want you here or anything, but – well, we do need to get the bedroom ready for when the baby comes.'

She hated herself the moment she said it. The girl's face tightened as the truth dawned on her and quickly Joanna added, 'Don't think we want to rush you away. I just thought that you might like to be doing something different from working at the fish shop. Perhaps something where you could live in?'

Maisie stared at the ground, a small girl, chastened, her world disintegrating around her. Joanna's stomach constricted with remorse. She stood up and squeezed Maisie's shoulder. 'Just forget that I said anything. If ever you want to, you let me know if you feel you would like to move on. Otherwise. . . .' She was lost for the right words.

In silence, Maisie picked up her handbag and slipped past her, climbing the stairs to her room.

'Damn it.' Joanna knew she had handled it badly.

'Well?' James came back into the room carrying a flat paper bag. From its shape Joanna knew that he too had bought a new record. As he went to the radiogram and lifted the arm, he said, 'What's this?'

'A present from Maisie. I think it's meant for you.' He gave a snort of amusement. She said, 'The girl doesn't want to go. We can't make her. We can't just throw her out.'

James didn't reply but there was something prickly about his movements that filled Joanna with panic. Just supposing. Might he, could he get so fed up with the situation that he would be the one to leave? They hadn't made love for weeks. Other men left for less reason than that. Quickly she moved across to him and slipped her arms about his shoulders. Already a conflict was beginning to rage in her soul. 'Don't worry,' she said. 'I'll make sure that something is settled before the end of the month.'

PART TWO

Nine

George Draper always relied on the cockerels to rouse him but as he started awake on Sunday morning, he immediately realized that he had overslept. His head felt like a scarecrow's: stuffed with straw. Suppressing his first instinct to leap out of bed, he took a deep breath and let the shock of his sudden awakening trickle through him then drain away like dammed water. The air felt hostile and he pulled the eiderdown up around his ears, squinting at the clock.

It was 6 a.m. He was already half an hour later than usual. There, what did a few more minutes really matter? Closing his eyes he listened to the ticking moments with the pleasure of a man who has just discovered some half crowns amongst a handful of pennies. Hazily he recalled that he had heard the first crow but it had been too early to get up. He must have fallen back to sleep. The cock birds didn't know about the clocks going back. Summer time was over. Unlike him, they went on in their own sweet way.

Even as he thought about it he heard the bird crow again. That was the old feller. A fine cock he'd been in his time, chest puffed out like a general and feathers fit to grace a prince. There was an answering call, one of the youngsters staking out his territory. George thought: the old boy has had his day really, p'raps it's time for the pot. It was a shame but everything comes to the end of the line and he couldn't afford to carry any passengers through the winter. A chill that came not from the autumn weather touched him.

George wriggled down in the bed, stealing a few more seconds of warmth. It wouldn't hurt to get up late this once. Neither Harry nor Jim, the hired hands, were coming in this Sunday so no one would be any the wiser. As he allowed himself to experience the decadence of lying abed, a ripple of anxiety threatened him. He didn't want anyone to think that he was losing his grip. A fierce argument raged in his head. Dammit. None of the livestock were shut up so why shouldn't he get up late if he wanted to? He was the gaffer. It was up to him what he did – except that if you changed the pattern of a lifetime someone was bound to think that something was up. He wasn't sure which part of himself was the winner – or loser – so he called the debate a draw.

Although it helped to have lighter mornings in the winter, interfering with the clock threw everything out of gear. He really must be getting old. The only other times he hadn't felt inclined to get out of bed was when he was a young man, in his prime, with Rose soft and yielding beside him. Now he who had been getting up at five o'clock in the summer mornings for as long as he could remember, sensed a different weakness of the flesh begin to consume him.

Everything lay heavy upon him. Winter was coming and with it a whole new set of problems. Every year it seemed to get harder. Lambing, ploughing, milk yields, egg quotas, calving, sowing, reaping, it just went on and on. A visual calendar unfolded as the year flickered through his mind. What with the government pushing you all the time to produce more, he couldn't see how it was going to end.

George turned over and allowed himself five more minutes. After all, he thought again, it was Sunday. His mind wandered back to the farm. Much of the pleasure had gone out of it these days, not that he would – or could – do anything else. It was his life and his father's before him. A pity they no longer had a son to carry on the tradition. The thought had caught him unawares and acid burned in his chest. Water under the bridge they said, but it wasn't. The hurt still lurked there, deep as a well. He felt its too familiar pain, Ned being taken like that, right at the end of the war.

Since then he'd never quite got his heart back, never been able to pursue things like he had before when there had been someone to hand it on to. Now he supposed it would go to his nephew, Ian. Not a bad lad, Ian, but not like your own son. He remembered then that his nephew would be arriving in a couple of weeks, coming to start work. His thoughts soured. The lad had been to take some fancy college course. George knew he'd arrive full of half-baked ideas when anyone with any sense knew that you could only learn a job like farming by being on the land.

His thoughts threatened to grow bitter so he distracted himself with itemizing all the things he had to do this morning; but his mind wandered again. Since the war there were things going on in the farming world, under the surface, difficult to put your finger on, but the world was definitely changing. All this form filling wore him down. Take this new Egg Marketing Board. You couldn't even sell your eggs to who you wanted to now. They demanded them all and set the price. Government gone mad, it was. In spite of himself he wondered if young Ian had done something about form filling on his fancy course.

George squinted at the crack in the curtains where a shaft of grey light reached the end of the bed. With a sigh he rubbed the sleep from his eyes and stretched, easing himself up. 'Time to wake up, Mother.'

At his side, his wife Rose pulled herself up with a little grunt and dangled her legs over the side of the bed, rubbing her knees to ease the stiffness. 'It's late. Why didn't you wake me?'

He stared with rueful tenderness at the plump outline of her shoulders in the winceyette nightgown. 'Legs bad old girl?' he asked.

'They're playing me up something rotten.'

For a boyish moment he wondered what she would do if he reached over and pulled her back to bed – *Get off, you daft bugger!* It would be good to capture the spontaneity again but he was afraid he would look foolish so he gave her rump a regretful, comforting pat, then slipping out of bed he followed her example and began to dress.

There was a definite chill in the air and the lino struck cold against his feet. Soon it would be time to wear his long johns out. Rose was struggling with her suspenders. Her joints were bad, especially in the morning. Proper misshapen her fingers were. She'd even had to take her wedding ring off. Usually she liked to get up first so that she didn't have to rush.

Downstairs, George cleaned out and stoked the range while Rose filled the kettle for a cuppa. He could see that she had difficulty in lifting it. He thought to himself: I'm going to have to do something about this. Perhaps we should get a girl in to help. Rose wouldn't like it, mind. She was used to ruling over her own kitchen, but come winter, what with the extra work, what with the lambing and like, she could do with some help. A good strong lass, that's what it needed, someone sensible. His thoughts returned to Ian's imminent arrival which would mean extra washing and cooking. His resolve hardened. He didn't know of anyone off hand but he would ask around. As his collie dog Gypsy pushed her nose into his hand, put out by his late arrival and asking for his breakfast, he made up his mind. He wouldn't say anything to Rose, just stick an ad in the *Clarion* and see what came up.

Joanna lingered over breakfast. She felt lazy, a sleepy lethargy that stretched right through her limbs, but accompanied by a sense of wellbeing. Last night, in spite of their visitor, in spite of the half-open door, she had instigated a particularly pleasurable session of love making. At first James had been hesitant and she had sensed his grievance but it didn't take long to win him round, and in spite of the fact that they had taken care not to be too noisy, they had both gushed out the tensions that had been mounting over the past weeks.

James was absorbed in the *Manchester Guardian* and Joanna flicked idly through the *Clarion.* She turned to the entertainments column, wondering what film was on at the Regal. Perhaps they could persuade Maisie to go that evening and have a quiet time to themselves.

As she turned the pages, her eye caught the *Situations Vacant* heading. Folding back the paper she scanned the list. 'Listen!' She looked across at James to get his attention.

Wanted, reliable girl to help with house and farm work. Must be honest and hard working and willing to live in. Fair wages offered.

James raised his eyebrow questioningly. 'You thinking of moving out?'

She grinned. 'I meant Maisie, silly. She said she wanted to work on a farm. This sounds just the job.'

He shrugged. Clearly last night's togetherness had taken away some of the tension but the situation still had to be resolved. At that moment, they heard Maisie coming down the stairs, her footsteps muffled on the carpet, her step light and unobtrusive.

'Good morning Maisie. Sleep well?' Joanna smiled at her, a welcome designed to reassure her that she was not in the way.

Maisie nodded and following the direction of Joanna's gaze, went to put the kettle on the stove. Mouse-like, she seated herself at the table and helped herself to a bowl of cornflakes, glancing across at James as if her eyes were cased in iron and he was some sort of magnet.

Joanna took the plunge. 'What do you think of this?' She read the advert out loud. When she finished, Maisie stared at her, expressionless. Joanna put the paper aside. 'I wondered if you might be interested. You said you'd like to work on a farm.'

Maisie looked away, her face a mixture of emotions: anxiety, curiosity, the earlier hurt and rejection still barely concealed. Joanna reached out and touched her hand. 'You don't have to, you know. We want you to be happy. We want you to be doing something you enjoy. You don't really like the fish shop – do you?'

Maisie shrugged.

'Well then.' Joanna felt triumphant. 'I'll write to them if you like. I'll come with you if you get an interview. Shall we give it a try?'

For several days nothing was said about the vacant situation but its very existence hung like a swarm of bees over Maisie's head.

The idea of leaving the Camerons filled her with dread. Just as all her uncertainties were beginning to settle this blow sent her toppling back into the abyss, down there where the locked casket stood, bringing her face to face with its secrets. *Serves you right. What did you expect? You didn't really think you could stay here – did you?*

She didn't say anything. In any case, what could she say? I don't want to leave? I don't care if I am in your way, I'm going to stay. No. She had no choice. If they didn't want her, then. . . .

Quickly she switched her mind away from that particular pain. Why had she told Joanna that she wanted to work on a farm? Just when everything was all right, just when she didn't have to speak and everyone was nice at the fish shop she was going to have to leave. It would mean new people, new things to learn. Living with Joanna was like being in the haven she had always dreamed of. And now they were throwing her out. She tried to find comfort by thinking that they were doing it for her own benefit, because this was what they thought she wanted. Why couldn't she tell them the truth? The catalogue began to scroll through her mind: No more wall-to-wall carpeting, no papered chimney breast in the living room, no electric kettle, or *bath robes.*

A bitter sweet pain wrenched her heart. No radiogram – no more *Mr Wonderful.* Perhaps she would never see him again.

Not for one moment did she imagine that James might actually like her, not in *that* way. Against Joanna she wouldn't stand a chance, but just to be there, to wash his dirty dishes, to be able to look at him. That had been enough. She'd read a book once where the heroine had loved a man without ever letting him know and then, just at the end when it seemed that she would lose him forever, he had had an accident and she had been the one to look after him. He told her then how much he had always loved her.

The significance of the story brought Maisie face to face with her true feelings. She was secretly, hopelessly, in love with James Cameron. He could never, ever be hers unless Joanna died and if that happened she would know how to comfort and care for him. At the wickedness of the thought, she knew that she would have yet another guilt to endure. It was all part of her punishment.

As she waited miserably in the hallway for James to drive her to work, she heard the rustle of paper outside, then the clang as the letter box lifted and several envelopes fluttered to the mat. As she picked them up she noticed that one of them had scrawly, old-fashioned writing. She knew immediately what it was. It was the farmer, writing to Joanna. For a moment she was tempted to put it into her handbag and then throw it away, but supposing he wrote again, or came round to see why she hadn't replied? With a sigh that did little to ease her gloom, she marched back to the kitchen and placed the letters on the table. Before Joanna could comment she stomped out and hurried outside, shutting the door harder than she intended, wondering if this might be the last day ever that James took her in the car.

When she came home that evening, the letter was on the dining table. Maisie ignored it but she had hardly got her coat off before Joanna said, 'Guess what, Maisie, that farmer and his wife would like you to go for an interview.'

She shrugged, blinking her eyes to show her unwillingness. Joanna sighed and sat down at the table. 'I know it won't be easy for you, but I think at least you should try. I'll come with you. If the place is awful or the people aren't nice, then of course there's no question of you going there, but otherwise. . . .' There was a sharp edge to her voice, warning. As Maisie folded her headscarf and put it on top of her handbag ready for the morning, Joanna added, 'The interview is on Wednesday afternoon so you won't need to say anything at work.'

To Maisie's amazement, on Wednesday Joanna announced that she was going to drive James to work so that they could have the car. It had never occurred to her that Joanna could drive. In a strange way it was something else that made James more unattainable. Of course he would only want a wife who could drive. No one in Maisie's family had ever owned a car.

'It's quite a long way out,' Joanna explained as she reversed the car on to the road. 'No bus service to speak of.'

The thought of being isolated in a strange place only added to

Maisie's misery. She wondered what she could do to make sure that the people didn't like her. If she didn't say anything, perhaps they'd think she was daft or mad or something and say that they didn't want her.

They drove out of the village in silence. Maisie didn't take much notice as to where they were going. At Joanna's suggestion she had changed into a Gor-ray skirt that had been Joanna's and the pink jumper with the hole that had now been mended. The wind was coming from the north-west, gusting and spiteful.

'You'll be glad you're wearing something warm,' Joanna remarked, partly to break the silence. Since the accident she had grown used to Maisie's lack of communication but today there was something accusing about it. Her hunched, resentful demeanour spoke louder than any words.

As the country roads gave way to lanes and finally to rutted trackways, several times they got lost. Still some of the signposts had not been replaced since the war and the farmer's written instructions appeared to have omitted some important pieces of information.

Passing between steep banks topped by hawthorn hedges, they suddenly emerged into open countryside. Grey stubble clothed the wheat fields and the pastures looked almost black in the damp October light.

'Look!' Joanna slowed down and nodded across the valley towards a hazy collection of low buildings. 'That's it. I'm sure of it. He said to look out for a black barn.'

Sure enough, through the mist they could make out a long wooden building, coated with tar for protection, contrasting starkly against the grey stone of a farm house. Other sheds and cow byres clustered around the yard.

In spite of herself Maisie could not help but look. On the higher ground behind the farm, creamy dots splashed the hillside, the reverberating call from the sheep echoing across to them. 'You'll like that,' Joanna said in a voice that brooked no argument.

When George came in for breakfast, the frosty atmosphere that had permeated the house for days continued to hang over the kitchen. By contrast the waft of heat from the range swept him in with a welcoming glow. Outside it was grey and damp, a portent of a long winter to come.

Rose was frying eggs, her back to him and she did not look up or speak. He wished now that he had mentioned the advert to her before, not waited until it actually appeared in the paper.

'Look at this, Mother.' He had presented it to her with the air of one bestowing a surprise. Surprise it was, but clearly not a welcome one. Rose handed it back, her mouth as tight as a heifer's bum.

'What do you think you're playing at?'

Amazing how she could still make him feel like a young boy. Not meeting her eyes, he said, 'Well, what with young Ian coming to live I reckon as how you'll need some help.'

'If I want help I'll ask for it. Besides, what's the point of taking on Ian if it means taking on someone else to look after him?'

He didn't have an answer to that so he simply said, 'Well, we might not get any replies.'

But get replies they did, or rather two. The one was clearly unsuitable. You could tell that immediately from the tone of the letter. *I must have a room near the toilet and I don't like to be disturbed after nine o'clock.* He and Rose were in agreement that they didn't want someone dictating to them like that. What they still couldn't agree on was that they needed anyone at all.

The other letter was a bit of a mystery. It came from a lady with good handwriting and posh blue note paper. *I am writing to you on behalf of one of my ex-pupils,* it started. She went on to explain that this young girl had suffered a bereavement, as a result of which she was very withdrawn but that in every way she was an excellent, trustworthy person, hard working, capable and that because she had always wanted to work on a farm she would not be afraid of taking on any kind of duties they asked of her.

'Sounds rum to me,' was Rose's only comment when he rather shamefacedly handed her the letter.

'Well, you wouldn't want somebody noisy, would you?' She couldn't miss the opportunity to say that she didn't want anybody at all. In the end he had got mad.

'Look here, Mother. How are you going to help with the farm and look after me'n Ian? Not with your legs like they are. A strong youngster could do the washing and fetch and carry, make life a lot easier for you. You'd be a proper lady.'

He knew that was the wrong thing to say straight away.

'And what am I supposed to do all day – sit around like some useless ornament?'

' 'Course not.' Silently, he thought: Give it a rest, Mother, but he knew better than to say so.

'Besides,' Rose was in full swing now. 'Where is she going to sleep? You can't have her'n Ian down the corridor together.'

He suppressed his first thought of 'why not?' saying instead, 'I can always put a bolt on the door if the young girl feels nervous.'

Rose gave him one of her looks. 'It's young Ian I'm thinking of. Girls these days are as bold as brass. What would your sister say if the lad ends up in trouble? I'm not having that.'

Perhaps he should have given up then but he couldn't stop himself from saying, 'There's no harm in writing though, is there? Inviting the girl along and seeing what she's like.' Rose didn't grace his suggestion with a reply but in a rare fit of defiance he wrote back anyway.

As he slid into his chair to wait for his breakfast he glanced up at the clock. In another six hours they would be here.

'You're late.' Rose plonked a plate of eggs and bacon in front of him with a remonstrative thud. She glanced across the table, adding, 'Ian's nearly finished.' Her look evolved into one of approval as the young man opposite wiped the last of the bacon grease from his plate with a hunk of bread, pushed it into his mouth and washed it down with the dregs from his tea cup. He stood up as he did so, the quicker to get back to work.

'Thanks, Auntie.' He hunched his shoulders into his jerkin, wiping his mouth with the back of his hand and transferring the damp smear across the thigh of his trousers. 'Well, I must be getting on.'

He nodded to George who grunted as he passed and followed the lad with his eyes as he made for the door. George felt a moment of undefined irritation, with Rose for being so partial in her approval and with himself for feeling affronted by it. Since Ian had arrived the boy could do no wrong and, coincidentally, it seemed that George could do no right. He ate in silence, hurrying to escape from the frosty atmosphere.

'See you later, Mother.' He delivered his empty plate to the sink and in response Rose clattered the frying pan into the water. Gloomily he registered that the remark had not even solicited an acknowledgement. Rebellion swelled in him. Dammit. He was only doing this for Rose and she was behaving as if he was planning on installing the girl in her place as some sort of concubine. Wickedly he allowed himself to imagine a buxom, corn-haired beauty placing his breakfast in front of him. 'There you are Mr Draper, my dear. Just you enjoy that.'

Outside it felt almost as if the air was being sprayed from a gigantic perfume bottle. Fine droplets of mist fought to defy gravity, hanging in the air and coating the yard with a grey veil. Across the farmyard young Ian was on a ladder, repairing the rotting wood at the top of the barn door. He worked methodically, a measured, rhythmic pace that suggested he could keep up the momentum all day. George's feelings towards his nephew softened. He was a good lad, a hard worker. Willing too. It wasn't his fault that Rose had gone all gooey-eyed over him.

He studied the youngster's outline with an appraising eye. He wasn't very tall but his lithe, sturdy limbs gave him a presence that would have been absent in a taller but thinner man. He allowed himself the semblance of a grin. The boy was a bit like a young carthorse really, powerful but at the same time graceful. He couldn't help but admit that Ian reminded him of Ned, in build, features and in temperament. It was a bittersweet realization.

They spent the morning working around the yard, and at one o'clock went back to the house for dinner. As George followed Ian inside he thought how quickly his nephew had settled into the routine – boots off outside the door, jacket hung on the hook in the porch, hands washed in the big sink where Rose did the washing, wiping them on the roller towel, then padding in stockinged feet to take his place at table with his back to the window. That had been Ned's place once. Now it was as if Ian had always been there. Life was full of surprises and this was one that certainly George hadn't expected.

He consumed his bacon pudding and potatoes and cabbage, keeping his thoughts busy with farm work, not wanting to think about Ned and Ian, or the inteview to come. Jam roly-poly and custard followed. 'Thank you, Mother, my favourite.' It was a noble effort but Rose was immune.

When Ian got up to return to work, George hovered uncertainly, wondering whether he should get changed. Apart from farm hands he had never employed anyone before. The young girl was being brought by her ex-teacher and in spite of telling himself that he was the gaffer and wasn't impressed by teachers, he still wanted to do the right thing.

He glanced at Rose to see if she was going to make any comment but she was busy clearing the table and stacking the crocks in the sink. That done she glanced at the clock, took off her apron and hung it behind the door. She behaved as if he wasn't there.

They both looked up as the sound of a car reached them. George began to feel panicky. What should he ask? He had been relying on Rose to do the talking. Now he wasn't even sure if she would stay in the room.

Outside, the dogs were barking like demented football fans. Through the window he saw Ian go across towards the gate, presumably to let the visitors in.

'Well?' Rose gave him a look that said: What are you waiting for? Hastily finding his best shoes he tried to put them on but his work socks were too thick. Too late he realized that he had the choice of either bare feet or stiff, muddy socks. He settled for the socks, hoping they might not notice. By now the voices were very close as Ian led the party up to the door. Lifting the latch he stood back and ushered the two women inside. 'Some people to see you.'

'Come along in.' To George's relief, Rose came up trumps. He noticed then that she had put the kettle on the range. He thanked the Lord that she wasn't going to be awkward. As they all four sat at the table, relief washed over him.

His eyes were drawn to the older woman, although older was hardly the right word. A pretty bit of a girl, no more than five and twenty and in the family way too by the look of it. He felt tongue-tied and forced his attention to the other, younger, woman. By contrast she looked little more than a child; short, skinny and wearing a tailored skirt and nice pink jumper, both of which looked too big for her. She sat with her eyes rooted to the table and her arms clasped about her as if for protection.

Rose was asking questions. It was the pretty woman who answered. The other one, the one they were supposed to be interviewing, was like a statue. George had doubts. Serious doubts. The girl acted like some sort of simpleton whereas what they wanted was a sensible body who could be relied upon to work unsupervised. He was about to take charge of events, make it clear that they wouldn't be palmed off with just anybody, when he heard Rose say, 'Well, how about a month's trial? See if we suit each other?'

He glared at her in amazement. Ignoring him, she said to the daft girl, 'What shall we call you?'

'Her name's Maisie.'

George couldn't believe what he was seeing. Talk about women being contrary. One minute Rose was washing her hands of the whole thing and now she was making firm arrangements for the girl to start work. He wondered if she might be doing it to punish him, teach him not to interfere but surely she wouldn't be that daft?

'Hang on a minute,' he started but he might as well not have spoken. They were all getting up from the table. Everything was settled. He gave himself up to fate.

As the door closed on the visitors, Rose came back with a self-satisfied smirk twitching about her lips.

'I suppose you think that's funny,' he said.

She gave him a withering look. 'Funny or not, that's what you wanted wasn't it? Someone quiet? Someone who wouldn't cause trouble with our Ian? Well now you've got your way. Perhaps next time you'll leave the running of the house to me. Anyway, the teacher seems very nice. Very responsible. So. . . .' She gave him an *I'll show you* stare before adding, 'So, like it or not, the girl's starting on Monday.'

Ten

For Maisie, events were moving so fast that she felt as if she were being swept along by a landslide. She had seen a landslide once along the grey, clay-clogged cliff tops, near to where they lived. Great shards of earth had broken away and tobogganed helplessly down the slope, uprooting a cottage and sending it slithering down the cliff face, ripping it in two as easily as torn paper. At the time she had wondered at the frightful power of nature, blind as a steamroller, immune to the lives of people in its path. Now, upon a whim, her life too was about to be turned upside down.

She passed the return journey and the rest of the evening in silence. Back at the cottage James and Joanna risked a few whispered comments which she knew were about her, then behaved with false jollity, pretending that everything was like it had always been. The hurt surfaced again. They were traitors, both of them.

When at last she went to bed, Maisie closed the bedroom door and her sense of unfairness fermented until it all spilled out in a good cry. She didn't do so easily. It was frightening to cry. She hadn't done so for years; not when Dad died, not even when the news came of the explosion. No, it was long before that, long ago in the times before *the terrible thing*. As her sobs gathered momentum, the danger signals went off, warning that the tidal wave of the past was threatening to engulf her. With a desperate effort of will she managed to rein in her grief, turning, instead to present matters.

Only one day remained before she would be leaving the cottage forever, never to lie in the comfortable bed again, never to watch her favourite programmes on the telly – never, ever, to see James. Traitor he may be but she could not stop loving him.

The sense of self-pity gradually evolved into one of injustice. It was just not fair! Whatever had happened in the past, surely it was time for God to forgive her and stop punishing her like this? I hate you, she thought. The admission of such a suicidal feeling stunned her with its daring but God gave no sign that He was moved by her rebellion.

After the cry she felt – not better, but at least she had not been washed away in a flood of past losses. Empty, exhausted, she fell at last into a dreamless sleep. When she opened her sore, tired eyes it was already daylight and as she pushed herself mechanically from the bed she remembered that today was Saturday. She would be going to the fish shop for one last, nostalgic morning.

The betrayal of leaving weighed heavy but Joanna had telephoned Mr Stephenson at home and explained everything to him. When Maisie arrived at the shop, instead of being angry with her everyone was kind and sympathetic, saying that they would miss her. The morning ticked by minute after painful minute, dragging her away from the safe shore of the familiar routine. As she hung up her apron for the last time, Mr Stephenson handed her her wage packet. There was an extra ten shillings inside. Mrs Harrison even gave her some nice soaps, saying, 'Be sure to come and visit us when you are in town.'

In town. She felt as if she was going to the moon. In all probability, although she had been born in the village, she would never come back here again. As she opened the door one final time, she longed to say that it was all a mistake and that she didn't want to go – but if she did stay, where would she live?

Burdened by defeat she forced herself to step outside. Mr Stephenson was pulling down the Saturday afternoon blinds as if saluting her departure. She was on the verge of running back inside when she noticed Joanna waiting for her across the street. Dredging up her courage she turned her back on the Fish Emporium and crossed the road.

Joanna greeted her with the words, 'Hurry up, there's something we've got to get.' She turned down the High Street and as Maisie's misery temporarily suppressed, she followed behind. To her surprise they stopped outside the shoe shop which was about to close for dinner.

'This won't take a minute,' Joanna said and to Maisie's consternation the shop assistant brought her a pair of wellingtons to try on. 'You must have boots to work in,' her teacher insisted. 'Come the winter you'll be ankle deep in mud.'

It wasn't a comforting thought. Maisie knew that she should say thank you but somehow she couldn't. All the time the knowledge that Joanna was abandoning her poisoned her thoughts. How could she be grateful for that? Silently she clutched the wellingtons and without waiting for her mentor, set out for the cottage that over the past few months she had thought of as home.

Her final evening at the cottage was even worse. James went out with some friends and she and Joanna were alone. Maisie longed to sit and watch the telly for the very last time but there was a lot to do. Joanna insisted on organizing her packing. As Maisie looked hopelessly at the collection of blouses and socks and skirts that had been packed for her from the house at West Street, Joanna said, 'Perhaps it's time to have a turn out.' As she spoke she held out a pile of neatly folded clothes, saying, 'Some of this should come in useful.'

For a moment Maisie forgot what was happening as she examined the stack of slacks and thick jerseys, just right for working outside. But then again, the kindness of the gesture reminded her that this was the ending of an era, one that she had wanted to last forever. At the bottom of the pile was a brown duffel coat that Joanna sometimes wore to go for walks.

'Keep you warm,' she said and, as Maisie looked up at her, 'You will come and see us, won't you?'

Somehow Maisie managed not to cry. Now that she had once given way to the emotion, she felt that if she should let it happen again, a waterfall vast as Niagara would come spilling over and splash down on to the rocky road ahead of her, taking her with it. When she climbed into bed that night she resurrected Rupert the Bear and cuddled her face into his threadbare body. He at least would never abandon her.

James and Joanna both came in the car to take her to the farm. During the journey Maisie sat in the back and studied James's head with the shrewd eye of a sculptor. The curl of his hair, the line of his neck and jaw, the wrinkling of his cheeks as he turned now and then to smile at his wife – they were perfect. In contrast, Maisie felt ugly, excluded, as if Joanna and James were both part of a conspiracy to get rid of her. With uncharacteristic determination she thought: One day I'll find a man like him – only better! She sat up taller until her head almost touched the roof of the car.

As the journey progressed she recognized various landmarks that they had passed on their previous visit. All the time they were drawing nearer and nearer to the farm, closer to the moment when they would have to say goodbye. Desperately she clung on to her resolve not to mind.

At last the car made its way down a narrow lane and there it all was, the farmyard with its black barn and where the black and white dogs had barked and jumped up at them, the barn where the young labourer had been standing on a ladder and had come to let them in. 'The gaffer's expecting you.' That was what he'd said. Gaffer. She didn't realize at first that he meant the boss. Anyway, he had been talking to Joanna, not to her. She wondered whether, when they had gone, she might find herself alone with him and then he'd be forced to talk directly to her. Worse, she would be expected to answer. A tremor shuddered its way through her entire frame.

With an effort she diverted her thoughts to the *Gaffer*. Now that she thought about it, Mr Draper seemed quite nice. He was really quiet, like her in fact. Her confidence rose by a degree. Mrs Draper was a bit more uppity. She had looked at Maisie a lot and asked loads of questions in a probing sort of way, but she didn't seem too bad really. Anyway, there was no time to think about it because James had already parked the car and was taking her cases from the boot. As Maisie watched him she remembered

Mrs Draper's words: . . . *for a month, see how we get on*. . . . Supposing they didn't? Why hadn't she thought of it before? She looked round to ask Joanna but already she and James were striding towards the farmhouse. Anyway, what was the point of saying anything? They didn't want her back.

Mrs Draper came to the door as they approached along the bumpity brick pathway. 'Here we are then.' She stepped back into the kitchen and waited for them to follow. Maisie brought up the rear, slipping in behind them and looking around the room with new eyes. It was big, low, the ceiling stained haddock-yellow by years of smoke from the kitchen range. Beneath her feet the uneven flagstones were gilded here and there with mats, some rush ones near to the door and some once-cheerful rag ones, now faded into a more uniform mustard brown by years of muddy stockinged feet.

'Would you like a cup of tea?' Mrs Draper glanced across at the huge black kettle that nested on the top of the range.

'No thanks. We've got to be getting back.'

Maisie saw James's conspiratorial glance and felt the betrayal all over again. As Joanna came to hug her goodbye, she stiffened, holding back. She saw a flicker of pain cross her ex-teacher's face. 'We do care about you, you know,' she said. Her expression seemed to be asking for forgiveness but Maisie had nothing to offer. Standing back, Joanna added, 'Whenever you get a weekend off, be sure and come to see us.' As the impossibility of such a journey dawned on her, she added, 'Of course, I'll come and pick you up.'

Maisie was aware of James, the merest warning flicker of his eyebrows that spoke volumes. She remained silent. Moments later they were in the car and Joanna was waving through the window. Maisie did not bother to respond.

'Right, my dear. Come along now. I'm sure if you pull your weight and try your best we'll get along just fine. Did you have a good journey?'

Maisie nodded and Mrs Draper caught her breath as if she had been about to say something then thought better of it. In the end, she said, 'Right, bring your bags and I'll show you to your room.'

Silently Maisie followed her to the staircase and waited while Mrs Draper pulled herself up step by painful step, using the bannister as a hoist. At the top she stopped and rubbed her knees. 'The screws are a terrible thing,' she admitted. 'I hope you never suffer from it.'

As they made their way down the dark, narrow corridor, Mrs Draper said, 'Your room's just here on the right. Opposite is young Ian.' She drew in her breath. 'I'm sure you'll keep yourself to yourself.'

Who was young Ian? Their son? It had never occurred to her that anyone else might live in the house. She felt suddenly uneasy as if the longed-for privacy was about to be invaded. Rose Draper said, 'Ian's gone home this weekend to visit his parents. He'll be back first thing tomorrow.' She opened the door now facing her and waited for Maisie to pass her.

The room was brown and square and featureless. A single bed blended in with the dark stain of the wooden floorboards, the brown-grey swirls of the bedside mat. Against one wall a tallboy in some dark wood sported only a china candlestick, and on the wall above the bed an embroidered picture announced that *God is our Refuge.* The likeness to Mum's bedroom at West Street was uncanny.

'Right then. You get along and unpack your things. Supper will be in about half an hour.'

Left alone, Maisie sank gingerly on to the edge of the deep gold-brown stripes of the bedcover, bouncing gently to see what sort of response she got from the mattress. It felt oddly familiar, not like the accommodating springs on her bed at Joanna's but more like the grudging resistance of the bed at home. Home. West Street. All gone. Swallowing hard, Maisie stood up and began to unpack her things.

As their car drew out of the farmyard, Joanna and James experienced a liberating sense of freedom. As James put his foot down too hard on the accelerator, skidding in the ruts that meandered up to the road, Joanna clung to his arm and breathed in an exhilarating cocktail of togetherness.

'What shall we do tonight?' She asked the question, imagining them alone at last in the lounge, the radiogram playing some sweet jazz, James downing a pint, reading the Sunday papers, remarking on items of interest in the news. She meanwhile, would change into her quilted dressing gown and curl up on the sofa, her toes enticing him with red polish as she wrestled with the crossword, consulting him about particularly tricky clues.

As they put distance between themselves and Maisie, a creeping sense of anticlimax began to seep in. They hadn't washed up before they left home. Normally Maisie would have done so. Secretly Joanna had been enjoying the Sunday serial on the television while pretending that she was only enduring it for Maisie's sake. Now she would miss the end. True, they could wander naked around the house, could make love as often and as loudly and wherever they liked, but the very freedom took away that indefinable thrill that had accompanied their clandestine unions with Maisie across the corridor. For some reason they had pretended to themselves that Maisie would have disapproved, would have lain there like some maiden aunt, shocked and outraged by their behaviour. In reality the girl had probably been either dead to the world, or perhaps even envious of the fleshly delights that were so far denied to her.

When the car finally came to a halt outside the cottage, the place looked somehow bereaved. Joanna glanced at James to read the same message in his eyes. Guilt, that treacherous rogue had robbed them of the very pleasure they had so long dreamed of.

Eleven

IN THE BEDROOM that evening George went through the business of sorting out his clean clothes for work. For the most part Sunday was no different from the rest of the week in that the livestock still had to be attended to, and the harvest certainly didn't pay attention to observing the Sabbath, but habit had dictated that he started every Monday with clean clothes. Likewise, Monday was Rose's wash day when she boiled up the copper, stripped off the bottom sheet and replaced it with the top one, then dumped the dirty linen with George's underpants and vest, her vest and knickers plus other odds and ends and the roller towel from the kitchen into the sudsy water for a good hot soak.

The atmosphere in the bedroom was not cordial. Rose still maintained a disapproving silence so that the everyday noises of drawers opening and floorboards squeaking took on a jolting, intrusive quality. George decided to take the bull by the horns.

'Well, what do you think?'

'What about?'

He bit back his irritation. 'The young maid. Be all right will she?'

Rose sniffed. 'How am I supposed to tell until she's been here a while?'

George decided not to answer but after a moment, Rose added, 'She don't speak. Really don't speak. When that young woman said she was quiet, I thought she meant shy but the lass hasn't said a word.'

He tried a joke. 'Well, that might be a blessing.'

Rose wasn't amused. 'You try working with someone that don't say anything. It was bad enough at supper and you were there then.'

George forbore to point out that at supper Rose hadn't been speaking either – at least, not to him. As he sank on to the bedsprings and slipped his feet between the seasonally cold cotton sheets, he said, 'Well, p'raps she'll come round in time. Give the girl a chance.'

He settled down to sleep. 'Did you tell her what time she's to get up?' he asked into the darkness.

Rose hesitated. 'I've told her seven. That'll give me time to get going.'

George sighed with exasperation. 'What's the point of that? The idea is that she gets up and does the jobs, not you. At this rate you'll end up making more work for yourself.'

Rose did not answer, and much as he would have liked a bit of a cuddle he thought he'd better not risk it. 'Anyway,' he said, trying to take charge of a less than perfect situation, 'just make sure she pulls her weight.'

He felt the rise of the bedcovers as Rose shrugged her shoulders. Turning her back on him and maintaining a distance as she curled away, she said, 'I've told her a month. After that. . . . .'

Maisie slept badly. She didn't have a clock and all night she dreaded oversleeping. Somehow, as the haze of morning pierced through her curtains, she fought the overwhelming need to escape into sleep and managed to drag herself up and dress and be ready for work. As she went into the kitchen she saw by the mantel clock that it was a quarter to seven. By this time, however, the big table was already laid for breakfast and the kettle blew smoke kisses like Indian signals from the kitchen range. Rose was nowhere to be seen. Maisie lingered uncertainly in the doorway, feeling like an intruder. She was about to go back upstairs to the comparative safety of her room when Rose walked in carrying a metal canister. 'Here, put this milk in the jug.' She gave Maisie a cursory nod.

Looking around she spotted a large earthernware jug on the table and taking the container awkwardly from her employer, she unhooked the lid and poured the still warm contents into the jug.

She wasn't sure what she was expected to do next. She had the impression that Rose didn't know either and that she didn't really welcome another woman in her kitchen. Looking round for something to occupy her, Maisie noticed some other jugs and bowls waiting to be washed up so she sidled over to the sink. It was huge and deep, much bigger than Mum's. A white metal bowl lay on the draining board and carefully Maisie placed it in the sink and turned on the narrow, copper tap from which a jet of cold water cascaded.

'Water's boiling in the kettle.' Rose indicated the range. She gave Maisie a nod of satisfaction for using her initiative and encouraged, Maisie lifted the kettle and struggled across to the sink. Gone were all the luxuries of Joanna's cottage. It was just like being at home again.

Meanwhile Rose busied herself cooking breakfast. She seemed to be doing a lot – a whole pan full of eggs and about eight rashers of bacon, fried bread and black-bellied mushrooms that gave off an almost sensual, earthy smell.

'Here, girl, you can slice up some bread.' Rose pointed Maisie in the direction of the larder where she found a round, wooden breadboard and a big crisp bloomer loaf in the tin marked *Bread.* Under Rose's sharp eye she carried them to the table, found a bread knife and began to slice.

'Nice and thick now,' Rose advised. 'Them men'll be hungry as hunters.'

Men? How many would there be? Rose answered her question: 'I've laid up for the four men. We can have ours afterwards.'

At eight o'clock the sound of male voices just outside the window announced their arrival. George came in first heading for the sink, closely followed by the young man who Maisie had seen before and who she guessed must be Ian. She risked a look at him. He was probably not much older than her, with light brown hair and very pale honey-coloured eyes that complemented the light gold shade of his lashes. He in turn looked across at Maisie and her face instantly began to flame.

Two older men, both similarly dressed in brown cords, thick twill shirts and jerkins, brought up the rear. Once the business of washing their hands was complete, they silently padded across the kitchen floor and took their places at the table. Something about their brownness, the measured tread of their gait, reminded Maisie of cows at milking time, each heading for their own particular stall.

Once they were seated, George said, 'This here's young Maisie, come to help mother out.' Three pairs of eyes turned in her direction, two mildly curious – and once again she thought of cows with their large bovine acceptance – the third, darting a glance at her with those questioning amber eyes and then, as if what they saw was not particularly interesting, returning to concentrate on buttering a hunk of bread.

To hide her embarrassment Maisie busied herself making tea in a huge brown pot with a chipped spout. She wasn't sure how many spoonfuls to put in, so she fell back on her mother's maxim of one for each person and one for the pot. Inside it was black from years of usage. Mum had had a theory that you shouldn't scour out a teapot because it spoilt the flavour. Clearly Mrs Draper shared her view.

As the men ate they talked about the farm, about a cow whose milk yield had dropped right off, of the need to shift the muck pile, of Len Bottomly who had just bought a fancy white French bull which was supposed to sire good meat stock. She felt reassured by the soft burr of their voices, the sound of ordinary working, country folk, unlike the clipped, educated tones of James and Joanna.

Comparing the two households like this gave her a momentary feeling of ingratitude. The Camerons had been kind to her. They couldn't help it if they were posh.

Again she glanced at the kitchen clock. James and Joanna would only just be getting up. Joanna would probably come down in her dressing gown and make toast and coffee while James showered and shaved with his electric razor then dressed in a suit with a white shirt and tie. They had a special breakfast set of plates, cups and saucers, jug, sugar basin and cereal bowls, all with a pattern of ripe wheat on them. Mrs Draper was slapping the breakfast on to thick, plain white plates. The huge brown jug stood on the table full of milk as golden as mimosa, straight from Mr Draper's cows. The milkman didn't need to call here. In a moment of nostaglia she imagined telling Joanna all about it but her thoughts were cut short.

'Come along, lass, get these plates given out.'

Maisie jerked out of her reverie and hurried to do as she was bid. As she did so, each man sat back for her to put the plate down in front of him and looked up into her face. She was covered with embarrassment, most of all when she got to Ian who had a bedroom only yards away from hers.

'Thanks.' He grinned at her. 'All right then?' She didn't meet his eyes but hastened away to fill the bowl with washing-up water ready for the dishes.

'We'll wash up after we've had ours,' Rose intervened.

In an agony of shyness, Maisie stood near to the sink, like a rabbit scared out of its burrow, avoiding the men's gaze as if they might capture her with their stares and mesmerise her.

With their plates wiped clean and two cupfuls of tea inside them, at last they got up to leave. Finally she had something to do and gratefully she began to collect up the dishes. At the door, Ian looked across to the table.

'See you later.' She pretended not to hear.

The day seemed endlessly long but Maisie hardly had time to draw breath. While they washed up, the sheets had been soaking and as soon as the dishes were all put away, Maisie helped Mrs Draper to swizzle the heavy laundry around with a long stick, its end bleached white with years of use. Then came the heavy business of lifting the dripping sheets out of the copper into a small galvanised bath and thence transporting them to the sink where they were rinsed.

'Three times,' Rose instructed. 'I like everything rinsed three times to make sure all the soap is out.'

As Maisie heaved them out for the final time she longed for

the gentle activity of the fish shop. 'Two kippers Mrs Benson? A nice jug of winkles?' It all seemed so far away.

While Rose supported the sheets, Maisie turned the handle of the mangle then between them they shook the linen out and folded it before carrying it out into the fenced-off garden at the back of the cottage and pegging it on to the washing line. Finally, the clothes prop was heaved up to hoist the laundry as high as it would go to catch the wind.

'Right. You take the kitchen mats outside and give them a good shaking and I'll start the pastry.' So it continued, cooking and scrubbing, washing and ironing, peeling and churning. By the time tea-time came around, or what Joanna would have called dinner, Maisie could hardly keep her eyes open. Dimly she wondered what Joanna would he watching on the telly.

There were only the four of them for tea, Mr and Mrs Draper, Ian and herself. Mr Draper and Ian talked about the farm – well, argued really, Ian saying that at college they had been taught to do things one way and Mr Draper saying that he'd been doing it his way all his life and he wasn't going to change now.

'Can you make custard?' Mrs Draper's question caught her out and she felt herself blush again because at that same moment there had been a lull in the men's conversation and they both looked at her. Keeping her eyes averted, she nodded and Rose sat back. 'Right you are then. Eggs in the larder, some milk still in the jug and sugar in the jar. You'll find that little saucepan's best. It doesn't stick.'

To her relief, George started to tell his wife and nephew about a neighbour who had got into trouble with the police for letting his sheep get out on to the upper road for the third time that year, so that Maisie was able to do things in her own way. Furiously she stirred the hot milk into the egg mixture in case it should curdle but to her relief a thick smooth custard emerged.

Rose had risen from the table and was dishing helpings of blackberry crumble into bowls. 'Good girl.' She handed Maisie yet another jug into which to decant the custard and took the dishes to the table.

To tell the truth, Maisie was already full up with potatoes and cabbage, carrots, sliced pork and apple sauce, but she forced the pudding down.

'Well, how do you feel after your first day?' It was the first direct question that Mr Draper had addressed to her and in her panic she nearly choked on a blackberry seed.

'Steady on, lass.' George patted her on the back and through watery eyes she caught Ian's grin. Mortified with embarrassment she accepted the glass of water that he handed to her, the only comfort being that she had avoided answering Mr Draper's question.

About nine o'clock, while Mr Draper and Ian went out to check the livestock for the last time, Mrs Draper made some cocoa. 'We'll all turn in now,' she announced. 'Market tomorrow. An early start.'

Earlier than seven o'clock? Maisie's spirits plummeted. She wanted to ask if she was expected to go to market too and if so, what she was supposed to do, but Rose added, 'The men like to be gone by seven so we'll have breakfast ready at half past six. While they're away, you can collect the eggs. Ian usually does that but he won't have time in the morning.'

At that moment Ian walked in. He smiled at Maisie. 'Got to look around proper,' he advised. 'Most of them lay in the hen house but a few pick some strange places. Make sure you check behind the water butt, there's a chooky there going broody.'

Maisie thought of Grandad's hens in their run in the back garden. After the explosion they had mysteriously disappeared. The neighbours had said that gyppos came and took them away. Maisie hoped that they had looked after them properly. In her heart she knew that they would have wrung their necks and eaten them.

At last she was able to leave the kitchen and make her way to her room. Earlier in the day she had filled the jug ready for her toilet but she was too tired to wash. Anyway, her hands had been in water for most of the day and her face felt stretched by the steaming it had received as they had washed and cooked.

Just as she was slipping her nightie over her head she heard footsteps in the corridor and she remembered Ian. Wildly she struggled into the nightdress, panicking in case for some reason he should walk into her room, but the footsteps went straight on by. There was no lock on the door, which would have made her feel safer, but within moments of climbing into the bed she was dead to the world.

Twelve

Ian had always considered himself to be lucky. It wasn't so much in the material sense as from an in-built awareness that life had been kind to him.

His was a loving family. His mother and father had always been interested in what he did, coming to watch him play school football matches in the pouring rain, or applauding him when he spent his pocket money on six ducks and proceeded to sell their eggs to make a profit in order to buy a bike. In the end it was they who forked out for a new Raleigh, complete with the latest drop handlebars for his thirteenth birthday. Even when he elected to go to the new Agricultural College rather than leave school and work for his father's haulage business, they hid any disappointment they might have felt and expressed pride in his abilities.

When his Uncle George offered him a job he knew that indeed he was fortunate, although the pleasure was tempered with a large dose of undefined guilt. Twelve years ago, just before Ian's eighth birthday, he had been shocked and shaken by the death of his cousin Ned. Ned had always been his hero, the older brother he didn't have. When Ned had joined the army, Ian longed for the time when he could follow suit. At school he sat in the classroom and day-dreamed of the heroic things that Ned would be doing, teaching the Jerries a lesson, but that was before he understood that war meant people not coming home any more, or if they did come back being changed in some way, as if they had inadvertently stepped off the path that was their life and were unable to find the way back. Sometimes he felt angry with Ned, thought of him as a fool for volunteering when, being a farm worker he could have stayed out of it. In his heart he didn't believe it, but in some way it eased his own guilt at still being alive. Besides, it didn't make him feel quite such a traitor when he wondered whether Uncle George might one day pass the farm on to him.

The thought of running the farm in his own way filled him with pleasure. For the moment he would have to keep his thoughts to himself, keep his mouth shut about the old fashioned way Uncle George and Jim and Harry went about things. Given a free hand he knew that he would soon make it more efficient, get rid of the acres of wheat and borrow enough money to extend the milking parlour, get a better milking machine, increase the herd. Borrowing money was something Uncle George was dead against, but everyone did it these days. Anyway, that would have to come later.

Ian's only regret at being on the farm was that it was so isolated. Coming straight from college he missed the companionship of his mates, the fooling about, the trips to the coffee bar in town, or to the pictures, and the Saturday night hops at the Trocadero. In the privacy of his bedroom each evening he kept up with the latest pop records by listening to Radio Luxemburg and planned to buy himself a motorbike so that at weekends he could get into Thorley for a bit of a night out and a laugh. Yes, he missed the fun all right.

One of the beauties of college had been that just along the road there was a Domestic Science College with a seemingly inexhaustible supply of girls.

For some reason, girls liked him. He didn't think he was great-looking or anything, although he was all right – reasonably tall and not too fat or bald or covered with spots or anything. He thought it was probably because he liked a joke with them and didn't push things too far too quickly. He'd only been all the way once and that was with a bit of a tart called Jenny. She'd shocked him really, undoing his trousers and putting her hand inside, calm as you like. Until that time he'd always been hesitant, wondering whether he dared risk touching a girl's breast or letting his hand slide up above her knee. Not with Jenny though. She'd whipped off her knickers and sat astride him and, slightly fuddled with brown ale, he'd let nature take its course. Afterwards he wondered what he'd do if she came and said she was in the family way, or assumed that they were engaged or something. Filled with remorse because his mother would be shocked at his behaviour, he agonized about whether he might have caught something. But when nothing happened on any of these fronts, he enjoyed the knowledge that he was now a man and knew all about it.

One thing was certain, he wasn't likely to be getting up to anything on the girl front while he was at Uncle George's, at least, not until he had some transport.

Last Friday after work Uncle George had driven him in the truck to Thorley so that he could catch a bus home. On the way he'd suddenly said, 'Got a bit of a lass coming to help out your Auntie. She's having the room opposite yours. Your Auntie's worried about you being so close.'

Immediately Ian's senses quickened, his imagination way ahead of him as he saw himself tippy-toeing across the corridor and into the arms of a big, rounded, hungry girl, all tits and kisses.

' 'Course I won't, Uncle George,' he said aloud, interpreting his uncle's question.

'That's what I told her. Women do worry.'

That was the end of the conversation, but over the weekend, while Ian had been delivering some gates for his dad in the firm's pick-up, and later on, having a beer in the Stag with a couple of mates who still lived locally, he let himself dwell on the possibilities. A girl in the house. Right opposite his room!

On Monday morning, Uncle George had sent Harry to pick him up at the bus stop in the truck. They'd made small talk until Ian managed to ask, casually, 'Seen the new girl?'

'What new girl?'

'The one helping out Aunty Rose.'

'Don't know nothin' about it.'

He'd had to curb his impatience a little longer until at last, it was breakfast time.

What a let down that had been. Until he saw her he'd forgotten about the two women who had visited the farm the week before, not made the connection. He wondered what it would have been like if it was the older woman who had been employed. Proper pretty she was, sort of sophisticated. For a while he diverted himself by imagining chatting her up, but sadly she was not the sort to take a job helping out a farmer's wife.

As he tinkered with the tractor he thought that the new girl, Maisie, was a queer little thing, small, skinny, more like Orphan Annie than Brigitte Bardot. She seemed timid as a mouse and just about as grey and uninteresting. That first evening, passing her room on the way to his own, he laughed at himself for ever having imagined creeping across for some illicit nooky. Undressing, he put his clothes on the chair ready for the next morning. It wouldn't have been so bad if they could just have been pals, listened to the latest hits, talked about films, but this one was dead strange. She didn't talk at all.

Settling down to sleep, Ian consoled himself with thoughts of the BSA he was definitely going to buy, doing some mental arithmetic and as the sheep replaced pounds in his counting, he drifted away.

Maisie soon discovered that each day on the farm had its own routine. To herself she identified them as much by their physical sensations as by name. Monday was wash day which meant heavy, choking steam in the low-ceilinged lean-to tacked on to the back of the farmhouse kitchen. It was a day for scalding your hands in the hostile, sudsy water, for pulling shoulder muscles as you heaved the great dripping weight of the washing around.

Tuesday was market day, so that meant you had to get up even earlier, although on the plus side it meant being allowed out of the house to collect the eggs. Outside, she loved the sense of freedom, no matter what the weather. There was a magic in the fresh, pearly-shelled eggs that she located in the nooks and hidey-holes Ian had told her to look out for. She liked Ian. He was quite nice really, often smiling at her but he never tried to talk to her or anything which was a relief. Often the eggs she found were still body warm but sometimes, if she was late making her collections, they took on a cold, dead quality, their wholesomeness further desecrated by being coated in drying chicken droppings. This change upset her. From fertile, vibrant wombs they quickly degenerated into cold, barren tombs. It left her with a painful sense of the perfidy of life.

Wednesdays meant giving one of the rooms a good clean out, churning up a dust which tickled her nose with insidious animal hair that – in spite of Rose's insistence that neither cats nor dogs were permitted over the threshold – managed somehow to coat every mat and to make tidal inroads, washing up like detritus along the skirting boards. The tangled density of the dust and the sticky grasping of spiders' webs filled her with abhorrence.

Most of Thursdays was taken up with cooking – bread and pies leaving a floury legacy to clean up afterwards, puddings tempting her with nibbles that always left her wanting more: *don't eat those, young Maisie, there won't be enough to go round.* Thursdays also meant butter churning (more arm aching), and bottling or salting down any left-over fruit or veg that happened to be in season.

On Fridays, Rose sometimes went into town to do an egg run so Maisie was left in charge of feeding George, Ian, Harold and Jim at breakfast. The responsibility was overwhelming – would she break the egg yolks? Burn the toast? Fail to crisp the bacon? Would the older men insist on talking to her until she felt mad with embarrassment? The very thought of running the kitchen kept her awake for most of the night before. In fact, most nights there was something that crept into her sleep and filled her mind with anxiety for the day to come.

On Saturdays and Sundays she was invariably sent out to help with the milking – not actually milking the cows, but fetching buckets of soapy water to wash their udders and then to swill the milking parlour down, plus keeping an eye on the old milking machine to see that it didn't jam. This was because Harold and

Jim each had a day off at the weekend and every third weekend, Ian went home from Friday night until Monday morning. She hadn't had a weekend off yet. Rose had stipulated once a month, and anyway, she didn't have anywhere to go.

In some ways the weekends were the best of all; rubbing her cold hands against the living flanks of the milking cows, basking in the warm satisfying contact with these living beings.

'Mind 'er, she kicks like a good 'un.' Maisie soon learned which cows were placid and which were not. She loved their huge eyes, the large pink moistness of their noses, the huge exploring litheness of their tongues. At first she had been intimidated by their bulk, fearing that they would trample her underfoot as they picked their way along the slippery aisles to the milking stalls, but she soon learned to stand her ground. There were some who were her favourites and she gave them names – Bramble and Forget-me-not. Their brief liaison was made more intense by the knowledge that one day soon they might be gone. 'Don't worry, I'll save you,' she whispered into Bramble's velvet, fur-lined ear, hoping that somehow her friends would be spared the seasonal cull, but she knew that sooner or later the time would come and that she would be able to do nothing. She tried not to dwell on the fact that either they or their children were certain to end up in various forms on her dinner plate.

Sometimes she felt angry. Why had nature made things like this? Cows were good, gentle creatures, loving mothers, providers of rich, nourishing milk for their children – and this was their downfall. To survive, the answer seemed to be not to be noticed, not to draw attention to yourself and what you could do. Armed with this thought, Maisie tried even harder to be invisible.

It was on her third Friday morning that the postcard arrived from Joanna. It was posted in London and it featured a red double decker bus and a policeman in a shiny helmet, with the words *Welcome to London* emblazoned across the front.

'Letter for you.' Rose held it out as she came back in from her visit to Thorley with a consignment of eggs for the grocer's. Strictly speaking they were breaking the law now, not handing them over to be tested and sized and sorted centrally, but as long as Mr Walsh at the grocer's was prepared to take them then, as Rose declared, she saw no reason to change the habit of years.

Maisie had just been washing up last night's cocoa mugs. Wiping her hands on her apron she took the card, her heart beating fast at the thought of someone bothering to write to her, cheeks flushing hotly at being pushed into the limelight. She tilted the card towards the light from the window and started to read:

> *Hope you have settled in OK. We are having a long weekend in London. Once the baby comes we won't be able to go anywhere. We have visited several museums and galleries. The pavements are NOT paved with gold! Hope to see you sometime,*
>
> *Love Joanna and James.*

'Who's that from?' Rose interrupted her confusion. Silently Maisie held the card out but apart from glancing at the picture, Rose placed it unread on the table. Her sniff implied that she didn't hold with the frivolity of postcards.

Maisie kept her eyes lowered. Love from Joanna and James. Love from James! For a moment a magic carpet whisked her into the air until she realized that the writing had not changed and that it was Joanna writing on behalf of both of them.

'Come along then, girl, get that table laid.' Again Rose brought her back to earth but while she was getting cutlery and crocks from the drawers and cupboards, she drew pleasure from the knowledge that one day soon she might be able to visit them.

The day however, had other surprises in store. At supper that evening Maisie couldn't help but notice an air of unease about Ian. Usually he was the first to finish his meal, sitting back and waiting patiently for the rest to catch up so that he could tuck into his pudding. Tonight, it was different.

'Nothing I like better than cooking for someone who appreciates it,' Rose was fond of remarking at regular intervals. Maisie wondered if she was having a dig at her, or even at George, but they both did justice to the solid meat and two veg, the puddings and pies that Rose dished up most evenings. The only thing

Maisie didn't like was macaroni cheese but she still forced it down, afraid to give offence. In fact, she had noticed that the jumpers that were Joanna's cast-offs were beginning to be filled out and that the slacks and skirts she wore for work no longer sagged at the seat.

For the most part, when they were at the table Maisie tried not to look at any of them but as Ian sat opposite her, she couldn't help but be aware of him even though she tried never to meet his occasional, friendly gaze. Tonight, however, she was aware that he seemed to dawdle, chewing his meat with a thoughtful air, now and then stopping as if he was about to say something only to think better of it.

When at last he had ladled the last spoonful of Apple Charlotte into his mouth and swallowed it down, he broke the silence.

'I was wondering, Uncle George, do you think that I might, on Saturday evening like, perhaps borrow the truck to go into Thorley?'

Before George could answer, his wife jumped in. 'Wanting to go out are you? When George and I were your age we had to walk. Didn't matter where you went, you had to get there and back on foot.'

An expression of defeat began to spread across Ian's face but at that point his uncle observed, 'Don't forget the lad's got to get up early of a Sunday morning. If he has to walk back from Thorley he'll be half-dead by getting-up time.'

Rose shrugged her shoulders as if she had had her say, and washed her hands of the subject. George turned to his nephew.

'Seeing it's only once in a while I can't see that it would do any harm. Where are you going, the pictures?'

Maisie felt a pinprick of envy. She hadn't been to the pictures in ages. She loved losing herself in the dark, drawn into the screen life with all its glamour and drama.

'I thought I'd go to the Town Hall, see what the dancing's like.' Ian's cheeks darkened a shade or two.

'Got a date, have you?' asked Rose.

'No.' He shook his head.

'In that case you could take Maisie with you. Do her good to go out.'

George and Ian and Maisie all stared at Rose with varying degrees of shock.

'Mother!' George frowned at her in disapproval. Ian's face froze into a non-committal mask and Maisie wished that she could be anywhere but there in the room with them.

Rose flashed George a look. 'It would do the girl a power of good,' she repeated. 'You don't mind keeping an eye on her, do you Ian?'

'Er, no Auntie.' He studiously avoided Maisie's eyes and she floundered around for a way out but could not think of one.

'He doesn't have to stay with her all the evening,' Rose continued, speaking as if neither of them were there. 'As long as he sees her home safe.'

There didn't seem to be anything else to say. Maisie's hands trembled as she cleared away the dinner plates. Humiliation descended upon her like fog, blotting out everything else. Ian must be dying of embarrassment being lumbered with her like that, and as for the actual evening. . . . In response to the thought of the dance hall with its crowd of strangers, of a nightmare journey sitting next to Ian in Mr Draper's truck, of not knowing how to respond when he tried to talk to her, bile rose foul and acidic in her throat. Of course she couldn't go. On the night she would pretend to be ill, a headache perhaps or a stomach upset, but even as she thought of it she knew that she wouldn't be able to carry it off.

'You could wear that pretty dress.' Rose had clearly looked in her wardrobe and seen the navy blue cotton dress that Joanna had given her. It was really pretty; tiny white polka dots, a full, calf-length skirt, sweetheart neckline and puffed sleeves. Maisie thought that if she wore it she would look like one of those rag dolls, all gangly arms and legs, a plain Jane trying to look like a princess. In any case, it was really too late in the year to wear it now. Rose seemed to pick up on her thoughts.

'I've got a nice little angora bolero in white. Never been worn. It would look just the ticket.' She nodded as if agreeing with herself, saying, 'You go and enjoy yourself, young lady.'

Once again Maisie slept badly and throughout Saturday she seemed to make endless mistakes – forgetting things, putting things in the wrong place, burning the sausages for tea. Rose got quite cross with her and for a blissful moment she wondered if, as a punishment, her employer might decide not to let her go out after all. *Up to your room young lady and stay there until you learn how to do the job properly.* That's what Mum might have said, but not Rose. Instead, she relented. 'Come along, lass, stop day-dreaming about this evening. Look, you'd better leave the cooking to me. Dinner will be about half an hour. Why don't you go and wash your hair? Make yourself pretty for the dance?'

Hair. That was another worry. In the weeks since Maisie had been on the farm her hair had grown quite dramatically. When she was at work she always pinned it out of her face with a couple of kirby grips, but she couldn't do that to go to a dance – to a dance! At the prospect her legs betrayed her and she sat down quickly.

As Rose chivvied her out of the kitchen, Maisie felt like a woman going to her execution. Unsteadily she climbed the stairs, carrying a kettle of hot water to wash her hair with, still at a loss as to what to do with it, for when it was clean it was even more unmanageable, all wispy and flyaway. She would look like a scare-crow. The diversion of worrying about what she would look like was only marginally better than thinking about how she should act and what she would actually do when she got there.

Ian and George were outside. As she poured half the hot water into the bowl she could see them from the window, heaving pitchforks of hay on to a cart to take across to the cows. For a moment she was distracted by the contrast between them; Ian all boundless energy while Mr Draper moved with a slow, tired rhythm. There was something timeless about it, flowering youth and fading age. Maisie wondered if she might write a poem about it. At the same time the lines of a letter she might send to Joanna began to form in her mind, the sort of letter that was written by somebody clever and famous and recorded for posterity – not her though, definitely not her. Her body slumped with the weight of her dilemmas as she turned back to the wash stand.

As she did so she noticed the white bolero on the bed where Rose must have left it. To her surprise there was a small package in tissue paper laid on top. Curiosity got the better of her, and putting the kettle on the marble of the wash stand she went across to investigate. The tissue paper parted with a pleasing rustle revealing a pair of the sheerest, finest nylon stockings she had ever seen. Carefully she picked them up, examining the embroidered patterns on the heel and the black seams along the back. They weighed next to nothing. Holding them to the light she could see through them and delicately she fingered the material. Rose must have put them there but however did she come to own something so frivolous? As she stood there, Maisie remembered that among the things Joanna had bequeathed to her was a pale blue suspender belt. Could she, would she dare to wear it?

A trickle of excitement started around her midriff, suffusing through her body as in her mind the vision formed of a chic girl in a pretty dress, wearing nylon stockings and with her hair in a bouncy ponytail. Taking a deep breath, Maisie struggled out of her blouse and set about taking the first step towards the metamorphosis.

Once her hair was washed, she brushed and brushed it until of its own volition, it lay sleek against her head. Then, before it could dry and fly about, she secured it firmly with an elastic band. A small, wavy ponytail reflected back at her in the mirror. Industriously she washed herself all over with one of the soaps that Mrs Harrison had given her as a farewell gift from the fish shop then, washed and dried, she set about the business of transforming herself into a teenager.

'Maisie! Tea's ready.'

Her heart thumping ridiculously fast, Maisie descended the stairs. She felt acutely embarrassed. Dressing up in pretty clothes was for other people, people like film stars and Joanna.

As she stepped into the kitchen, Rose was in her accustomed place, dishing up piles of mash on to four plates. 'Have you brought the kettle back?' As she spoke she glanced up then looked back in disbelief. 'Well I never! You men, just have a look at this.'

Maisie's face flamed as, in slow motion, George and Ian turned their eyes in her direction.

'What a little humdinger!' George declared. 'Wish I was going to the dance meself.'

Ian nodded his head but at what, Maisie was not clear. Perhaps he wished that George was going too. To give herself time to recover she sidled over to Rose and helped to take the plates across to the table. As she ate other worries assailed her. What should she do about paying? Surely there was a charge to go in? What would she do if Ian asked her to dance? Her mind flew back to *Rock Around the Clock* and the smooth, swinging jive with all its complicated movements. Would Ian dance like that, or did he do the waltz and the quickstep like the older people did? Either way, it was a mystery to her, another agony that she would have to endure.

Somehow she forced the last forkful of tea down and with her last swallow and an intake of breath, she prepared to say something, anything to let them know that she couldn't go. Her throat felt dry as the Sahara and somewhere it constricted so that not even the tiniest whisper could escape.

'Off you go then.' Rose's voice was abrupt, matter of fact. 'Don't be out late now, you two. You've both got to get up in the morning.'

For a moment Maisie stared at her employer like a rabbit faced with a weasel then, with an impending sense of doom, she rose from the table and set out to meet her fate.

Thirteen

As Maisie tottered into the yard a cold blast of air assaulted her. She was glad that Rose had insisted that she wear her duffel coat, even though it looked ridiculous over the light cotton dress. The truck was waiting outside the door. Ian was already in the driving seat and the engine was running. She could feel his impatience.

'Hop in.' He put the engine into gear as Maisie scrambled up beside him, aware that in so doing she was showing an embarrassing expanse of leg. He did not appear to notice.

As they jolted down the track, Ian whistled to himself as if he could hear a tune running though his head. He made no attempt to talk and for this Maisie was absurdly grateful. All the while she tried to think of something to say to make him take her home again but between her tongue and her brain the vacuum remained. It was hopeless. Giving herself up to the ordeal, she let out her breath in a long sigh. Gradually, in response to the swaying of the truck, her heartbeat slowed to a less erratic thumping.

It didn't seem to take any time to reach Thorley, and almost before she knew it Ian was manoeuvring the truck on to the parcel of unmade up land that served as a car park behind the Town Hall, applying the brakes and turning off the engine in one smooth movement.

'Ready?' He eased himself from the cabin while she fumbled

with the handle and dropped in an ungainly fashion to the ground. It was further down than she expected. Following behind him she crunched her way across the gravel towards the imposing, porticoed entrance to the Town Hall. As they approached the steps, she was relieved to see the entrance prices written up outside. In her purse she had half a crown and some shillings and sixpences. Extracting the half crown she held it out to Ian. With a shrug he took it. 'Thanks. I'll buy you a drink.'

A drink! Here was another dilemma. What should she ask for? Lemonade would sound silly. Silently she practiced in her head '*Gin and orange? I'll have the same as you?*' This was another time when the need to say something was paramount but nothing would come. She prayed that he wouldn't ask.

The Town Hall was diversely used as council offices, theatre, venue for the horticultural show and public meetings. Various posters bore witness to forthcoming events. In the foyer young people mingled, their voices rising in volume as the numbers increased. Girls were queueing to hand in their coats while the boys gathered in groups, hands in pockets, heads thrown back in laughter as they shared some secret joke.

'See you in a mo.' Ian sidled in the direction of the Gents, leaving Maisie stranded. She sought refuge by joining the queue. In a panic she glanced round to see what the other girls were wearing. There was nothing that she could pick out as being the fashion. Tight black skirts, floral circular skirts, jumpers, blouses, occasional narrow trousers imitating the 'drainpipes' that some of the boys sported. She consoled herself that her dress didn't look too out of place.

Across the foyer, Ian emerged from the men's toilets. He wore casual trousers and a sports jacket. His hair was slicked back and he looked at home in this environment. The realization added to Maisie's sense of isolation.

As she shuffled forwards in the queue, she noticed a pretty girl with her hair in a sleek French pleat at the bar. As she wriggled on to a stool her tight black skirt rode up nearly to her knees, revealing slim, shapely legs. Maisie watched in fascination as she first took out a compact and patted her cheeks with powder, then produced a lipstick which she applied with great concentration, pressing her lips together to distribute the vivid pink evenly, her bottom lip transforming into a full, provocative pout. Finally she took out a cigarette case and proceeded to light a Du Maurier, lifting her head and blowing a long, cool column of smoke. Maisie had seen such scenes at the cinema, where beautiful, sophisticated girls sparred with American detectives. Surreptitiously she exhaled, pursing her lips and letting imaginary smoke escape. With a jump she realized that she was at the head of the queue and awkwardly she handed over the brown duffel, aware once more of its incongruity in this setting.

In silence she took the ticket and, relieved of her burden, looked around for Ian who was now strolling across to the bar. As she went to join him, he turned to the girl on the stool and started to talk to her. Maisie halted in embarrassment. The girl tilted her head back, looking at him from under her lashes. The gesture was pure Lauren Bacall. Swept along by the tide of dance-goers, Maisie began to feel that she was drowning. Just as she looked around for the exit, Ian noticed her and called her over.

'Here, Maisie. This is my cousin Dolores.' Smiling at Dolores, he said, 'And this is Maisie what I work with.'

Maisie couldn't look at Dolores. She was too beautiful. Instead she glanced somewhere in her direction and nodded her head, aware that the other girl was staring at her. From the corner of her eye she saw the slightly raised eyebrows, the dismissive gesture.

'Buy me a drink, Ian?'

'What will it be?'

Dolores stretched on the stool like a sleek tabby. 'Gin and orange.'

'Same for you?' As an afterthought Ian turned to Maisie.

Relieved of the responsibility of deciding, she nodded. As he fought his way across to the bar, Dolores studiously ignored her. In spite of the hubbub all around them the silence felt oppressive. Feeling increasingly humiliated, Maisie stood awkwardly next to the stool, focusing on some distant, unseen place across the hall. Long minutes passed before Ian returned with three glasses, seemingly oblivious to the tension. Maisie sipped the syrupy measure, her nostrils crinkling at the scented fumes of the gin, concentrating hard on the glass to keep her hands from shaking.

In silence she followed Ian and Dolores through the door and into the dance hall itself. Inside, the air was thick with smoke. Specks floated in the haze highlighted by the gently revolving glass ball in the centre of the ceiling. Maisie gazed at it in wonder as it cast delicate bursts of light on to the dance floor. For a moment her embarrassment was forgotten.

Through the gloom she could see three musicians at the far end of the hall on a raised stage. They were dressed in black suits with bow ties. As she watched, they began to play: a pianist, a trumpeter and a paunchy man with Brylcreemed hair, who began to croon into a microphone, his body bent over the instrument as if embracing the girl of his dreams. '*You are my sunshine, my only sunshine. You make me happy when skies are grey.*'

A few older couples began to take to the floor, gliding in time to the music and leaning back so that they could still talk to each other. Maisie found herself singing along inside her head. It helped to blank out the world around her.

Dolores found a table and insinuated herself into the corner, crossing her long legs and lighting another cigarette. Without looking at Maisie, she proffered the cigarette case in her direction. For one daring moment Maisie was tempted to take one, to rest it delicately between her lips and draw long and sensuously on it, but her nerve failed. She shook her head.

Dismissing her, Dolores turned away and concentrated on her cousin, leaning forward and holding a conversation that was drowned out by the quick step the trio were now playing.

Maisie gazed around, trying to breathe normally, hoping that in the mêlée no one would notice her. Ian fetched a second round of drinks although she had only just forced down the last gulp of the first one. She didn't like the sickly sweet texture, the acid aftertaste of the gin, but she was too embarrassed to say so, so she obediently accepted the glass, swallowing it like medicine.

After a while the band stopped playing and there was another stampede for the bar. The interval lasted for about twenty minutes during which time Maisie excused herself and went to hide in the ladies. There were four cubicles and perhaps a hundred girls, all waiting, chatting, giggling. It was impossible to stay inside longer than it took to empty her bladder so she sauntered back, relieved to find that both Dolores and Ian had disappeared. Maisie seated herself and concentrated on a puddle of beer on the table in front of her, wondering if she should use her hankie to wipe it up.

Her companions came back just as the trio took their places once more on stage. Stepping up to the microphone, the singer took off his jacket and loosened his tie. Round and about there was a tangible change of atmosphere, a rising tension.

'And now, ladies and gentlemen, what you've all been waiting for.'

As the singer spoke, a drum began to beat out a pulsing tattoo and there was a mass exodus from the chairs and the bar as people hurried on to the floor, quickly becoming engulfed in the swaying, swirling morass of bodies. Maisie was astonished. Here was *Rock Around the Clock* taking place in the Town Hall.

'Coming?' Ian grabbed Dolores by the hand and moments later they were dancing. Maisie was transfixed as Ian the farm hand, Ian the lifter of bales and wielder of axes metamorphosed into a gyrating, sinuous performer. He was at least as good as the people in the film. Better. Expertly he swung Dolores round, flicking his wrist to turn her this way and that, pulling her to him and pushing her away, spinning her around, lifting her and setting her on her feet so that she kept pace with the insistent rhythm of the music. How did they know what to do? What sort of message was he giving to her that she anticipated his every move? Maisie felt an engulfing sense of envy begin to claim her.

The dancing continued for ages. Whenever it threatened to stop, cheers and cat-calls had the trio playing again. People glowed with their exertions. Their eyes were bright with pleasure, their cheeks red with the excitement. When at last the final beat of the final bar was played out they returned to their seats, exhausted, exhilarated, all the tensions of the evening lifted.

The trio now returned to their earlier style, a long, slow foxtrot. Dolores wandered away to the ladies. 'Repair my face,' she announced.

As the dance came to an end, the singer moved again to the microphone. 'And now, something for all the young men, dedicated to all the young ladies. Come on lads, don't be shy, find yourselves a partner.' Smoothly he began to croon. *Why this feeling? Why this glow? Why this thrill when you say, 'hello?'*

Mr Wonderful! Maisie's chest tingled with longing, longing for James, for the sight of him, the sound of his voice, the need just to hear his name. It was an exquisite pain, enfolded in the routine of life at Joanna's, the fish shop, her room which would by now be the nursery. The sense of loss was profound.

Everything around her faded into darkness. Would James, could he be playing the record she had given him now? At this very moment? Perhaps he would turn to Joanna and say, 'I wonder how Maisie's getting on. Isn't it time we had her over for the weekend?' Next weekend would be her first weekend off. Two whole days, stretching ahead with appalling emptiness.

'Want to dance?' The vision was shattered. She jerked round to find Ian already standing beside her. His expression told her that he was doing his duty, ensuring that he could tell his aunt that he had looked after her during the evening, seen that she wasn't left out or anything.

Maisie shook her head but he was already moving on to the dance floor and she had no choice but to follow him. Turning, he placed one hand on her waist and clutched her other hand, then began to shuffle around the floor, all the time looking over her shoulder, scanning the direction Dolores had taken. Round about them, couples had moved indecently close, girls were buried in prolonged embraces, hands rested on thighs, pulling partners ever closer.

'Enjoyed it?' Ian made an effort.

Maisie nodded. Being so close to Ian had all her senses on a razor's edge. He felt hard, strong. The lingering scent of soap mingled with fresh sweat. His easy movements brought his body into contact with hers. It was a feeling that was frightening in its ambiguity.

She longed to say, 'Look, you don't *have* to dance with me. This song reminds me of someone special. I don't want to share it with anyone,' but of course she said nothing.

As the song came to an end, the singer hardly paused for breath. 'And now, the last waltz, ladies and gentlemen. Come on, you young men, let's not have a single lady sitting out.'

Maisie and Ian were still stranded on the floor. Maisie felt his anguish. He glanced several times in the direction of the ladies and even at that moment, Dolores emerged only to be swept on to the floor by a boy in a huge draped jacket and a greased quiff of hair. Ian's face remained stony. It was not hard to guess what he was wishing. With the air of a man bravely facing disappointment, he began to push her round the floor once more.

Maisie thought, 'Look, go and find her if you want to. I don't care if you'd rather be with someone else. It's all the same to me.' She endured the humiliation, looking down at her feet, watching their uncertain progress.

As the waltz drew to a halt, the gathering came up for air. Ian was still glancing around him. He hesitated and his expression was shamefaced.

'Look, here's the key to the truck. I'll see you back there in about fifteen minutes. All right?'

Even as he spoke, he pushed the key into her hand and fought his way through the throng. Moments later he was extracting his cousin from the other man's hold.

A knot of exclusion formed somewhere under Maisie's ribs. As she looked around, it seemed that everyone without exception was waiting for somebody else. Only she was the odd one out, the misfit, the weirdo. Fighting down the misery, she joined the queue for the coats, shutting out the babble of voices, the overexcited laughter.

Armed with her duffel coat she trudged out into the crisp night and made for the truck, determined not to feel anything. In silence she sat in the cab, the words to 'Mr Wonderful' circling in her head.

Ian was longer than fifteen minutes. Including the time she had spent queueing up for her coat, Maisie reckoned that he had been at least half an hour. She sat in the passenger seat, growing colder, aware that the car park was now nearly empty. There were no lights and it began to feel threatening. Just as she was wondering how long it would take her to walk home, she heard the crunch of gravel and saw him coming towards the truck, his hands deep in his pockets, his shoulders raised in a self-satisfied pose. Opening the door, he climbed in, and picking up the key which she had placed on the driver's seat, he started the engine.

'Sorry if I was a long time.' Even in the dim light of the car park she could see the smug grin. He was feeling very pleased with himself.

It took several attempts to get the truck to start. Outside, frost iced the hedges. Ian began to whistle again jauntily, congratulating himself. When he stopped humming the silence once more felt oppressive. Maisie stared ahead, watching the road as if she and not he was the driver. If it hadn't been for her, she knew that he would have stayed much longer. She could just imagine him saying, 'I'm really sorry but I've got to go. My Aunt's lumbered me with that dumbo.' She blinked to dispel the self-inflicted pain. What had they been doing anyway, him and Dolores? Kissing? Petting? She shut out the images. Could you do that with your cousin?

When they reached home, he drove across to the doorway again and leaning across her, opened the van door.

'It's raining out,' he observed. 'Don't want you getting wet.' The thought crossed her mind that he was being nice to her so that she wouldn't tell his aunt what he had been up to. Well, she wasn't likely to say anything, was she? A sniff of self-derision immersed her.

Silently she slipped from the cab and let herself into the house. The evening had been awful. Even worse than she had expected. It hadn't seemed quite so bad when Ian was just sitting there, or standing at the bar. It was even tolerable when he began chatting up Dolores, but once he got on to the dance floor, once he showed his true colours, his experience, his joy in being there, her presence had turned into a nightmare.

As she hung her coat on the hook in the hallway the desire to leave the farm began to suck her under. It didn't matter where she went, but even as the first thought came it was shadowed by a second. There was only one place she wanted to be – at Joanna's.

Perhaps she could run away? Tomorrow she would be working with Ian in the milking shed. Even if she got up really early he would soon realize that she had disappeared. She knew he wouldn't care or anything, but he'd still think it was his duty to tell his aunt and uncle. She'd hardly have a few miles start before they started to look for her, Ian driving the truck, hunting her down. Panic at the thought of a chase began to claim her.

For a moment she seriously thought about leaving immediately, as soon as Ian had gone to bed, but outside it was raining. Outside it was so dark that once you left the yard you wouldn't be able to see your hand in front of your face. Once outside the farm yard she would have no clear idea of the geography, no idea where the road led. No, she would have to be patient. She comforted herself with the firm decision to write to Joanna and hint that next weekend she would be free, free to visit. Surely she would understand and respond?

Outside she heard the sound of footfalls, the stealthy opening of the front door and in response she jumped. By the time Ian entered the hall, she was already upstairs and in the safety of her room.

Fourteen

'LOOK AT THIS.' Joanna held out Maisie's letter.

James was halfway through breakfast, a copy of *World Water* propped up against the milk jug. For once, the meal was a leisurely affair because Bill Cox, a colleague, was collecting him half an hour later than usual to visit a suspect water main in the next county. Left to himself, James would gulp down his toast standing up and be ready to leave by now.

'What does she want?' He ignored the profferred letter and Joanna bit back a lightning flash of anger.

'She doesn't *want* anything.' Her next words were much harder to get out. 'It's her first weekend off next weekend. I think we should invite her over.' She saw the smirk, the 'I knew it,' expression on his face and she felt angry again because Maisie hadn't asked to come and he was being unfair to her. Still he did not take the letter and she let it slip to the table, her resolve hardening. As she poured him more coffee, he dragged his gaze from the magazine.

'Where are you going to put her then, the nursery?' There was accusation in his tone, implying that the newly transformed nursery was sacrosanct, a place fit only for babies.

'We could put a camp bed in the study.' What she meant, was *your study*, the small, downstairs room that he had purloined as his office. Memory came to Joanna's rescue and she added, 'After all, you won't be using it this weekend, will you? Didn't you say you are working all day on Saturday?' She'd caught him there. He didn't reply and she knew that he didn't quite have the nerve to voice his true feelings: that is, that he didn't want anyone touching his things. She'd noticed it before, the little boy streak in him, not wanting to share his toys.

'Invite her if you want to.' He stood up and pushed his plate away. 'I'm going to pop up and check on the greenhouse.'

The greenhouse contained the skeletal remains of last summer's tomatoes and two buckets planted with potatoes that, in happier times, James had put in, in the hope of having a crop for Christmas dinner. Joanna had seen the telltale cigarette stubs carefully heeled into the earth outside the greenhouse door. What he really meant was that he was feeling tetchy and that he needed a smoke to calm him down.

She felt heavy, acknowledging the same thought that came to her every morning and a dozen times during each day: that by getting pregnant she had spoiled everything, made impossible all those dreams they had confided in each other, the hundred plans for the future when anything had seemed possible.

It felt worse because most of the time James tried not to show it. The nursery was a dream, wallpapered with a neat little teddy bear pattern, with James's own cot beautifully re-painted and stencilled with rabbits and foxes in little country cameos. He had made a built-in cupboard for baby clothes, and the bath unit was his own design. When visitors came he showed it to them with enthusiasm but after a while she realized that what he was doing was showing off his expertise, his ingenuity, and that the baby was incidental to it all.

She got up and began to clear the table. As she moved the jug, the magazine James had been reading slipped down flat on to the cloth. It was then that she saw he had it open at the *Situations Vacant* page and with a neat, precise, engineer's cross he had marked an advert for a senior engineering post in newly independent Rhodesia. The memory of long, distant talks seared her, of her and James seated in smoky pubs, or in post-coital closeness in his old Morris Oxford.

'*Water's a problem everywhere. They always need engineers. We could go anywhere we liked.*'

'*And I would be able to teach. . . .*'

Plans, day-dreams, pipe dreams, ashes.

At that same moment she heard the sound of a car outside and James poked his head round the door. 'Bill's here. Don't worry about cooking because I don't know when we'll be back. We'll get something to eat while we're out.'

Her imagination was at work again, torturing her. Like James, Bill was married. Like Joanna, his wife was pregnant, although with a second child – unplanned apparently. Men *did* talk. Joanna visualized them sitting in a pub, commiserating, two men feeling cheated, disappointed by the unfulfilled promise of wedded bliss. She did not dwell on her own expectations.

'See you sometime.' James's parting kiss was the same as usual, warm against her mouth but it did nothing to melt the glacier closing around her heart.

It came as something of a shock to George to realize that Maisie's trial period was nearly up.

'What you going to do about the young maid?' he asked Rose as he came in on Monday morning to change his socks. He'd been down to the lower field with Ian and it was waterlogged. Careless like, he'd gone in over his boots. Leaving Ian to get on and clear the ditch, he thought he'd have a quick cuppa before trying to sort out the blockage in the petrol pipe on the tractor.

'What d'you mean, what am I going to do about her?' Rose heaved the kettle on to the range and went back to the sink where some dishcloths were soaking.

'Well, are you going to keep her or not?' He had seen Maisie outside, struggling to get some bits and pieces on to the line. It was blowing a fair old gale out there.

Rose spooned tea into the pot and poured on hot water. She was a long time answering. 'She's a good worker,' she offered.

'You ain't still worried about her'n Ian are you?'

' 'Course not.' She gave him a disparaging look, as if any anxieties on that front had been his, not hers. 'No. It's just that it would be nice to have a bit of company about the house, someone to talk to proper like. When she doesn't say anything it makes it uncomfortable.'

George forbore to point out that at the beginning Rose hadn't wanted anyone in her domain at all. He slurped his tea appreciatively.

'Well, it's up to you.' Putting the cup aside he dropped his sodden socks in the hearth and stretched his toes towards the heat to let them dry. At that moment the telephone rang and with a sigh Rose went to answer it. As soon as George realized that it wasn't for him, he pulled on dry socks and beat a retreat. He still wasn't any clearer whether Rose wanted the girl to stay or not. In his view she was a blessing; no trouble, trustworthy and it was true, not likely to cause a problem with young Ian. Anyway, whatever he said, Rose would have her own way.

As Maisie came in from hanging out the shirts and pants on the line, Rose was in the act of replacing the telephone receiver. Her face was slightly flushed as if she had been talking to someone important or famous.

'That was Mrs Cameron. She rang to invite you over for the weekend. She's going to pick you up at five o'clock on Friday, and bring you back at tea time on Sunday.' The mention of returning Maisie brought Rose naturally to George's question. If Maisie came back then that would mean they intended her to stay. She hadn't really thought it through. She tried to imagine what it would be like if the girl wasn't there. Immediately she realized how much Maisie did around the house, and if her presence was a bit like being haunted, then that was the price she had to pay. Aloud, she said, 'You realize it's a month since you came here? Well, Mr Draper and I have talked about it and we are prepared to let you stay on.'

In response, Maisie nodded. She wasn't sure what she felt. Everything was such a muddle.

Rose returned to the subject of Joanna's call. 'It's really nice of her to take such an interest in you. Such a nicely bred young woman, and she and her husband are doing so well for themselves.'

By drawing attention to the difference in their backgrounds,

Rose only added to Maisie's confusion. Now that her wish to visit the Camerons was about to be granted she began to backtrack. It really was posh there. Perhaps she would be better off staying where she was.

Since Saturday, the ordeal of the dance had shrunk to more manageable proportions. In the house the routine went on as before. Ian treated her as he always had done, not taking much notice of her but friendly whenever he had reason to speak. At first he had seemed a bit sheepish but Maisie guessed that once he was certain she wasn't going to mention his little adventure with Dolores he settled back into his old ways.

Like her, Ian was going home for the weekend, while Jim and Harry were working. If she stayed at the farm it wouldn't be too bad. She could still help Rose in the house but spend more time outside visiting the cows and helping with the chickens. But then she remembered her room at Joanna's, and the telly and all the other luxuries, not least the presence of James, and thought how wonderful it would be to experience them all again.

She had a sudden moment of revelation – that perhaps everything in her life was already mapped out for her and if that was the case, then no matter what she did, however hard she tried to avoid her destiny, things would turn out the same. She made a decision. She would go to Joanna's, and on Saturday morning she would walk down to the Fish Emporium and just see what happened. If they made her welcome, said how much they missed her work and wanted her back, then she would let them know that she might be able to do so, provided they found her somewhere to stay. If on the other hand they didn't, then she'd bow to the inevitable and come back to the farm, back to Bramble and Forget-me-not, back to collecting eggs. Yes, this was it, Fate must be guiding her life. That was surely the answer, to give yourself up to it. She decided there and then that from now on, following her fate would be her guiding rule.

The weekend visit was not a great success. When Joanna arrived to collect her, Maisie was shocked by the change in her. It wasn't just her altered shape. There seemed to be an air of neglect about her. Joanna's thick black hair, once so stylishly cut, looked straggly and in need of a wash. The smock that she wore had tea stains on the front and with disbelief, Maisie suspected that she had started to bite her nails.

As they drove home, Joanna fell back into holding a one-sided conversation, not asking Maisie direct questions but starting off with 'I expect', or 'It must be. . . .' This way Maisie could agree or disagree without having to actually say anything. She felt a rush of tenderness towards her teacher for remembering.

To her surprise she wanted to ask questions but the habit of not doing so had now become so ingrained that nothing would come. She wondered what James thought of the change in his wife. For a wicked moment, dressed in Joanna's cast-off skirts and jumpers, Maisie wondered if he would look at her with new appreciation. Ever since the evening of the dance she had continued to wear her hair in a pony tail and today she wore the nylons that Rose had given to her. The thought of the black seams snaking their way up her legs released a tremulous moment of awareness, a new appreciation of the possibilities that might one day come her way. She nursed the day-dream that James was bound to notice.

When they got to the cottage, however, a disappointment awaited her. James was going to be out for the evening and he was working all the next day as well, probably late into the evening. In fact, it began to seem unlikely that she would see him at all.

Another disappointment awaited her. Instead of sleeping in 'her' room, she was consigned to the little study downstairs. There was some consolation in being surrounded by James's papers and things, but she had really looked forward to reliving the pleasure of her own bedroom.

Joanna served up beans on toast for tea and seemed quite happy to sit in front of the telly all evening. Maisie couldn't help but notice how untidy everything was. By the look of things, the hoover hadn't been out of its box for ages. The realization took her a step further, tipping the balance irrevocably. No longer was she the child and Joanna the grown up. Joanna needed looking after. She resolved to give the place a good going over next morning.

In fact, by the time she had done so she realized that it was too late to go to the fish shop which closed at midday on Saturdays. Remembering her new philosophy, she suppressed the feeling of regret. Perhaps she wasn't meant to go back there. A loud voice seemed to be telling her that she was needed right here at the cottage, but when she finally caught up with the object of her dreams on Sunday morning, it was clear that James had no wish to share the house with a third party.

'How are you doing then, Maisie? Enjoying that job of yours? Good job you found somewhere to go. As you can see, there's not much room here any more.'

James had changed too. He looked harassed, tired. His face seemed to have drooped in some undefined way, taking away the sharp, aristocratic line of his features. There was an angry red spot on his chin. With shock it dawned on Maisie that like her, he was only human.

After a strained lunch on Sunday, he agreed to drive back with them to the farm. Maisie knew that he was making an effort. Not for her, but for Joanna. Most of the journey passed in silence and she was relieved when they arrived.

As they made their farewells, Maisie thought that she detected tears in Joanna's eyes.

'Take care. Be sure to keep in touch, won't you?' They were the words that Joanna had used that first time when they had abandoned her at the farm. Now Maisie heard the plaintive note in her ex-teacher's voice, the need for a friend. Returning Joanna's hug, she nodded.

James was still in the car. He poked his head out of the window and gave her a dry sort of smile. 'Look after yourself then, kid. Keep in touch.' He echoed his wife's words and Maisie felt none of the anguish that would once have enveloped her when she realized how empty was their meaning.

In the farm kitchen, Rose was sitting near to the range, darning a hole in the elbow of George's jumper.

'Had a good time?' She looked up briefly from her task and

nodded towards the range. 'Put the kettle on, there's a good girl.'

Half past five on Sunday evening. Maisie fell easily into the routine of the farmhouse. With a bittersweet regret, she thought: I've come home.

PART THREE

Fifteen

THE OLD HORSE stood in the gloom of the cow byre. Slowly his head drooped lower and lower until his nose came to rest on what remained of the rancid straw. His nostrils twitched with misery and with an effort he lifted his head away from the acrid fumes, but the weight seemed too much for his long, thin neck and his head dropped again. This time he could not find the energy to raise it.

Painfully he eased the joints of his feet one by one. His fetlocks were swollen and his overgrown hooves made it difficult to stand comfortably. Dimly he remembered the hiss of steam and the smell of singed hoof as the farrier pressed new, hot iron shoes to his neatly trimmed feet. Then there had been comfort, a joy in his step as he cantered the length of his paddock, newly shod, groomed and fed.

Miserably, he kicked at his belly in a vain attempt to stop the irritation as lice burrowed into his dusty coat. The hair on his flanks had grown long and matted, except where he had rubbed himself sore in an attempt to get rid of the torment.

His eyes closed and somewhere inside of him he relived the pleasure of munching his way through a bucket of chaff and barley. '*Here we are me old laddo,*' the gruff, comforting memory of the old man's voice filled his head. *Duke* the old man called him, *Dooky.*

The farmer always used to come at this time of the evening,

before the darkness set in, enveloping the world. Then, Duke had enjoyed the nightly privacy of his stable, the crisp golden straw, the aromatic sweetness of hay, with mice making timid sorties for the dropped crumbs of cereal. In winter the old man covered Duke with a hessian rug: *To keep Jack Frost at bay*. The old horse let out a long, resonating echo of despair.

When the old man stopped coming the old lady had shut him up in the barn. Day and night he saw no one. It was dark and draughty. Beneath the layer of old straw the earth floor turned to ooze and he stood in the soupy mud while his feet grew smelly with fungus.

Once a day she threw a couple of slices of hay over the door. When he moved hungrily to eat it she eased the door open a crack and struggled in with half a bucket of water. If he turned to look at her she shouted, 'Geddup, you devil!' Fear made her harsh.

Almost before she reached the other side of the yard he would drain the bucket dry. He wanted more, more of everything, food, water, light, bedding. Kindness. Company. He was lonely. He was cold. As winter advanced he waited only to die.

Sixteen

ON FRIDAY MORNING George got up even earlier than usual. He didn't gain much because outside it was pitch black, but in so doing he reasoned that at least he wouldn't have to rush at the last minute.

The evening before he'd given Ian his orders for the day. He had to be careful here because Harold and Jim had both worked for him on and off for donkey's years and they didn't take kindly to being told what to do by a slip of a lad, but he knew that sooner or later Ian would be taking over from him so, one way and another, they'd have to get used to it.

In a strange way, acknowledging the inevitability of Ian as his heir had the opposite effect from what he would have expected. It spelled acceptance, a coming to terms with the fact that Ned would not be coming back. For a while he dwelt on the feeling, giving himself up to a different future. Ian might have some fancy ideas but he was a good lad at heart, keen, reliable. This new future wasn't too hard to take.

As he climbed out of bed the revelation of last night was still with him but now wasn't the time to dwell on it. He forced his thoughts back to more familiar ground.

Once they had done the routine work of the morning, Harold and Jim could make their way across to Spinners and begin grubbing out the old hedgerow. That, or depending on the weather, digging out the ditch that ran along its outer length. The field didn't drain well so at this time of the year it stood fallow. Come April he'd layer the hedge proper, then the bullocks could be turned out to get some weight on them. Meanwhile the animals stood in the yard, churning up the mud, costing him a fortune in hay.

As he pulled on the thick socks that Rose had knitted him in easier times, before her joints got so bad, he drew comfort from the knowledge that Ian could busy himself in the office, get those milk returns up to date.

Although it was a Friday, George put on a clean shirt and cords. He was going across to Dunsbury Dew where there was a farm clearance. It meant extra washing because Rose would insist that he still changed all his clothes again on Sunday but at least she had help now. Anyway, you had to be a bit tidy because at a farm sale you never knew who you might meet.

Last night Rose had trimmed his hair. She'd been his barber ever since they first married. He sniffed as he pulled his braces up. None of this poncing off to the hairdressers, especially not these days when you were as likely to get a girl as a feller. It weren't natural having a bit of a girl fiddling about with your thatch.

Downstairs, everything was quiet. He raked the range, coaxing it back into life and flung in some kindling to get the kettle boiled, then he went to the larder and helped himself to some cold bacon and bread and butter. It was a breakfast that was familiar from childhood, before the luxury of fried eggs and sausages, bacon and mushrooms. There was something pleasant in knowing that forty years ago his old dad would have been sitting at the same table, eating just what he was having now.

Outside the air was spilling over with damp. To his relief the cattle truck started at the second try. In response to the sound of the engine, the farmhouse door opened and Rose appeared in the yard. He hadn't expected her to get up so quickly. Stopping the truck, he pulled down the window and waited as she approached.

'What you taking that great thing for?'

'You never know.' He touched his nose mysteriously.

She gave him one of her looks. 'Don't you go coming back with a load of rubbish. I know you, George Draper.'

Grinning, he pecked her on the cheek. As the truck drew away he savoured the sense of liberation, patting the fat wad that was his wallet, nestling in the inside pocket of his jacket. No good going without a few bob. You never knew what you might find.

The sale was well attended. Rumour had it that a company from up north had bought up the farm but they had no use for the antiquated equipment. They already owned the neighbouring farm. Greedy, that was. The little man was in danger of being pushed out. George chose not to dwell on the prospect for the future. Perhaps he should get out of farming altogether, but at his age that was easier said than done.

When he reached his destination it was already busy. Parking up he waved to one or two familiar faces, suddenly comfortable in the knowledge that he was at home here, in his own element. As he wandered amongst the crowd he saw a few items worth going for – if the price was right, mind. There were several job lots too with some odd bits and pieces. He quite liked some of the older stuff, bit of a collector really.

His eye was caught by an old governess cart. That took him back a bit. They'd had something similar once when first they were married. He had a mental picture of Rose driving their black mare, Bessie; a young, vibrant Rose, pretty as a picture. The Rose of today was stout and tormented with the screws but she was a good old gal. He'd not change her. He'd sold the cart when they'd got their first motor, that old Wolsey. That was about the time the horses went and he'd bought the old tractor. Idly he looked the cart over. Quite a bit of worm in the shafts and a couple of spokes missing but nothing that couldn't be put right. He was good with wood, though he said so himself. It wouldn't take too much to do it up.

'*What dyou want that for?*' He could hear Rose's voice, gently chiding, pretending a despair that was part of their love. '*Whatever am I going to do with you, George Draper?*' Sometimes she was sharp these days but that was because of the pain. He never took it to heart.

The bidding was swift for there was a lot to get through. George couldn't believe how the time had flown. He got the governess cart for thirty bob. His initial delight began to pall as he queued up to pay. Rose was right, what *did* he want it for? Oh well, it was too late now. He hoped it would fit into the back of the truck.

Altogether he'd done well. He'd picked up a chain harrow and a pretty good lathe. And he'd got one of the job lots, quite a mixture of tools and some old bits of horse harness. In total he'd spent eight pounds, twelve and sixpence. Better not tell Rose, wouldn't she moan!

He watched as the auctioneer's assistant wrote it all in his ledger, handing over one five and four one pound notes and scooping up the change. The man nodded to him. 'Got transport?'

'Ay. I reckon the trap will just about fit inside.'

'What about the horse?'

George frowned. 'What horse?'

'The one that goes with the trap.'

His brow creased with disbelief. 'I didn't bid for no horse.'

'You didn't have to. It was a job lot.' The clerk held out the catalogue and under *Governess Cart, good condition,* was the single line: *Chestnut cob, no vices.*

George's heart beat faster. Goddang it he didn't want a horse. 'Where is it?' he asked, feeling a fool.

'Round the back in one of the barns. Bit of a plate rack.'

Pocketing his receipt, George made for the barns. The sun was behind them and inside it was like the black hole of Calcutta. As he peered in he sensed rather than saw a movement. He could dimly make out a shape, hardly a horse really, more like a skeleton. By God, he'd been caught here!

Going back to the auctioneer he waited until no one was within hearing, then he said, 'Look, I don't want that horse. No good to man or beast is that. Why don't you give the hunt a ring and they can take it for the dogs?'

The auctioneer gave him a look that said it wasn't his job. Aloud, he said, 'Can't do that. We want everything cleared out today. You'd better take it with you and ring them yourself.'

With a grunt George went to collect the rest of his gear, humping it up into the truck with the help of one of his cronies. 'Push that cart back a bit,' he called. 'I've got a bloody horse to get in yet.'

Before anyone could comment he went back round to the barn. There was no halter, but a length of rope hung on a cobwebby hook outside so he helped himself and opened the barn door. 'Come on you old codger, let's get you out of here.'

As the animal stumbled across to him his heart plummeted. Poor old devil. What a state to be in. He'd been around livestock all his life and there was no mistaking the degree of neglect here. He reached out a hand and touched the horse on the nose. It did not respond. Its eyes were vacant, a long way away.

'Right, laddo,' he ducked briefly to check the horse's sex and proceeded to fasten the rope around its head, making a loop to go over the distinctly Roman nose. Shakily it followed him out, blinking its amber eyes against the unaccustomed light.

'What the devil you got there, George?'

Some of the blokes gathered round, ready for a laugh.

'Running that in the National, are you?'

'I bought it for the kennels,' he said, hoping to hide his embarrassment.

They had to drag the old boy up the ramp. He wasn't unwilling, his legs were simply too weak to make the incline.

Several of the men turned sober. They didn't like neglect. Others covered their discomfort by joking.

Once the animal was aboard, George pushed up the back of the truck and fixed the pins in place. He'd better drive slow or else the old feller might fall over and knock everything else flying.

Rose and Ian were in the yard as he drove in. Uh-uh, he thought. What's Rose going to say? He'd already prepared a speech about the cart, but the horse was a different matter. Best try and distract them with the other bargains.

'What you got, then?' She came across, resting her hands in the small of her back, easing her aches.

'This 'n that.'

Harold came to help him unlatch the back of the truck. 'Now don't start going on,' he warned as the ramp dropped down.

Harold was the first inside. 'Good God, Gov, what the devil you got here?' He untied Duke and pulled him towards the slope. At first the old horse held back but he didn't have the energy to resist so he stumbled down the ramp, his back legs buckling.

'Oh, George!' Rose turned dismayed eyes to him. 'If that ain't a waste of money I don't know what is.'

'He didn't cost me nothing,' he defended himself. 'He was just thrown in with some other stuff.'

'Well if he didn't cost nothing to buy he's sure as hell going to cost to put right. Just look at him. He needs a hundredweight of grub inside him for a start.'

George couldn't argue. She was right. He was going to cost – delousing for a start, then the blacksmith to sort out those hooves, a good dose of worming, not to mention fodder. 'I'll phone the hunt. For the hounds.' He fell back on his original plan.

'I'll have him.'

The three of them turned as one to see Maisie standing by the gate. Her expression was stricken, her eyes glued to the horse as if she was mesmerised.

'You don't want him,' Rose warned, barely hiding her amazement that Maisie had uttered a word. 'Besides, what you going to keep him with? He'd cost a fortune.'

Maisie came towards them but her eyes were still on the horse. If she heard what Rose said, she didn't show it. Going up to him she lay a gentle hand on his bony head. He seemed to lean against her as if for support.

'We'll talk about it tomorrow.' George was in equal parts amazed and grateful to Maisie for intervening. He was tired and they still had to unload the truck. To Harold, he said 'Take him round the back. Clear that loosebox out and put him in there for tonight.'

Before Harold could move, Maisie had taken the lead rope and was gently coaxing the old horse, forward. He seemed to draw confidence from her and tottered a few, faltering steps in the direction of the stable.

'I'll give you a hand.' Ian came to stand on the other side of the cob and together they led him round the corner. George was on the point of reminding Ian that he still had to hay up the heifers for the night, but something kept him quiet.

He looked across at Rose and they both raised their eyebrows in mute question.

Rose drew in her breath. 'Don't forget, there's still the table to lay, the stove to stoke and the bread to cut,' she called out to her assistant but already Maisie was walking away, her head bent close to that of the gelding. With Ian obscured by the old horse's head, they seemed enclosed in a world of their own.

George came to stand beside his wife and together they watched the retreating figures. In unison they shook their heads and he voiced both their thoughts.

'Well, if that ain't a sight for sore eyes, I don't know what is.'

Seventeen

AS THEY REACHED the stable yard, Ian released his hold on Dooky's rope and went ahead to open the door of the loosebox. The bottom dragged across the uneven ground, setting Maisie's teeth on edge, the hinges squealing with unaccustomed use. Already there was a tightness in her chest, a sense almost of disbelief. She reached out and touched the old horse just to convince herself that he was really there. He closed his eyes and his breathing was laboured. For a terrible moment she thought that he might collapse and die.

'Look at this.' Ian forced the door open a few more inches. Clearly the stable had not been occupied or many years, for inside was an assortment of old drills and hoes, sickles and sacks, all generously coated with dust and cobwebs. More spiders' webs hung in drapes from the rafters.

'Tie him up there.' He emerged with a film of cobweb clinging to his hair, a rusty bucket and a sack in his hands. As Maisie hesitated, he gave an impatient sigh and putting the objects down, took Dooky's rope again, secured him to a ring set in the wall outside the stable door.

'Don't you know anything about horses?'

Maisie shook her head, her ignorance shaming her. Ian changed his tone. 'Well, d'you know how to tie a sheep shank?'

Again she shook her head. It was clear that he was quite at home with horses but her further humiliation was tempered with a moment of envy, a mourning for the childhood she might have had, one filled with farms and animals, one with enough money to allow her the freedom to play the piano, to have ballet lessons, to go on holidays, to own her own horse.

Immune to her thoughts, Ian went through the motions of the knot, showing her how if a horse pulled back it would tighten, but in an emergency it could quickly be released. Maisie practised a couple of times, her fingers clumsy under his scrutiny, but he nodded his approval before disappearing back inside the box where he began dragging the rest of the equipment out into the yard.

All the while, Maisie stood near to the horse, staring at him with such intensity that it seemed as if her willpower alone would prevent him from toppling over. He looked so thin and frail.

She felt afraid. Somehow, at the sight of the old animal, something inside of her that was stronger than all her carefully constructed defences had burst through and forced her to speak. Now she felt exposed as a hermit crab without a shell, having nowhere to hide, no way of protecting her raw, tender feelings. Once more she was out there, back in the world of speech. Endless dangers lurked.

'Get him a bucket of water. Not too much though.' Ian burst into her thoughts, casting an expert eye over Dooky. He ran a firm hand down the animal's neck. 'See how his skin has lost its stretchiness?' He pinched a line of flesh along the horse's shoulder. As he let go the ridge of skin remained. 'That's dehydration, that is. We did it at college.' He nodded as if to confirm his own diagnosis.

Hastily Maisie ran to obey, her respect for Ian growing by the minute. When she had half-filled a bucket, she lifted it up so that the horse did not have to bend. With a short-lived flash of spirit he pushed his muzzle into the pail, sloshing the water in his haste and began avidly to syphon it up. Ian stood and supervised, watchful as a gold merchant guarding his raw materials.

'That's enough for the moment. Give him any more and you'll make him ill. Come on, you can give me a hand with clearing this junk.' He looked around him. 'Better still. if you carry on clearing out the box, I'll go and find some straw.'

As she worked, Maisie talked to Dooky inside her head. Gradually she managed to convince herself that she could not have actually spoken out loud at all. Surely she hadn't? As doubts resurfaced, she reassured herself with the thought that even if she had, no one had been paying attention. In any case, the physical effort of giving voice to her thoughts would be too much. Even if she wanted to speak now, she was sure that she could no longer do so.

In silence she communicated with her new companion. 'Don't you worry now. You've got me to look after you. I won't let anybody hurt you. I'll help you to get better.' She smiled to herself, aglow with newly found love.

Dooky twisted his head round to gnaw at a particularly irritating itch on his hind fetlock. With a struggle he managed to balance on three legs. He looked ungainly, as precarious as a not-very-proficient tightrope walker. For a moment he wobbled dangerously and Maisie drew in her breath, waiting for the dramatic fall, but just in time he managed to place his fourth foot back on the ground and regain his balance. Maisie saw then that his hooves were so cracked and overgrown that he could not rest his feet flat on the ground. Undiluted pain for his misery engulfed her.

A thousand questions raced through her head. How much would it cost to take him to the blacksmith? What did he need to eat? More important, would Mr Draper agree to let her have him or would he want to sell him? She had three pounds saved up. Would that be enough? She comforted herself with the thought that if she offered to work extra hours, perhaps he would let her have the stable in exchange. But what about everything else? One problem dominated the rest – to find the answers to her questions, she would first need to ask them.

At that moment Ian came back wheeling a huge barrel piled high with straw. By now Maisie had removed all the junk and swept out the stall. Great clouds of dust filled the air.

Ian tipped the straw into the cubicle and grabbed a pitchfork. 'This is how you need to put the bed down – see? It's important that it's thick enough so that he doesn't sink through to the ground beneath.' Expertly he shook the straw out, layer upon layer so that when he prodded it with the prong of the fork it did not strike through to the floor below. Maisie nodded and he handed the fork over, leaving her to continue while he fetched more bedding. By the time they had finished, Dooky had a bed fit for a Derby winner.

A wooden rack ran along the back of the stable wall and Ian filled it with packs of hay. Maisie watched him, breathing in the scent of crushed grass and clover, warmed by the way that as he came out, he patted the old cob compassionately on the rump.

'Eat up then, old man.' He turned to watch.

Dooky pulled a few strands of hay into his mouth and chewed with difficulty, his teeth grinding against the stalks. Ian frowned. Reaching for the halter he slipped it over Duke's head and brought him back to the door and the fading light. 'Here, hold on to the rope. Lets have a look at those teeth.'

Expertly he forced Duke's mouth open, grabbing his tongue so that he could not close it again, slipping his hand confidently into the chasm. The horse's eyes widened, the whites showing his alarm, but he did not struggle.

'Here, have a feel of this.' Ian turned and grabbed Maisie's hand, sliding her fingers into the gap between the teeth and the cheek. His grasp was firm and confident and she felt an alarming mixture of fear and excitement at his unexpected touch.

'Can you feel those lumps along the inside of his cheek? That's where he keeps biting himself. Now, run your finger along his teeth – that's right.'

Maisie did so, confident that Ian would not allow Duke to close his mouth and in so doing, bite her. The edges of his teeth were razor sharp. She winced as her finger was snagged.

'See? The poor old devil can't eat much with teeth like that.' He shook his head.

She wanted to ask what could be done but he saved her the trouble. 'They need a damn good rasping.' He was thoughtful. 'I've seen it done often enough, but never tried it myself.' He shrugged, leaving the treatment of Duke's teeth in the balance. Released once more, Dooky tottered back to the hayrack.

Already the sky had grown dark and Ian glanced up before saying, 'I'd better get back, I've still got work to do.' Maisie too remembered her unfinished tasks.

They were about to leave when George himself came across to see what they were up to.

'How is he?' He looked over the door and shook his head at the state of the old animal. 'A crying shame.'

'Can we make him up a feed?' Ian asked.

'I suppose so. There's a sack of oats in the barn. And some barley.' From his hesitation, the tone of his voice, it was clear that George was reluctant to waste too much of his stores on a lost cause.

'His teeth are in a state.' Ian rubbed his hands together to instil some warmth into them. The wind had come round to the east and was slicing though his jerkin.

George turned to Maisie. 'Go and get an old saucepan and put a couple of handfuls of barley in with some water and give it a good boil. When it's cool, mix it with some oats and a good handful of bran. You can give him half tonight and the rest in the morning.'

Maisie ran to do as she was bid, exhilarated at the prospect of doing something for her new found friend. In the barn it was already dark but she fought down her fear of the mice and rats that rustled day and night in the nooks and crannies, and poked in the sacks until she found what she wanted. On a shelf there was an assortment of old pans and taking one, she put in the barley and made for the house.

During her absence Rose had started the tea and had already laid the table. Steam erupted from a saucepan on the range and spat and danced across the black hot plate. Rose didn't look too pleased.

'You took your time. Whatever have you been up to?'

In answer, Maisie held out the saucepan for inspection before going to the sink and covering the contents with water.

'Don't you go thinking you can spend all your time over at that stable,' Rose warned. 'And don't go getting ideas about keeping that horse, neither. I meant what I said. You can't afford him.'

Thankfully, the telephone rang at that moment and Rose went off to answer it. By the time she came back, the barley was bubbling away and Maisie felt it was politic to do some work so she began to slice some bread.

A moment later, George came in. 'Got that barley on?' He walked over and peered into the pot, assessing its progress.

His wife had something to say. 'Don't you start littering up my kitchen with horse food, George Draper. And don't you go putting ideas in the girl's head, neither.' Rose could be formidable when she chose. With a sinking heart, Maisie feared that her employer's disapproval could push George into sealing the horse's fate. She kept her back to them, swilling the teapot under the tap then placing it near to the range to warm.

'Don't go on now, mother. That poor old hoss needs one good meal inside him.'

Rose didn't answer and Maisie had the feeling that her friend was being given the equivalent of a condemned man's breakfast. She drew in her breath, preparing herself for the fight to come. No matter what the cost, she would find a way to save him.

As she fetched some butter from the larder, George lifted the lid off the pot of barley. 'Here, lass. This'll do. Remember what I told you. Half tonight and half tomorrow morning with a handful of bran. By the time you get over there it will have cooled down.' Sensing that Rose was about to remonstrate, he added, 'And don't go spending half the night over there. It's already past time for supper.'

Maisie carried the precious barley over to the barn and ladled half of it into a bucket, adding an equal measure of oats and bran and mixing it all together, watching the steam rise, thinking how wonderful it would feel to the horse as the warm mixture worked its way down to his stomach.

As she crossed the yard, she encountered Ian coming to check on Dooky again.

'What you got there?'

She held the bucket out for him to see and he peered at it with a professional eye. 'That's more than enough. Don't want to give him colic.'

He looked up from the bucket to Maisie. Just as she went to walk away, he said, 'Didn't know you could talk. I thought you were really dumb.' Maisie felt her cheeks grow hot. She looked away, despair claiming her as she realized that she must indeed have spoken out loud.

'Why haven't you said anything before?' Ian followed her to the stall. She shrugged, wishing that he would go away but he was not to be deterred. 'You going all silent on us again?'

Opening the door she went inside, sensing escape in the near darkness. Duke, resting at the back of the stable, his nose inches from the ground, smelt the long remembered aroma of cereal. Somehow he found the energy to come across to her.

'Here you are, my love.' Maisie formed the words in her mind, putting the bucket on the floor and rubbing a loving hand down his neck.

'Come on then.' Ian stood back and reluctantly she came out of the box while he closed the door behind her.

There being nothing else left to do, he started back across the yard, Maisie following behind. She felt breathless, almost overwhelmed by the turn that events had taken. Halfway across she wanted to turn back, to go and look at the horse again, just to convince herself once more that it hadn't been her imagination and that he really was there.

A picture began to form in her mind of herself riding him; not the poor emaciated skeleton that he was now but a sleek, muscular, transformed horse with flowing mane and tail, neck raised proudly, head tucked in, legs moving with a strong, floating gait. She, Maisie, would sit astride him, flowing with his every movement, a natural horsewoman, admired by everyone around: *There they go! What a wonderful sight!*

'Come on!' Ian had reached the porch and deposited his boots. He held the door half open, waiting for her to follow suit. Shamefaced she struggled out of her wellingtons and followed him inside.

George was seated in his stockinged feet in the big wooden chair close to the range, a mug of tea in one hand and the *Farmer's Weekly* propped up on his knee. He laid the magazine aside. 'Got the vet coming in the morning to that heifer,' he said to his nephew. ' 'Spose we could get him to have a look at the old boy. If not, the knacker's coming after lunch. . . .' He didn't finish the sentence.

Maisie's chest grew tight and her limbs began to tremble. He was suggesting the unthinkable. Somehow she would have to get there first, see the vet and find out what it would take to make the horse well again. The horse. He had to have a name. That would make him more real, more permanent. She went through all the names she had ever heard before: Prince, Dobbin, Rocket – that had been the milkman's horse – Major, Black Beauty, Ginger, Merrilegs. . . her mind scrolled through the cast of characters in *Black Beauty*. Albert, Duke . . . she began to smile as she knew for certain what he should be called – Mr Wonderful.

'For goodness sake, Maisie. What's the matter with you? Just get and drain those potatoes, will you? My poor old hands are giving me gyp.'

Maisie hastened to oblige, storing Mr Wonderful away into that secret, precious part of her where all the good things lived. She felt restless, impatient, hardly able to wait for the next morning so that she could visit the new object of her dreams again.

She was up long before it was light, dressing stealthily and creeping down the stairs, praying that the farm dogs would not set up a hullabaloo and alert everyone as to her intentions.

Outside the air was like steel; cold and sharp and hostile. Hunching her shoulders against the wind she skittered across the yard, avoiding the mud where she could, until she came to the stable.

Mr Wonderful stood with his head framed in the doorway, his chin resting on the top of the door, his eyes half-closed.

He jerked awake as he heard her approach but immediately was distracted by something biting him and he swung round to nibble his flank.

In her pocket Maisie had an apple, one of those fallers that were in a pile just outside the back door. Remembering the state of Mr Wonderful's teeth, she bit a chunk from the apple and held it out to him. The feel of his muzzle against her palm was as gentle as a kiss. He blew softly into her hand then retrieved the slice and crunched it. Avidly he ate his way through the rest of the apple and when it was gone, snuffled around for more.

'That's enough for now. We don't want to make you ill.' She didn't know whether too much apple would be bad for him. Mum had always said that too many apples gave you the colly-wobbles.

In the corner of his box the water bucket was empty. She wondered: should she fill it up? As the unanswered questions began to mount she was aware of a quick lance of light as the farmhouse door opened and then closed. Looking round she saw a silhouetted figure emerging. Moments later, Ian hurried across the yard to join her.

'Guessed I'd find you here. How's Caesar?'

Maisie raised her eyebrows in question and in answer, he said, 'With a Roman nose like that, what else could he be called?' He reached out and slipped his hand under Mr Wonderful's mane, saying aloud, 'Not too bad. You can always tell how cold a horse is by feeling under there.'

Maisie reached out and did likewise.

'Right, then. Fill up his water bucket, and let's get his breakfast. And here he produced something from his pocket, waving it in the gloom. 'I found this brush. You can give him a bit of a groom, get some of that loose coat out.' As Maisie took it, he added, 'There's an old horse blanket in the barn. We'll hang it outside to air a bit then he can wear it at night if it gets too cold. All being well Uncle George might let you turn him out somewhere during the day.'

Maisie's spirits soared. Ian was talking as if the horse was already hers and as if he would be allowed to stay.

After Mr Wonderful had munched his way through his breakfast and had a long drink, Ian brought him outside and tied him up. He showed Maisie how to pick his feet out, explaining the importance of removing impacted dirt and stones. Duke's feet smelt like a damp cellar and Ian tutted at the terrible state of his hooves.

'Take a month of Sundays to put them right.'

At the gloomy prediction Maisie became aware that she was like a thermometer, her hopes and fears rising and falling like mercury, according to Mr Wonderful's prospects.

Ian picked up the brush. 'Give him a bit of a groom now. Nice steady strokes.' He demonstrated before handing the brush over. 'When you've finished, put him back inside – and don't be long or Aunty Rose'll have your guts for garters!'

Maisie grinned, the shared joke warming her through. For a while she had forgotten that Ian was a young man, that he was the nephew of her boss, that she had endured a humiliating evening with him at the dance, and that in normal times he viewed her as something of a joke. For a while they had been two people sharing a cause.

Meticulously she worked her way over Mr Wonderful's shaggy, louse-ridden coat, amassing a pile of ginger hair, stirring up a scurfy film over his skin. Here and there insects made a dash for shelter and she shuddered.

When there seemed no likelihood of making him look any better, she picked the hair out of the brush, kissed Mr Wonderful on the nose and returned him to the box. 'I'll be back later,' she mouthed into his ear. The feel and shape of it reminded her of Bramble and Forget-me-not. It reminded her that it was Saturday morning. She remembered that this was her day for helping in the cowshed.

Already daylight was winning the battle for supremacy. If she didn't hurry she would be late and that would give Rose another excuse to say that the horse must go. Giving Mr Wonderful one more hug she ran back across the yard and into the house to light the range.

The vet came at around half past ten, just as she was helping to swill the milking parlour down. George broke off from what he was doing and went across to meet him, then together they set off for one of the out buildings where the sick heifer was isolated from her companions.

As she swept, Maisie fretted. Supposing Mr Draper forgot to

mention Mr Wonderful? Supposing the vet took one look at him and advised that he should be shot? She needed to be there to plead his cause, to promise that whatever it cost, she would pay for the treatment that he needed.

There was a clatter in the lane outside as the milk lorry came to pick up the churns. Peering out, she saw Ian helping to heave them into the back of the pick-up. He did so with an easy rhythm that belied their weight. She thought how strong he looked; agile, full of restless energy. In response, an unnamed feeling started somewhere inside of her, part sadness, part magic. For a few seconds Ian had a conversation with the driver of the milk lorry. Both men laughed and Ian stood back and waved the vehicle away.

Coming back into the yard, he came across to the milking parlour, just as George and the vet emerged from the shed. Maisie felt her face grow hot, afraid that he might tune in to her recent feelings.

'Go on.' Seeing her agitation, he took the yard brush from her. 'Go and get the horse out so's the vet can have a look at him.'

Maisie didn't need a second bidding. George and the vet were in low voiced conversation as she passed them. Seeing her, George glanced in the direction of the stable.

'While you're here, Mister, just take a look at this old hoss, will you? I got the knacker coming later but I'd like your opinion first.'

'Not going back into horses are you?' The vet was a small man, skinny, with sharp features and a narrow, sensitive face. His grey eyes reflected the morning haze. He wore a warehouse jacket over his tweed suit, and gumboots.

'Not likely.' George encouraged him to start walking.

'Lots of men are. There's many a time you can use a horse when you can't take a tractor on to a wet field.' Glancing quickly at his pocket watch to show that his time was limited, the vet followed George across the yard. Maisie was already at the stable, struggling to secure the rope around Mr Wonderful's head. She hadn't yet mastered the knack of looping it over his nose and passing it behind his ears to hook through the nose-piece, thus making a secure halter.

'Bring 'im out.' George sounded impatient and clumsily she did as he asked. As they came through the door, Mr Wonderful stepped on her toe and she gave a yowl of pain. Mr Draper grinned. 'Got to get used to that with hosses. Just be glad he ain't got shoes on.'

Maisie hobbled out, aware that the vet had screwed his eyes up and pursed his lips in a way that said what he saw was bad news.

He walked around Dooky, mentally recording his failings, pressing his flanks, feeling down his legs, all the while shaking his head. After a moment he looked in his mouth.

'He's not that old,' he conceded. 'About twelve I'd say. He's taken quite a hammering though. Those hooves are a problem to start with. With the state of those feet it's hard to say how much damage his legs might have suffered. No point in asking you to trot him up, he'd probably drop dead.' He sniffed as he said it, dismissing Mr Wonderful.

George nodded. He looked impatient. It was clear that with every observation the vet was hammering a nail into Mr Wonderful's coffin.

But the vet hadn't finished. 'Clearly he's suffering from long-term neglect. His kidneys are probably shot to buggery – excuse my French.' He glanced at Maisie as he spoke, then turned to George. 'If you want my opinion I'd get him out of the yard as soon as you can. He's alive with vermin. You don't want that spreading.' By his manner the consultation was at an end.

'Please!'

Something about the tone of Maisie's voice made both men stop. She struggled for something to say, anything that would save Mr Wonderful's life.

'Can't you give him something? I – I'll pay.'

The vet looked at George and George looked uncomfortable.

He turned to Maisie and spoke slowly, as to a not very bright child. 'I'm sorry, gal. It's probably a kindness to put him out of his misery.' He looked to the vet for his support.

'But he's not old. You said so!' Maisie too turned to the vet, sensing that he was her best bet.

He shrugged. 'I can give you some louse powder, get rid of

that itching. God knows how long it will take for his skin to recover, he's been bitten raw in places.' As Maisie stared at him, willing him to continue, he added, 'And some jollop to drive the worms out.' He shrugged as if that was the best anyone could hope for, a bit like giving someone with a fractured skull an aspirin.

George started to shake his head, but seeing Maisie's expression, the desperation in her eyes, he weakened. 'I'll have to stop it out of your wages,' he warned. 'You do understand that?' She nodded vigorously. Making up his mind, he said to the vet, 'We'll give him a week or two, just to see how he goes. If he picks up I might be able to sell him. Someone might want him.' From his look it was clear that he didn't think that it was remotely possible.

The vet went back across to his Jeep and returned with a tin and a bottle. 'Right, give him a good dousing down with this powder, do it in the open air or you'll get it up your nose and it's poison. And tonight, give him a good feed and a jolly good jollop of this in it. It'll clear him out good and proper. Oh, and you'd better get him to a blacksmith as soon as you can, get those hooves sorted – although I can't see him walking into the village.' He looked at George and with a sigh, her boss said, 'I suppose I'll have to take him in the truck. I reckon it's the only way.'

Relief flooded over Maisie. For the moment at least, Mr Wonderful was reprieved. She put him back into his box and then, remembering that Ian was doing her work, hurried across to the milking parlour. Inside it was thoroughly washed and swept and empty.

She found Ian across in the barn. 'Well, what did he say?' He put down a pitchfork and waited.

Maisie struggled with her throat. For an eternity words teetered on her tongue. Already she had broken her vow never to speak again by pleading Mr Wonderful's cause with Mr Draper and the vet. There seemed to be no going back. With a rush, she said, 'He's given him some medicine. For worms and fleas.' She blushed as she spoke, her words hesitant, like those of an infant newly come to talking.

Ian nodded, apparently immune to her struggle. She detected

his satisfaction, then his brow clouded. 'Who's going to pay?'

Maisie looked away. 'Me.'

'You got any money then?'

She told him about the three pounds. From his look it was clear that he knew it would never be enough. As she waited for him to confirm her worst fears, he said, 'If you promise to pay me back I might be able to lend you some.'

She nodded her head vigorously, gratitude bringing tears to her eyes. She wanted to thank Ian, to tell him how much she appreciated his kindness – to her and the horse – but other, more complicated feelings got in the way. As she stared at him, her silence was consumed by something far crueller than gratitude. With growing agony she realized that for the first time since the explosion she had something to care for – and something to lose. Her feelings for Mr Wonderful were not like the fantasy love for James that had only been in her head, but for a real flesh and blood creature that needed her – and a real flesh and blood man who was kind and compassionate and *there*. Ignoring Ian's cry of surprise, she turned away and began to run, out of the farmyard, up the lane and into the open countryside.

Eighteen

'DID I DREAM it or did that girl actually say something the other day?'

It was not the first time that Rose had asked the question but somehow, something always seemed to intervene and she never quite managed to get a satisfactory answer.

She spoke, with a tone that implied that she knew very well she had not dreamt it. Maisie was upstairs making the beds and George and Ian were in the kitchen grabbing a quick cuppa when she raised the subject again.

Other than on that one occasion when Mr Wonderful had arrived, on the day of vet's visit, and very occasionally when she was alone with Ian, Maisie had reverted to her usual habit of silence. If Rose or George asked her something, she either showed them what she was doing, nodded, shook her head or shrugged her shoulders. There was something about her manner that defied anyone to ask questions. Like a tortoise, it seemed that at the least sign of intrusion she would pop her head back into her shell and be unreachable. Even Rose, never one for being shy about coming forward, hesitated to ask outright why she had been silent all this time, when it was now obvious that she could speak.

'You must have imagined it.' Ian, thumbing through a motorcycle magazine, looked longingly at a picture of the BSA he intended to buy. In another two weeks he should just about have enough saved up. Indeed, he had even put in an order at the garage at Thorley and they'd promised to get one delivered in time for Christmas. As long as Uncle George paid him on time he should be able to pick it up on Christmas Eve. He glanced across at George as he spoke, challenging him to comment on Maisie's recent outburst. George merely shrugged and picked his cap up from the table.

'Time to be going.'

'Where are you off to?' Ian followed him out of the kitchen and into the inhospitable gloom of the farmyard. Beneath their feet the mud gleamed slate-grey, nestling around their boots in cloying folds, reluctant to release its hold.

'Just out.' Something about George's manner stopped Ian from retreating directly to the barn. His uncle looked uncomfortable, shifty even, like a boy caught scrumping apples.

'Can I go for you?' he offered.

It was clear that his uncle was mulling something over in his head, deciding whether or not to come clean. Then, with a large intake of breath, he said, 'Look, I'm taking the truck down to Billingtons. I – I'm going to take the nag. I should have done it the day I bought him.'

Ian was aware that his mouth had dropped open. For a moment he couldn't quite believe that his uncle meant it. 'You can't,' he said. 'You can't do that to Maisie.' Knowing his uncle's weakness, he added, 'She says she'll pay for whatever the horse needs. There's no need to take him to the knackers yet.'

George sniffed with irritation. 'You know as well as I do that he ain't going to come right. Even if he did, the lass hasn't got that kind of money. It's a kindness to the horse. Besides, what does she want him for anyway?'

All the time Ian was shaking his head, waiting to interrupt the older man's flow of excuses. As soon as he could get a word in, he said, 'He doesn't take up any room. You don't use that stable and there's that patch of ground at the back you never grow anything on.' He was aware that in pleading Maisie's cause he was beginning to sound like her. His tone hardened. 'Anyway, it isn't going to cost you, is it? Why don't you give her a chance?'

'Yes? And what about all the straw and hay?'

Ian snorted. The hay cost only a few pence and as for the straw, it was only a by-product of the wheat and barley anyway. As he opened his mouth to say so, his uncle added, 'And what about these trips to the blacksmith? What about the petrol? I haven't got time to keep driving him to the forge.'

'I'll take him then.'

'You've got work to do.'

'I'll take him on Saturday.'

George swallowed. 'I thought you were going home this weekend?'

'Well, I won't.' Before his uncle could say anything, he added, 'And I'll pay for the petrol.'

This set George off on a different tack. 'Don't you start spending out on him. And don't you start lending that girl money. She'll never be able to pay you back.'

Ian bit back the desire to say '*I don't care.*' It was all getting out of control. He felt embarrassed, a fool, but he couldn't bear the thought of Maisie's grief, of her pain if she found the old horse gone. Besides, there was something about Caesar, a sort of appreciation, something in the depth of his wide, amber eyes that implied gratitude at his change of circumstances. It would be wrong to deny him at least one chance.

'Don't you be a danged fool now.' George went through the motions, buttoning up an old army greatcoat that he wore for work, but he turned away from where the cattle truck was parked. Ian knew that for the moment he had won.

'It's only for a couple of weeks,' he called out. 'You agreed that with the vet.'

'I got work to do.' George let out a parting sigh, washing his hands of the whole affair, and went to take his frustration out by sharpening a riphook. Ian listened to the angry rasp of stone on metal. Once again, for the moment, Dooky was spared.

As Ian went back to work he wondered if his uncle wasn't right. He'd been looking forward to a weekend at home, a night out with the boys. He might even have borrowed his dad's car and driven across to Thorley Town Hall to see if Dolores was there.

According to Aunty Rose she was supposed to be engaged to someone who worked for the Council. Ian remembered the pleasurable gropings that had been cut short because Maisie was waiting in the car park. The prospect of experiencing them again had preoccupied him ever since that evening. If she was engaged though, that put a different slant on things. I'm damned if I'd want my girlfriend carrying on like that, he thought. He wondered what he'd do though, if the opportunity arose. Apparently her fiancé worked on the dustcarts, a big bloke. He nodded his head at the silent voice in his head, advising him to keep away. By sniffing around there, he was probably treading on thin ice.

Perhaps it was the thought of ice and, by implication, scenes of winter snow, for he found himself instead thinking about Christmas. Uncle George had given him Christmas Day and Boxing Day off which was decent of him. Harold was coming in one day and Jim the other because, after all, the livestock still needed to be attended to.

He wondered what Maisie was going to do. Perhaps she was going to stay with that posh teacher friend of hers. She'd have a pretty dull time if she stayed with his aunt and uncle – up the same time as usual, all the farm routine to get through, church after breakfast, cooking a chicken dinner, going into the front parlour to listen to the Queen's Speech – where it was cold enough to freeze your balls off as the fire was only lit there once a year – and there was nothing else to do but stare at the wallpaper. Then there would be the evening routine: cold meat and pickles, stilton and celery for tea, listening to the wireless and early to bed.

He and his parents had spent Christmas here once, the year that Ned had died. True it had been bad timing, but it was still bloody awful, Aunty Rose in mourning, Uncle George outside most of the day, and never a moment's respite for enjoying yourself.

Ian thought about the routine at home: the Christmas tree, lots of baking, presents for everyone, the neighbours and a few relatives round for sherry and mince pies in the morning, a dinner as big as Everest, afternoon in front of their telly – he didn't half miss the telly at Uncle George's. He catalogued the rest of the Christmas Day pleasures at home – silly games, Christmas cake and trifle, an evening playing cards, as much beer as he could drink.

He thought back to the day before and Maisie's sudden and weird departure, running off when he offered to help her out. She was a strange little thing, no doubt about it, like some small, hurt creature, a rabbit in a snare, a wounded pheasant, trembling and fearful. For a wild moment he wondered about buying her a Christmas present. He could just imagine the expression on her face, surprise, delight – or would she run away again like she did yesterday, as if he was offering her a threat instead of a gift?

For a moment he wondered about her family. Aunty Rose said that they were all dead. She'd made a mystery of it. Could it be that Maisie was a mass murderer, like that axe girl in a song he'd heard – Lizzie Borden? Supposing she'd bumped off her whole family? He grinned. His aunt and uncle had better be careful, not keep on at her like they did.

He settled back into the routine of work. There was no sign of Maisie until teatime. As he went into the kitchen he got the impression that she was trying to avoid his eye. Perhaps she felt embarrassed by her behaviour the day before. By the time the food was dished up however, and they were all seated at the table, things seemed to have got back to normal. No mention was made of the cob or his future.

In fact, it wasn't until Saturday morning that Ian said to Maisie, 'I'm going to take the horse to the blacksmith presently. Want to come?'

She nodded and her cheeks took on a rare flush of pink. Immediately he regretted asking her, remembering the silent journey to the dance, the frantic searching for anything to fill the chasm, but having committed himself it was too late to go back. When he mentioned it to his aunt however, she had other ideas.

'You know she can't come with you, she's working. I want her to go with George into Thorley and get me some shopping.

Besides, weren't you supposed to be going home?'

Ian shrugged. Her unwillingness to let the girl go made him stubborn. 'I'll be home for Christmas. It's not long now.' He knew that Rose was quietly fulminating away. He added, 'We can call in to the shops on the way back if you like, get whatever you want. It'll save Uncle George a trip.'

He watched a nerve pulsate in his aunt's cheek, sensed her reluctance to give way. He remembered what his uncle had said about him and Maisie having rooms so close. Surely his aunt didn't suspect that he was taking an interest in her – not in that way?

'I want some stockings,' Rose said by way of reply. 'They do good thick ones in Maidments. I want a pair of slippers too, for George, for Christmas.'

'We can get those.'

There was nothing else that she could say. Before he went to get ready, he asked, 'Are you going to get Maisie a present? For Christmas?' Rethinking what he had wondered earlier, he added, 'Is she staying here or going to her friends?'

'I suppose she's staying here.' Rose sounded put upon but grudgingly she added, 'I suppose she'll be able to do the fetching and carrying for me, save me a lot of work.'

The outing had been agreed upon but the question of Maisie's Christmas present remained unanswered.

Dooky wasn't very keen on going back into the cattle truck. He dug in his old, overgrown feet and resisted Maisie's attempts to pull him up the ramp. Even with Ian leaning against his rump he defied them until George came along, and together the two men looped a rope around his hind quarters, jerking and driving him forward.

'Ged up, you old bugger!'

Knowing when he was out-numbered, Dooky gave in.

'No one's going to hurt you,' Maisie whispered into his ear. She had started the day in her old trousers, wellies and a thick woolly jersey but once Ian had suggested the journey, she had hastily changed into a pair of navy blue slacks that Joanna had given her and the pink jumper. Mr Wonderful thoughtfully pushed her with his nose, depositing a spread of chestnut hairs on her leg. Carefully she began to pick them off.

With Mr Wonderful safely loaded, she climbed into the cattle truck, exhilaration at the prospect of the outing setting up a tightness beneath her rib cage. The day offered all kinds of treats – the visit to the blacksmith, the sortie into Thorley to do Mrs Draper's shopping, perhaps a chance to buy some Christmas presents for her friends – and just being with Ian. Catching a glimpse of herself reflected in the truck window, she reached up and patted her hair, smoothing a few renegade strands back into place. When she had changed her clothes, she had also taken extra trouble with her hair, tucking the ends under and securing them with kirby grips to make a fair attempt at a french pleat. Her reflection was reassuring. She had been worried about what Rose might say and prepared to justify her changed appearance because she needed to be tidy for going into town. In the event, however, the older woman did not comment.

As they drove away from the farm, Ian whistled to himself. Maisie guessed that it was a habit, one that she liked for it made him sound cheerful.

'I'm getting a motorbike,' he announced above the roar of the engine, slowing down to get the truck through the gateway.

Maisie looked round and raised her eyebrows, registering her surprise.

'Haven't told Uncle George yet.' He glanced at her and grinned. 'It means I won't have to stay on the farm every weekend and evening.'

The thought of Ian going out and about, probably into town and the dance hall, threatened her sense of well-being, but his next words restored the balance. 'I'll give you a ride if you like.'

She nodded her enthusiasm. Riding on a bike with Ian! The little narrow corner that was her normal life expanded its horizons. For a precious moment light seemed to stream into her inner world and she felt as if anything was possible.

When they reached the forge and Ian had parked the truck, Maisie scrambled up into the back and led Mr Wonderful out.

He seemed to sense why he was there and followed her willingly across to the yard towards the cavernous darkness where the fire glowed orange. An assortment of tools and rusty iron shoes formed weird sculptures, reflecting the undulating glow.

'God'n hell, what you got there?' The blacksmith came out into the light to get a better look. He was a scrawny looking man, with large, horse-like teeth and beneath the dark skin of his upper arms, sinews wrapped themselves around like well-established ivy.

'He belongs to the young lady.' Ian nodded at Maisie. Seeing the frozen set of her face, he added, 'She's got a kind heart, rescued him.'

'Rescued him?' The blacksmith didn't add whatever he was thinking but it wasn't too difficult to guess.

'Come on, let's have him here.' He examined Duke's feet, tutting to himself, pointing out to Ian the faults and failings. Standing up and stretching to ease the stiffness in his back, he said, 'Well, I can tidy him up, make him a bit more comfortable, but. . . .'

He worked with professional ease, cutting and filing, levering off great chunks of hoof with pincers. 'Can't take off too much,' he explained. 'I'll have to do it gradual. Can you bring him back in a few weeks?'

Maisie glanced at Ian and he nodded. 'How much?'

'Fifteen bob.' As Maisie went to look in her purse, Ian said, 'Er, what about his teeth? They need a good rasping.'

The farrier sighed. His manner implied that he wasn't used to practising his skills on such a lost cause but he grabbed hold of Mr Wonderful's nose and forced his mouth open. For an age he poked and prodded, then let the horse go. 'Looks like the Rocky Mountains in there.'

He returned with a long rasp, and while Ian hung on to Mr Wonderful, the blacksmith began to file away at his sharp molars.

Maisie screwed her face up in dismay. The sound, the thought of having her own teeth rasped, made her shudder. Mr Wonderful seemed to share her opinion, for he began to struggle until the blacksmith fetched a loop of rope tied to a stick and proceeded to twist it around the horse's upper lip until he was firmly secured.

Maisie wanted to protest, to tell them not to hurt him, but Mr Wonderful stopped struggling and his eyes took on a glazed expression. Patiently he stood there until the operation was complete.

All the time the blacksmith was working, Maisie tried to guess how much more it might cost. She had already paid the vet. Then she had given Mr Draper seven and sixpence for the stable, and for hay and straw and oats and barley. In her purse she now had seventeen shillings. It seemed certain that the treatment was going to cost more than that. Even putting aside any hope to be able to buy Christmas presents for Mr and Mrs Draper, for James and Joanna – and for Ian, it was clear that she would not have enough.

As the blacksmith flung the rasp aside and wiped his hands on his leather apron, he said, 'Right, that'll be twenty-five bob.'

She scrabbled in her purse, looking for non-existent money. Sensing her anxiety, Ian said, 'I'll pay for now. You can settle up later.'

He took a pound note and two half-crowns from his pocket and held them out to the smith.

As the man pocketed them he said, 'Right then, bring him back in a month. Don't leave it any longer.'

'We will.'

Duke felt his way back across the yard like a barefoot bather on a stony beach, adjusting to the newly exposed parts of his hooves, testing out his balance. Having got used to the feel, he walked straight into the box and began to nibble the straw that lined the floor.

Ian looked at her and nodded his approval. 'See, he's feeling better already.'

Maisie nodded, her pleasure still tempered by her lack of money. Wouldn't Ian be angry when he realized that she couldn't pay him back? As they climbed back into the cab, she said, 'I've only got seventeen shillings.' It felt like confessing a sin.

'Never mind. You can pay me later.' Gratitude flooded her.

With the seventeen shillings she still had, she would be able to buy something for them all, but particularly for Ian.

As Ian put the truck into gear, an unpalatable truth hit him. Now he was short by twenty-five bob. Once he had done his own shopping, with or without a present for Maisie, there was no way that he was going to have enough to pay for the bike.

Nineteen

JOANNA'S MOTHER HAD always been fond of saying that marriage was a compromise. At the time Joanna hadn't questioned it; indeed she somehow absorbed the idea that with goodwill on both sides, any situation could be resolved. With that confident thought, on her wedding day she embraced the future, certain that as far as she and James were concerned, compromise, co-operation – call it what you will – would come so naturally that they would hardly notice it. At the moment though it certainly didn't feel like it.

Last year they had passed their first Christmas together as a married couple with Joanna's parents, and with the unspoken assumption that the following year they would go to stay at James's family home. All had been well until Joanna's father had died the following February. His death had been unexpected; one minute fit and healthy, then mysterious pains in his stomach, a prescription for a peppermint mixture to help his digestion, mysterious attacks of vomiting, rapid weight loss, whispered prognosis, and death. Joanna had of course been upset. Among the myriad of implications, she had somehow assumed that James would recognize the need to spend another Christmas with his newly-widowed mother-in-law. When she raised the subject however, it was clear that he did not.

'My parents are expecting us. We can't let them down now. Not at this late stage. Why didn't you say anything before?'

He was right of course. She should have made it clear but it hadn't occurred to her that she needed to do so. The thought of her mother alone at Christmas dredged up a feeling of resentment at his insensitivity. She defended herself by accusing him. 'Well I can't leave her by herself, can I? How would you like it if it was your mother?'

He didn't reply and gloomily she realized that in this instance, her mother's maxim did not hold water. This wasn't something you could compromise over. Either you went to one house or to the other. You couldn't be in both places at once.

'Besides, your mother is coming here when the baby is born, isn't she?' James spoke as if the one thing cancelled out the other. By his tone, the prospect of his mother-in-law visiting did not hold any great appeal.

Joanna searched around for a solution. She wanted to shout at him not to be so heartless. Experience was beginning to teach her that trying to win arguments was fruitless. Always, with cold logic, he beat down her impassioned pleas.

Grudgingly he made the first move. 'I expect, if I ask Mum, she'll say to invite your mother over.'

That wouldn't do. Joanna's mum wouldn't want to go. They had already tentatively discussed it on the phone and Joanna was in no doubt that her mother would rather stay at home alone than feel like an intruder into her son-in-law's family celebrations.

Aloud, she said, 'I don't think that's a good idea. You can't expect her to behave as if nothing has happened. I'm sure she needs to be somewhere familiar where she can go off and have a good cry if she wants to.'

James's shoulders stiffened subtly, speaking volumes. Joanna was afraid that she was being unreasonable. His parents couldn't do more than invite her mother over. Surely though, for once they could forego the pleasure of their son's presence on Christmas Day, given the circumstances?

Joanna didn't exactly dislike her mother-in-law, but they weren't two of a kind. Mrs Cameron was upright, confident in her view of things. Away from his parents, James was open to change, willing to break with family traditions, but as soon as he was back in their sphere of influence, he seemed to revert to type, spouting the views that in other circumstances he would never adhere to.

Joanna thought that although her own mother often irritated her, she was softer, more accommodating. While she had been part of a couple she could compete comfortably with the Camerons, make her famous compromises, tread warily around issues on which they would not agree. She imagined her mother alone with James's dad, being bombarded by his rhetoric, beaten into verbal submission as he expounded his views on the colonies, on women working, immigration, young people today. It wouldn't work.

For a moment it was on the tip of her tongue to suggest that he went home to his family and she would go to hers but that was unthinkable. On top of everything else, what would the older generation make of that? Already his mother nursed doubts as to Joanna's suitability as a wife, especially for her beloved only son. Leave him alone to spend Christmas elsewhere and all her worst fears would be confirmed.

Joanna felt tearful. This argument, all the other niggling disagreements, seemed to be tied in with her pregnancy. Somehow she had lost her direction. It was as if the baby was turning her into someone else. She was expected to be happy, to want the baby, but she couldn't feel anything except resentment for this unborn wrecker of lives.

James was concentrating on wiring up an electric plug for the table lamp that he had bought for his office. As he screwed the Bakelite cover back into place, he said, 'For a moment I thought you were going to insist that Maisie came with us as well.'

His comment unearthed further guilt and she felt a flash of anger at him. Hadn't she, in some undefined way, taken on the role of Maisie's guardian? Didn't she now owe it to the girl to invite her over? Supposing the Drapers didn't want her there, what would Maisie do? But she couldn't challenge it. She didn't have the energy, either physical or emotional, to deal with any more uncomfortable scenes. Faced with an unsupportable sense of loss she began to cry, not quietly but in great, dam-busting sobs.

James put the plug aside and came to her. The cloud of discord evaporated and he put his arms about her.

'What is it love? What's going wrong with us?' It was the first time that he had acknowledged it.

Hungry for his comfort she sheltered in his embrace, closing her eyes, absorbing his warmth through the rustling of his nylon shirt. She tried to speak but the sobs formed too great a barrier.

Paternally James smoothed her hair. 'Come on, poppet. Let's sit down and see if we can't sort this all out once and for all.'

As her sobs subsided, she wiped her eyes and sat down at the table, kneading the damp cotton of her handkerchief. She had no idea where to begin.

'It's the baby, isn't it?' James sounded gentle, avuncular. 'What's wrong? What do you want to do?'

She shook her head because she had no answer. Another situation where compromise was useless. The baby was there, a fact, not something to make a choice over.

'Do you want to move away from here?' he asked.

Again she shook her head. Her failure to find the right words reminded her of Maisie, stuck in a tunnel of non-communication.

'What would make you feel better then?'

She shrugged her shoulders, another way of avoiding saying that she didn't know what she wanted, what to do.

James sighed. There was an edge of impatience in his action and afraid to lose her hold on this precarious closeness, she scrabbled round for some reasonable explanation.

For a moment he beat a tattoo on the table with his fingers, then he said, 'It seems to me that you would be better off going back to work. If we were both working we'd have enough money to pay someone to look after the baby. And clean the house.' He glanced round at the chaos as he spoke and further guilt heaped upon her.

Joanna tried to imagine having a nanny, someone starched and efficient. She visualized herself getting ready for school in the morning and giving her orders for the day. Already she could see the disapproval in the hired help's eyes, the barely disguised contempt for her inefficiencies. No. A proper nanny wouldn't do. She'd be too intimidating. What she wanted was someone kind and hardworking who wouldn't make her feel a failure. For a moment she wondered if her mother might not fill the role but she and James would never hit it off. Besides, her mother lived too far away and would never want to give up her independence to move in with them. No, the answer was obvious – Maisie.

In one of those now rare moments, James seemed to pick up on her thoughts almost before she voiced them to herself.

'I suppose we could ask Maisie to come back.' He stuck out his lower lip, drawing his mouth down in a rueful expression. 'She is good about the house – and I bet she'd be good with the baby.'

'Where would we put her?' Joanna remembered the scene about the study.

James shrugged. 'I could always move my office into work. There's plenty of space there. That's not a problem.' He grinned sheepishly at Joanna, acknowledging his earlier possessiveness over the room. She had a grim picture of the future, with James, now that his office was part of his place of work staying ever later, in fact hardly bothering to come home at all. Seeing her despair he cuddled her again, a big brother, half-mocking her foolish fears. He said, 'She can have her own wireless. Perhaps we could get her a telly?'

Joanna treasured his comfort. As she nestled against the hollow of his shoulder, she said, 'I'll have a word with my mum, about Christmas. As for the other, let's get the holidays out of the way first, then we can see.'

The question of where they were going to spend the festive season still hadn't exactly been resolved, but the prospect of a future that did not revolve around nappies and gripe water gave her an almost forgotten glow.

'Please, Mum, it's only for a couple of days.' Joanna was aware that her breathing had suspended as she listened to the crackling silence from the other end of the telephone line. After an eternity, her mother said,

'You don't understand. None of you do. I can't go there by myself, not without your father. He's the only one who ever looked after me, who really understood me.' She began to snivel. 'I want him back. It's so unfair.'

The sound was excruciating. Inside her head, Joanna replied, '*Stop bleating on about fairness. Since when has the world been fair? D'you think my life's fair?*' She placed her hand against the bulk of her belly. All the time the silence oscillated. To herself, she continued, '*Anyway, Dad didn't understand you, at least, he probably understood you too well. He just put up with you, didn't say anything because he couldn't stand your whining.*' Not for the first time she was admitting to her own feelings, that there were times when she didn't like her mother, was irritated by her, lived in terror that she, Joanna, would grow to be like her. In that same moment she knew that she was in danger of expecting James to be the same as her father. Before they married she had naively believed that he instinctively knew what she felt and thought. By the very nature of their closeness she saw them as one and without even thinking about it, she had assumed that James's role in life was to look after her and fulfil her dreams. Now, of course, she knew different. It was unrealistic to expect it to be so and yet . . . it wasn't James's fault but she couldn't quite forgive him for not being omniscient. Other thoughts conflicted. James was strong, his own person. She didn't want him to be otherwise, not a lap dog, a 'yes' man. The fact that she made these distinctions felt like a betrayal of her father, as if implying that he had been weak not standing up to her mother – and yet ironically that very 'weakness' had preserved her parents' marriage, keeping them together for thirty-odd years. She felt a flash of anger towards her mother for never having learned any of these lessons.

Aloud, she said, 'You won't be going there by yourself. You'll be with us. Please, Mum.' She heard the martyrish sigh, the unspoken 'poor me' resonating back to her, then her mother said, 'Next year I'll go away somewhere then you won't have to bother about me.'

'Mum!' The force of her irritation hit home. She could hear

her mother changing to 'brave face' mode. 'Anyway, how are you keeping?'

Joanna stifled her anger. 'All right. Only two weeks to go.'

'Have you decided what to call him yet?'

'Or her.' Why was everyone so obsessed with the baby being a boy? She said, 'If it's a boy we thought we'd call him after Dad.'

'That would be lovely.' She heard the catch in her mother's voice but knew that she was pleased.

She made arrangements for them to pick her up on Christmas Eve, made small talk to get everything back on to an even keel before hanging up. As she placed the receiver back on the cradle, the future seemed to open up before her; dark, narrow, unchanging. Joanna thought: perhaps this time next year we could go away somewhere, perhaps by then I'll be back teaching, perhaps we'll win first prize on the Premium Bonds – perhaps, perhaps, perhaps. . . .

Twenty

THE PROSPECT OF spending Christmas at the farm held few fears for Maisie. Since the age of ten Mum had stopped allowing her to hang up her Christmas stocking, and any presents she received had degenerated into useful things like vests and toothpaste. If there was little excitement at the thought of staying in the Draper household, then the experience would only be what she was used to.

Occasionally she had little regrets, wondering what it would have been like to go to Joanna's. It would probably be similar to some of the films she used to see, where a Christmas tree the size of Jack's beanstalk filled the hallway, smothered with lights and tinsel, and with a barrier of brightly wrapped packages circling the base – not that the Camerons' cottage was as big as the American mansions of the films of course. She adjusted her picture to something more Dickensian with roasting chestnuts and a table creaking under the weight of meats and fruits, puddings and cakes. That too would be wonderful, along with the telly, except that if James and Joanna were in a mood with each other then she would feel uncomfortable. She wondered what could have happened to make this change. They had seemed so enviably happy, the perfect couple in fact. Perhaps that was the trouble – aim for perfection and that stingy God would soon knock you back down to size. She pushed the uncomfortable thought aside. In any case, the farm held a much more immediate appeal – the chance to spend some time with Mr Wonderful.

Maisie had already prepared him a Christmas stocking of carrots, apples and sugar lumps. As a treat she planned to take him for a walk, knowing that he must be bored with his stable and the daily, few yards' ramble across to the paddock which his hooves had quickly transformed into a bog.

Just outside the farmyard gates were verges, still green with saturated grasses. Mr Wonderful would love to graze on the banks, pluck sprigs of hawthorn from the winter hedges and crunch them with his newly spruced-up teeth.

Ian was going home for Christmas and this left Maisie with a dilemma. With her seventeen shillings she had managed to buy all her new friends presents, which of course included one for Ian. She longed to be able to thank him for making it possible for Mr Wonderful to stay. Without him she would have made mistakes that would certainly have made Mr Draper get rid of him. As it was, in the time that he had been at the farm, there was a noticeable change in the old horse. Gone was the dead, matted look to his coat. True it was still thick and shaggy, still dusty and unruly, but lice no longer tormented him. Beneath the surface of his woolly hide, his body was taking on a vibrant if lean quality, giving him back some shape instead of the skeletal frame that had stumbled from the cattle truck on that so-important Friday.

Although his fetlocks were swollen in the mornings, Ian said that that was only because he had been standing still all night in his stall and it was nothing to worry about. Sure enough, once he had walked around his paddock a few times the swelling disappeared. By following Ian's instruction and cleaning his feet each day, his hooves no longer gave off the sorry smell of decay.

'I reckon you've done wonders,' Ian pronounced as Maisie fetched her companion in from the paddock before it grew too dark. 'Who'd have thought he would make it?'

Maisie looked at him to see if he was joking but his eyes were wide and clear and serious. He nodded as if to confirm what he had just said and Maisie turned away, hiding her confusion by picking pieces of straw and twigs from Mr Wonderful's mane. She felt ridiculously, gloriously proud. She hadn't done anything except follow the advice of the experts, but the fact that Ian approved gave her a priceless feeling of confidence. Apart from her love for Mr Wonderful, secretly she knew that she would do anything to keep Ian's good opinion.

Companionably they walked back to the house, and while Ian went upstairs to change his clothes prior to leaving for home and the Christmas celebrations, Maisie took over the task of preparing the meal. This time of the year they invariably had soup with bread and butter for supper, or 'tea' as Mrs Draper usually called it. Tonight it was beef and vegetable, made with good beef stock from a boiled up shin bone, pearl barley, onions, carrots, turnips and potatoes. On the range it simmered into a soft, tasty mush. By the time it was ready, Ian came back down carrying his suitcase.

'How many clothes have you got in there for goodness sake?' asked Rose. Maisie noticed that she was wearing an uncharacteristically vivid pinafore with red, green and black circles emblazoned across it. Normally, by this time of the evening she had cast her pinny aside, but tonight there were still the sprouts and parsnips to prepare for tomorrow's dinner, plus a good sage and onion stuffing to go with the capon that George had killed that morning. Somehow Maisie had managed to get out of plucking the bird. The sight of the quilt of white feathers, the goosepimply skin of the dead cock filled her with sadness. Even Christmas was a time of death.

In response to his aunt's remarks, Ian grinned. 'It's not just clothes I've got in here, Aunty, I've got presents as well.' As he spoke he opened the case and produced three wrapped packages, placing them on the kitchen table. 'Not to be opened until tomorrow, mind. Don't forget.'

With a frown he poked among the contents of his bag. 'Darn it, I've forgotten my razor.' Leaving the case open on a chair, he went back upstairs to fetch it, which gave Maisie the chance to sneak a look at the presents. One of them was for her.

Up in her room, wrapped in crepe paper, was the present that she had chosen for Ian: a jar of Brylcreem and a hairbrush and comb in a fancy box. It had cost more than she intended to pay but it looked so smart that she knew she would never find anything else to satisfy her. The only problem was how to give it to him without dying of embarrassment. Now was her chance. While he was upstairs she made a dash for her bedroom and just managed to beat him back to the kitchen where she slipped the box inside his open suitcase, hiding it among his shirts along with a card with a coach and horses, snow and glitter on it, in which she had written *Thank you, from Maisie.* There was so much more that she wanted to say but writing her feelings was as dangerous as speaking them. To her relief, when Ian came back he put the shaving things inside the case and shut the lid without noticing.

'Come along, Maisie. Get that soup dished up.'

She hurried to do as she was bid, the excitement of having a present from Ian competing with the pleasure of having one to give to him. As they ate, Mrs Draper said, 'After supper I'm going to cut your hair – both of you.' She looked across at George and then at Maisie. Ian opened his mouth to say something but realizing that his aunt did not intend to include him, he refrained.

Rose added, 'Your hair's proper shaggy, young lady. Time you had it tidied up.'

'Not too much off, Aunty, I think it really suits her like that.'

Maisie couldn't quite believe what she was hearing. She glanced at Ian and before she could look away, he winked at her. Already he had finished his supper and was waiting impatiently for George so that his uncle could run him into Thorley to get the bus home.

This wasn't the way Ian had planned it. For weeks now he had visualized arriving home on his own motorbike. He'd hinted to his parents about it, just to test out their reaction, and not wanting to spoil his arrival if the bike came as too much of an unpleasant surprise. His mum had of course expressed the fear that he would ride too fast and have an accident, but he had been quick to reassure her: '*I'm not daft, Mum. I've got no intention of killing myself.*' Anyway, he had had to ring up and tell them that he would be getting a lift from Uncle George after all.

He wondered if he would have some money for Christmas. If so he might be able to go and get the bike on his next day off, except that that was the day he had promised to take Caesar to the blacksmith again and he wasn't convinced that Maisie would have enough money, so once more he might have to pay. True, she had insisted on giving him half a crown towards what she owed him but the sad fact was, whatever she paid back, the horse was always going to cost more than she could afford. Oh well, he didn't mind nearly as much as he would have expected to. He liked Caesar. He was a game old chap. He liked Maisie too. What he didn't understand was why he felt so responsible for her. The feelings she engendered were too confusing to even think about so he reverted to contemplating the horse. Perhaps, come the spring, they'd be able to ride him, or even drive him in that old cart that Uncle George was doing up.

George pushed his plate away and wiped his mouth across the back of his hand. 'Come on then, lad. Let's get going.'

Ian stood up. 'Well then, have a good time, one and all.' After a moment's hesitation he kissed Aunty Rose on the cheek and looking at Maisie, he smiled. She felt unsettled inside, picturing the impossible, that she too might receive a kiss, but of course she didn't. His lips curved into a grin, revealing his white, regular teeth. For a dangerous moment Maisie wondered what it would feel like to have his lips pressed against her mouth but the thought was cut short because already Mr Draper and Ian were going out, calling goodbyes.

As she cleared the table she nursed an exquisite sense of longing, plucking cameo scenes from the air to fill her imagination. The package from Ian was square. She longed to poke it but Mrs Draper had placed the presents on the sideboard and she didn't have the nerve to go near them. What might it be? Her thoughts switched to Ian opening her present. What would he think? One version was a smiling, delighted Ian, thinking fondly of her, the other was of a frowning, dismissive Ian, thinking that she was a fool. Why did she never know how things would turn out?

Once the table was cleared and the dishes washed, once the

sprouts were done and the carrots and parsnips peeled, Mrs Draper fetched her scissors and instructed Maisie to sit on a stool next to her chair so that her head was level with Mrs Draper's chest. Maisie sat up very straight, aware of the softness of Rose's bosom, the faint smell of wintergreen. In spite of her sharpness of manner, there was something cosy about her employer and Maisie gradually allowed herself to slump back, her shoulder blades pressing against the older woman's knees.

'Mind out, girl. If you lean on me, my legs'll seize up. I get that stiff.' Chastened, Maisie returned to her former pose while Mrs Draper industriously brushed her hair out.

'My goodness, you've got a head of hair here, thick as a jungle it is.' Maisie wasn't sure if this was good or bad. She endured the tugs and jerks, listened to the clipped swishing of the blades and prayed that Mrs Draper would pay heed to what Ian had said. She didn't want her hair short, not any more.

Once, long ago, Mum had talked about her own hair when she was a girl, describing it as her 'Crowning Glory'. It conjured up a wonderful picture of innocence and beauty, but just tinged with a hint of danger. Please, God, Maisie thought, I know it's Jesus's birthday and all that tomorrow and that you must be busy, but could you just find time to make sure that my hair grows so that it's my crowning glory? As she formed the prayer, she wondered if she was being vain and instead, as a punishment, God – if there was a God – would make Mrs Draper cut her hair right up to her ears, and not even into a pleasing shape. This was the trouble with God, the source of His hold over you was because you never knew whether He really existed or not. Although she knew that He didn't, there was still that tiny corner of her mind that hoped that perhaps there was a good, kind, just God who would help her to make sense of everything that had happened. In spite of herself, she held her breath and waited.

'Right, get those locks swept up. As soon as Mr Draper comes back I'll do his, then I think we should all get to bed because tomorrow there will be a lot to do.'

Maisie stood up and risked a glance at the floor. To her relief the scattered hair was no more than an inch or so in length. She risked putting her hand up to feel her head and there was still enough left to tie back. Thank you, God. Thank you very much.

Once the evening routine was over, Maisie was the first one to go to bed. She found it difficult to sleep. Every time she surfaced, the thought of Ian's present filled her mind, startling her into instant wakefulness. She tried to be firm with herself, to decry the excitement, branding it as childish, but a physical trembling just beneath her ribs persisted. In the end she got up ridiculously early, creeping down the stairs with her presents for Mr and Mrs Draper, and her paper bag of goodies for Mr Wonderful.

Without the benefit of light, the kitchen seemed cold and cavernous. The merest glimmer of embers through the grill of the kitchen range gave the illusion of some small warmth and she made towards it. In the gloom she could still make out Ian's presents on the sideboard, but since last night the pile had grown. She crept over to investigate.

There was something that looked like a shoebox that she knew to be Mr Draper's slippers, and a soft, squashy package of about the same size that she had purchased at Mr Draper's request.

'*Get her something nice, lass. Something useful mind, but nice.*'

Maisie had chosen a blue bed-jacket with fluffy angora wool along the edges, guaranteed to please even Mrs Draper.

On the sideboard there was also a smaller, flatter parcel, soft to the touch, that she did not recognize and underneath it, an envelope. It was still too dark to make out the names on any of them so Maisie added her gifts to the collection and headed for the stable.

Mr Wonderful heard her before he could see her and called out, the resonating trill of his greeting intruding into the pre-dawn silence.

'Hello, my love. Happy Christmas.' Maisie felt the now familiar joy in placing her fingers on his long nose, feeling him lift his head in response and blow gently into the palm of her hand. 'Here, see what I've got for you.' She opened the paper bag and took out a carrot which he crunched with a pleasurable rhythm that made her realize that there was music in the strangest places. With a mouth still half-full of carrot he snuffled against her until she produced an apple, followed by two lumps of sugar.

'Aren't you a lucky boy? No more now or you won't want your breakfast.' She knew that this wasn't true. Mr Wonderful never refused food. He had been without it often enough to appreciate every grain, every blade that came his way.

It was still too dark to take him for a walk so she took the hessian blanket off him and led him across to his paddock where he immediately lowered his head and began the task of mowing the entire surface. Maisie watched his outline. Random feelings possessed her, not tied to any event or memory, simply sensations of tenderness, anguish, love, joy, all entangled in a confusing whole. She didn't know what they related to – her past? The tragedies that had taken all her living relatives? The arid life at West Street? The loss of James and Joanna? The dawning awareness of something out of reach and embodied in Ian? Or was it simply the presence of Mr Wonderful, his painful history, his miraculous progress, and the knowledge that for the moment at least, he was hers? For the moment.

She breathed in deeply, gathering her resources to push the feelings away. Light was beginning to paint a colour-wash over the skyline, putting the world into sharper focus. Across the yard she saw the dim outline of Harry, crossing to open the farmyard gate and let the cows in for milking.

'Mornin' lassie. 'Ave a happy one.' He waved to her.

Uncertainly she waved back. She should wish him a Happy Christmas, properly, but already the words had solidified in her throat and her mouth turned too dry for speech. Instead she waved again. Time to let the chickens out, to fill up water troughs and to distribute hay; time to clean out the range and get the kettle boiling and start a hundred other tasks.

She wondered when they would open their presents. Before breakfast? After church? She didn't want to go to church. Much better to stay behind and keep an eye on the dinner and take Mr Wonderful for his walk.

But go to church she did. At home, church had meant Sunday School and an occasional venture into the Methodist Chapel which her family claimed as theirs whenever they were asked to define their religion. She couldn't remember Grandad ever actually going to church and Mum had only done so under protest, showing her face at Easter, or at a special Mother's Day service. This sort of church was different. The vicar wore a fancy smock and sang some of the service instead of speaking in a normal voice. Meanwhile the congregation sang back at him. Maisie kept an eye on Mrs Draper to see what to do next, kneeling and sitting and standing without apparent reason. Fortunately the carols they sang were familiar to her so she was able to reproduce them inside her head. But all the while her mind was abstracted by the intensity of her earlier feelings, interspersed with unsatisfied curiosity as to what the parcels contained.

It was a relief when the service came to an end and they came back out into the churchyard, but that produced its own fears. Maisie did not like churchyards. Too many memories, her last visit too recent, too raw. She focused all her feelings on Ian and what he might be doing at that very moment, wishing with a sudden longing to be with him.

They ate their Christmas dinner as usual in the kitchen, only today Mrs Draper took off her pinny before sitting down. She had placed a vase with a sprig of holly in it in the centre of the table, and instead of a cup of tea afterwards, they had a glass of port.

'Put some colour in your cheeks,' Rose observed, half-filling the tiny delicate glass with its twisted stem and engraving around the rim. 'Not much now or you'll start acting silly.'

Maisie liked the rich, sweet taste and the feelings that followed, first a warmth in her stomach and then a vague, light-headed feeling. She would have liked some more but Mrs Draper didn't offer, although she filled both her own glass and her husband's. Maisie wondered how much it would take to make them 'act silly'.

Afterwards, when they had washed up and put everything away, they went into the sitting-room where Mr Draper turned on the wireless and added some logs to the fire. The room had a stillness about it as if it was used to sleeping and didn't take kindly to being disturbed. Everything had a dewy bloom to it and was damp to the touch.

Looking around, Maisie thought that the furniture looked too big for the room, a heavy, dark sideboard, a table under the window with sturdy, bulbous legs, two fireside chairs with brown moquette upholstery. On the mantelpiece, a photograph of a young man in uniform looked down at them. He had very short, brown hair and kind eyes in a young face. A hollow opened up somewhere inside of her – this must be their son, the one who had died in the war.

She tried not to stare at the photograph, not wishing to remind them by drawing their attention to it. Painfully she realized that he could not have been much older than she was now. The knowledge was made worse by the fact that he bore a strong resemblance to Ian. Supposing there was another war? Would Ian suffer the same fate? She sought protection in anger. Why did life always have to be so brutal? No God worth His salt would let it be so.

Maisie wondered if Mr and Mrs Draper blamed themselves for letting their son go. The thought was something of a revelation. Of course they couldn't be to blame. Things just happened. People never knew what might be the consequence of their actions. The thought played around the edge of her mind but she decided not to pursue it, afraid where it might lead. In any case, Mr Draper was tuning the wireless in for the Queen's Speech.

They had to stand up for the National Anthem which came as something of a surprise. At home it would never have occurred to Mum and Grandad to do so. Still, it gave her a chance to edge a little nearer to the fire, to feel a momentary shaft of warmth before Rose said, 'Sit down, girl and don't block the heat.'

After the speech, Rose and George both dozed in the fireside chairs. In spite of the coolness of the room, their cheeks were unusually bright and their eyelids had quickly grown heavy.

Maisie sat on a stool, afraid to make a noise that might disturb them. There was absolutely nothing to do. She glanced at the mantel clock. Nearly half past three. Through the lace of the curtains she could see that low cloud blanketed the sky. Already it was getting dark. Outside, Mr Wonderful was still in his paddock. He would be getting restless, waiting for his oats and barley. Then there was the milking, the chickens to feed. Harry wasn't coming back this afternoon. Maisie had been delegated to help with the daily routine. Quietly she stood up and tiptoed towards the door, intent on doing the job by herself. Wouldn't that be a surprise for Mr Draper, almost like an extra present?

As soon as she stepped outside she began to have regrets. Already it was nearly dark. By the gate, the cows gathered, impatient to enjoy the dual benefits of cow cake and mangels that waited in the feed troughs, plus the relief of having their udders emptied. Somehow they looked bigger today, less biddable. She had a nasty feeling that they might not obey her. When Mr Draper was there, or Ian or Harry or Jim, the cows did as they were told. Surely today they would sense that she was nervous, that she didn't really know what she was doing?

Then there was the business of having to milk Crumply, Violet and 332 by hand because they wouldn't tolerate the milking machine. Although she had had a go, it had felt different when there was someone there to put her right if she made a mistake. Supposing for example they kicked the pail over – or kicked her? Cows had very strong hind legs. She had a vision of herself sprawled on her back amid the sludge of the parlour floor, milk from the upturned bucket soaking her skirts. If things went dramatically wrong, they might lose the entire milk yield for the afternoon and instead of being pleased, Mr Draper would be furious.

Across the yard she could just see the dark outline of Mr Wonderful waiting to come in for his tea. She sensed his anxiety, wondering if once again he had been abandoned, but if she left the cows and went to see to him, it would soon be too late to do the milking at all.

Still there was no sign of Mr Draper. With an effort she blotted out a picture of the cows careering up and down the milking parlour, trampling the machinery and each other. Her mouth dry with anxiety, she waded across the yard and flung open the gate. Obediently the cows filed to their places and began to feed. So far so good.

Maisie worked methodically, trying to remember everything that the men had told her, putting into practice the operations that so far she had only witnessed. While Bramble was attached to the milking machine, she took a pail and stool and seated herself close to the undulating flank of 332. The cow munched placidly, her stomach playing a melody of its own. Maisie's firm but gentle pressure on her teat produced a fine stream of milk that resonated pleasingly into the bucket.

So engrossed was she with her work, that when a hand touched her shoulder she jumped violently, sending a squirt of milk across the aisle.

'Did I frighten you, lass?' George stood just behind her, his eyes still watery with sleep. 'You should have wakened me.' He screwed up his face as if to regenerate the slack muscles and went across to move the milking machine to the next cow.

As he came back, he said, 'You can leave that now, if you like. I'll take over. Go and see to that old hoss of yours.' As Maisie slipped from the stool to do so, he added, 'You'd make a good farmer's wife.'

Her thoughts propelled her across the yard. Mr Draper had finally said it, referred to Mr Wonderful as hers – '*that old hoss of yours.*' Surely that meant that now she would be able keep him? In its wake his last remark kept playing over in her mind – '*You'd make a good farmer's wife.*' If she had had doubts about whether her work was acceptable, now they were removed. More than that however: Mr Draper was actively saying that she was the sort of girl that a man would want to marry, the sort of girl that someone might fall in love with, not just any man but one who worked the land. . . . She shook her head, not wanting to be greedy over where her thoughts were leading her. Let the praise be enough in itself.

Mr Wonderful tossed his head impatiently as she tried to put his halter on, making it take longer than ever. He walked quickly, almost at a jog and as soon as he reached his stable, his head was straight in the bucket, syphoning up his supper.

Maisie allowed herself a few minutes to brush off his flanks and to ease the mud from his legs, picking the filth from his hooves. He lifted his feet automatically, intent on keeping his head in the bucket. When she had finished, she covered him with the rug, ran her hand over his head and started back for the farmhouse, a rare feeling of exhilaration carrying her along.

Rose was already setting the table for tea, with dishes of pickled cucumber and red cabbage, pickled onions and celery, a hunk of cheddar, plates of mince pies and sausage rolls.

'You cut that ham, Maisie. Nice thick slices now.'

There was far too much food for the three of them. As Maisie carried the plate of cold meat to the table she looked across at the presents, still unopened. Following the line of her gaze, Rose at last said, 'You can put those by our places. We'll open them after we have eaten.'

At last! She carried the parcels across, putting Mr Draper's slippers on the floor beside his chair, because Mum had always said that it was bad luck to put new shoes on the table, and the same probably applied to slippers. They each appeared to have three things to open, one of Maisie's being the envelope which she now recognized as coming from Joanna.

It seemed to take forever to eat their tea and even then Mrs Draper insisted that they should clear the table and put the left overs away and stack the dishes on the draining board. At last, they returned to the table and began the business of opening the packages.

George declared himself well pleased with the slippers. He put them on and stretched his legs out, wiggling his toes to show them both what a good fit they were. 'Thanks, Mother. Just what I wanted.'

Rose unwrapped the parcel containing the bed jacket and held it up to the light. 'A bit fancy, isn't it?' she sniffed, but Maisie could tell that she was pleased. She didn't actually say thank you to George, but he knew that she appreciated it really.

'Come along then, Maisie, let's see what you've got?' Maisie opened the parcel from Mr and Mrs Draper. Inside was a cotton apron. She suppressed any feeling of disappointment and held it against herself, showing that it was suitable. 'I thought that'd keep your skirts clean,' Mrs Draper observed and Maisie nodded her agreement.

Meanwhile, Mrs Draper had opened Maisie's gift, a bottle of Eau de Cologne. 'Goodness, I'll smell like a proper lady.' Rose put it aside without undoing the lid to smell it. At the same time, Mr Draper had unwrapped the penknife that Maisie had bought for him in the hardware store in Thorley.

'Thank you, lass. Just what I needed.' He pulled out the blades and rubbed them against the sleeve of his shirt to give them an extra shine.

In turn they both unpacked their presents from Ian, a pair of gloves for Aunty Rose and a lighter for Uncle George because he was always losing his matches when he came to light his pipe. '*Very nice.*'

Maisie opened Joanna's envelope, thinking that the rural scene on the front looked not unlike their farm in winter. Beneath the verse, Joanna had written, *Have a wonderful time. Two weeks to go before the birth – promise you'll come and see me then. Get yourself something You want. Happy New Year. Joanna and James.* As if the card wasn't enough, enclosed was thirty shillings. Maisie's mouth opened in amazement. This would go towards Mr Wonderful's keep.

Her employers were still watching her, waiting. Maisie took a deep breath and turned her attention to the remaining parcel. She didn't want to open it in front of anyone. Who knew what was inside? What might the Drapers read into the gift – whatever it might be? The longer she hesitated, however, the more significant the parcel seemed to become. Feigning casualness, she began to undo the string and fold back the paper. The seconds that elapsed seemed to last forever. Inside, a small, bright box greeted her with the words *Californian Poppy* written across it and a drawing of a vivid red flower. Perfume! Ian had bought her perfume. Her fingers fumbling, she took the bottle out of the box and unscrewed the top, allowing the scent to tickle her nostrils. It was wonderful, truly wonderful. And more was to follow, for beneath the perfume bottle was a small, compact book. Maisie picked it up and read the words on the cover: *The Observer Book of Horses.* Fancy Ian buying her such a present. She opened the cover and on the fly leaf he had written: *You won't find Caesar in here, but I thought you'd enjoy it just the same. Happy Christmas, 1957, your friend, Ian.*

Out of the corner of her eye she caught Mrs Draper's expression, a slight outpouring of breath that might have been relief. Clearly the perfume had worried her but the book had restored the balance. In that expression, Maisie could read it all – the book wasn't something romantic that young men gave to their sweethearts. She felt the merest regret, but all in all, this was the best Christmas that she could ever remember.

Twenty-One

IAN WAS REALLY pleased to get home. It wasn't until he saw the silhouette of the house that he realized how much he missed it. On the far side of the yard, the old barn where his father garaged his lorries sent out its own familiar shadow, and between the two was the backdrop of chestnut trees that had been his playground for as long as he could remember. It filled him with a sudden, throat-catching nostalgia. Those trees had been Indian camps, army lookouts, hiding places from enemy invaders, a hundred other imaginary scenes.

As he stepped though the front door, his Mum was waiting for him and he felt an endearing wave of affection as she hugged him to her. 'Happy Christmas, Son.'

Through the door into the sitting room, he could see that she had done her usual decorating job, only this year she seemed to have gone overboard with new tinsel and paper lanterns.

'Crikey, Mum, it looks like Piccadilly Circus in there!'

His Dad stood behind her, nodding a greeting. He looked as if he was in two minds whether to shake hands, but thought better of it, for which Ian was grateful. 'Hello Dad.' He nodded to his father then went to put his suitcase at the bottom of the stairs.

Behind him, his uncle accepted the invitation to come in for a drink before driving home. Uncle George was in a good mood. As he knocked back his brown ale, he gave his brother a favourable report on Ian's work. Ian saw the naked pride on his mother's face, the quieter satisfaction on his father's. Draining his own glass dry, he savoured the sense of well-being, looking forward to the next two days. When Uncle George made ready to leave, he wished him a Happy Christmas and took his suitcase up to his room.

It felt strange walking into the bedroom that had been his ever since he could remember. In some ways it was no longer his, but that of a young boy, a ghostly presence who no longer existed but whose belongings – books, Meccano, toy cars, lead soldiers, model airplanes – left a strange sense of continuity.

Ian sat on the bed thinking that everything in the room seemed smaller than he remembered it. Perhaps this was inevitable when you had started out as a toddler and ended up reaching five foot, ten inches.

It wasn't until he came to unpack his bag that he found Maisie's present. For a moment he couldn't think where it had come from then, opening the card, he smiled to himself. Maisie. For a moment he hesitated. Take the present downstairs and his parents were bound to ask who it was from. Of course it didn't matter, but somehow he didn't want them asking questions. There was something about Maisie that made it impossible to explain about her. Try to put into words the essence that was Maisie, try to describe the bizarre love affair between her and the horse, and he knew that his parents would never begin to appreciate the fragile nature of it. Speak about it and they would see it as a curiosity, something to smile about, some sort of a joke. He felt suddenly serious. Maisie. She certainly wasn't a joke. Wryly he thought that there are some things you should never try to explain to anyone, least of all to your parents. Putting the present back in the suitcase, he thought that he would open it tomorrow, on his own.

Going back downstairs, he could smell fresh pastry wafting from the kitchen. He went through to the living room and sat in the chair that had, from habit, been his. Strange how quickly you fitted back into the pattern of things.

'What's happening tomorrow, then?' he asked, settling down

to watch the telly with the anticipation of a hungry man who is at last to receive a decent meal.

'Granny and Grandad are coming for dinner.' Mum put a plate of sausage rolls on the coffee table within his reach.

He nodded.

'And Aunty Mildred.' Ian turned his attention from the television. Aunty Mildred was cousin Dolores's mother.

'By herself?' he asked casually.

'No. Uncle Raymond is coming. And Dolores, I think.'

Ian tried to deny the tightening sensation under his diaphragm. Immediately he thought, perhaps she isn't engaged after all. Aloud, he said, 'Alone?'

'What do you mean, alone?'

'I thought she was engaged or something.' He feigned indifference.

Mum placed another plate, this time of mince pies, at his elbow. 'I think she's got a boyfriend but his family live up north. I assume he's gone home.'

Conflicting emotions preoccupied him; one sensible, parental voice reminding him that if she was indeed engaged then he should put his earlier decision into practice. At the same time though, another Ian, the daring, fun-loving Ian, was thrilled by the thought that Dolores would be here alone – and available? He tried to be sensible, to fight the growing anticipation, but somehow it seemed to be running away with him.

That night he slept well. The first thing he knew was when his mother brought him a cup of tea at eight o'clock.

'Happy Christmas, dear. Time to get up. It's a fine, crisp morning.'

The bed was comfortable and he had no wish to get out of it. Vaguely he was surprised that his mother had woken him. She seemed anxious that he should get up, although long-gone were the days when he would wake up before daylight, open his Christmas stocking in a frenzy of anticipation and then pester his parents until they dragged themselves reluctantly from their bed to come and open the presents under the tree. Surely they didn't think he was still that desperate to do so?

'Breakfast in ten minutes.' Mum walked out leaving him little option but to force himself out.

When he arrived downstairs, everything was as usual; breakfast laid out in the kitchen, his dad already seated at the table. 'Happy Christmas,' he murmured, wondering how they managed to be so alert.

Once the food was eaten, they retired to the living room where Dad had already lit the fire and Mum proceeded to share out the parcels from under the tree.

Ian had the usual sort of gifts; socks, a shirt, a tie, some brilliantine. His parents usually gave him something substantial. This year he had hinted that he wanted some decent boots but there was no sign of them. For a moment he wondered if they were feeling the pinch and had cut back on presents. As Mum opened her last parcel she looked across at Dad and nodded.

'Right.' His father stood up. 'You'd better come with us.'

Frowning, Ian rose from the sofa. 'Better put your boots on,' his father added, stopping in the hall to change out of his slippers and to don his overcoat.

Ian followed suit, wondering what was about to happen. In silence, his parents led him across the yard in the direction of the barn. Once, some years ago, they had hidden a toboggan in the barn and by way of good fortune, the weather had obligingly snowed. His father slowed at the door, undoing the padlock with the key that hung on his watch chain. Putting it back, he seemed to brace himself before swinging open the door and stepping back for Ian to go inside. Still mystified, Ian gave him a grin and took a pace forwards. He could not quite believe what he saw, for there, parked between a pick-up and a flatbed trailer, was a BSA motorcycle.

'Wow!' He turned to his parents with delight, seeing enjoyment at his pleasure reflected in their faces.

'You will be careful, won't you?' Mum's anxieties surfaced.

He drew in his breath to say something but the enormity of the surprise, the pleasure of having this dream come true, was too great.

His father began to explain various features of the machine

and Ian tried to concentrate. The tank shone like jet, reflecting the silver embellishments on its sides.

'It's terrific,' he said at last. 'I can't believe it. Thanks.'

Before long he was taking his first, tentative turns around the yard, then with a rush of pure exhilaration, he set off onto the road, savouring the cold air that grazed his face, the heady sensation of speed, pressing against his body.

He rode for about half an hour, reluctant to stop. As he turned back, he passed his father in the car, on his way to collect his grandparents. He felt the bike wobble as he raised his hand in greeting – better be careful, and not let his father think that he couldn't handle the machine. Deliberately he opened up the throttle, caught up once more in the pleasure of the speed.

When he came back into the yard, he found some old flannelette sheeting in a box in the barn and began laboriously to clean the silver rims and spokes. As he worked, be blew gentle puffs of pleasure into the frosty air.

He was still fiddling with the bike when a car drew into the yard. Uncle Raymond and Aunty Mildred – and Dolores!

Wiping his hands on the cloth, he cast it aside and went across to meet them, taking care not to let his eyes drift in Dolores' direction. All the time, as he was wishing his aunt and uncle season's greetings and asking about their journey, he was aware of her presence, a sleek shadow just out of his range of vision.

'That yours?' She was the one to speak first.

He followed her gaze in the direction of the bike. 'Yup. Fancy a ride? He took in the glorious mass of her dark hair, the neat little waist, her long legs. Memories of the dance at Thorley swept him along. Had he really touched her breasts? Had she really touched him back? The answering hardening between his legs embarrassed him. Surely he must have imagined it?

Dolores nodded her agreement but at that moment his mother came into the yard and seconds later his father's car drew up. He went to help his grandmother from the back seat, guiding her to the warmth of the sitting room. Once they were settled, the sherry bottle came out, followed by more present-opening.

Dolores' mum and dad had bought him a pair of sturdy

leather gauntlets, just right for motorcycling. Clearly they had been in the know about the bike. From his grandparents he had a thick, hand-knitted scarf and socks. 'Thanks, Grannie, I'll be well set up now.'

He began to wish that he had bought something for Dolores, some perfume, perhaps. He didn't know what she used, but the scent of her skin and hair set off a chain reaction whenever he was near enough to get the faintest hint of it. An image formed in his mind of Maisie opening her present. What would she think? He wasn't aware that Maisie ever wore scent. She was more likely to smell of cows or horses, and yet there was a cleanness about her, a refreshing aura of soap and water at the end of each day.

When the present-giving was complete, the women retired to the kitchen to dish-up. Before long, Ian was seated at the table opposite his cousin, watching the way she forked sprouts and parsnip into her mouth, how her neat little tongue licked away a speck of gravy. In his heightened state of awareness, everything about her seemed provocative.

Once they had forced the Christmas pudding down and found the silver threepenny pieces hidden inside, the women once more retreated to the kitchen to wash up. Ian sensed Dolores' reluctance to go and help. In her vivid blue, woollen dress with fluffy edging at neck and cuffs, she didn't look cut out for washing dishes, but this was the tradition: women in the kitchen doing the domestic things, men in the sitting room, rearranging the furniture, filling the coal scuttle, stoking the fire. Once they were seated, the men made small talk about their work, told amusing anecdotes, wondered about the year ahead. When the women came back, Ian stood up to make room for his Gran.

'Thought I'd take Dolores for a spin on the bike.' He knew his cheeks were betraying him but he couldn't help it.

'Be careful.' The three women chorused as one, as if nature had programmed them to see danger everywhere. He saw another look pass between them, a knowing acknowledgement that it wasn't the bike alone that enticed them out. Their awareness further added to his embarrassment.

As they escaped outside, he felt incredibly light. Dolores wore nylon stockings and neat little boots. As he started the bike, she eased her skirt above her knees and slid over the saddle, her hands closing about his waist. It was magic.

For about ten minutes they rode along the country lanes, weaving between the puddles, increasing speed on the straight pieces of road, until they came to a gently undulating lane that ribboned its way down to a bluebell copse. Ian had come here often as a child. The congregation of broad-leafed trees made an airy canopy beneath which, even at this dark, damp time of the year, the ground was still dry and spongy beneath the feet.

Embarrassed, he slowed to a halt. 'Shall we go for a walk?'

Dolores signified her agreement by dismounting, smoothing her skirt down across her thighs.

Hand in hand, they climbed the stile into the wood and followed the path. Overhead, a blackbird warned of their arrival with a sharp expletive. Ian had no idea where the walk was taking them, not in the geographical sense, but as far as their personal journey was concerned. . . .

As the path opened into a natural hollow, he slowed down. Side by side they looked around as, like the pillars of a cathedral, the domed silence of the wood enveloped them.

'Aunty Rose said that you're engaged.' It was a clumsy opening.

Dolores still held his hand. She shrugged her shoulders before saying, 'You could call it that.'

'Where is he now?' He spoke to ward off the silence.

'Gone home to his family. He wanted me to go but I'd rather stay here.' As she spoke, she squeezed his hand and her hip moved closer to his.

Ian felt in danger of losing control. The degree of his passion was undignified. Make a wrong move and he might blow the whole thing.

He turned to Dolores and looked down at her upturned face, the slightly amused grin playing about her lips, mischief sparkling in her dark eyes.

'Have you got anything?'

He frowned his lack of understanding.

'You know, a rubber.'

His heart ricocheted. He hadn't expected this, this assumption that they should go the whole way. Shamefaced, he shook his head.

She gave a little sigh. 'We'll just have to be careful then. . . .'

Afterwards he replayed the scene over and over. Somehow or other, his unpreparedness seemed to have shaken his confidence. He was clumsy, embarrassing himself by coming too soon. It was messy, humiliating. Dolores wiped herself clean and handed him her hanky, shrugging philosophically. 'Hadn't we better be getting back? It's getting dark.'

On the way back he felt miserable, a failure. They did not speak.

The rest of the day passed in a fog of dissatisfaction. When they played games later in the evening he looked out for any indication that she might still like him; if he was the one she would choose to partner her in playing Charades, or in 'Guess Who I Am', but he couldn't interpret the signs.

The sleeping arrangements were complicated. Granny and Grandad had the spare room while Uncle Raymond and Aunty Mildred were sleeping on the put-u-up in the sitting room. Dolores was in the little boxroom that was almost above his head. In bed he tossed and turned, wondering if he should make his way to her and show her that he could be a better lover – except that he still didn't have a johnnie. He cursed himself. You could get them at the barbers. He'd seen the discreet displays on the shelf behind the counter. No chance that they'd be open on Boxing Day. He consoled himself by thinking that next time he went to have his hair cut, he'd certainly buy some. He put off the thought of the ordeal of actually asking for them.

Somehow he managed to sleep. By the time he got up next morning, Dolores and her parents had gone to watch the hunt meeting at the village pub. He felt some disappointment but it was tempered with relief that he didn't have to face her. Besides, he didn't like the hunt much anyway.

Somehow they made their way through the day. He felt sad that he couldn't really enjoy this time at home, not with Dolores there. Strange how much he had looked forward to it and how easily it had been spoilt.

Ian had to leave at about four to go back to the farm. He realized that he was looking forward to it. It wasn't until he was putting his presents and things back into his suitcase that he found Maisie's present. Sitting on his bed he opened it. The sight of the Brylcreem, of the brush and comb, made him smile. It was a big present from someone who had so little. He was doubly glad that he had brought her what he had.

When he said his goodbyes, he could hardly bring himself to look at Dolores. She still had that amused expression on her face, as if his poor performance of yesterday had only been what she expected. Hating himself for minding, he secured his case to the pillion where only yesterday she had perched her neat little bum, and, with relief, he rode out of the yard and back towards the farm.

Twenty-Two

JOANNA'S PAINS STARTED after dinner on Boxing Day. At first she put it down to indigestion because she had eaten too much and risked a glass of sherry. Gradually, however, she began to realize that these pains were different from anything she had experienced before, almost a prowling sensation as if a big cat was exploring the territory of her lower back expanding its claws, insinuating itself into narrow hollows. As the time passed she felt sure that they were becoming stronger and more frequent.

She didn't want to say anything, to cause a fuss. It was ages before she had a chance to get James on his own and then she tried to play it down. 'I think I might be. . . .'

James raised his eyebrows in query. He had eaten and drank well. He looked relaxed, accommodating. Across the room, Joanna's mother and mother-in-law were sorting out cutlery and putting it back into the heavy wooden box with the velvet lining, each knife, fork and spoon having its own particular place.

'It's probably nothing,' she backtracked, 'But I keep getting – you know, pains.'

He frowned, then gradually the significance dawned on him. 'You can't be, you're not due yet – are you?'

She recognized his response, the fear of the unknown, because that was how she was feeling too.

He opened his mouth to make an announcement but she stilled him with her hand. 'Let's just hang on a bit. We can be at the hospital in half an hour.'

Secretly she wondered if by then the baby would have arrived, in the front seat of the car, or in the foyer of the hospital. An answering gripe told her to get a move on.

Both mothers instantly went into midwife mode, treading carefully around each other so as not to be the one to interfere. James said, 'I'll run Joanna in. Perhaps you, Mum (he looked at Joanna's mother as he spoke), would like to stay here. I'll ring as soon as there is any news and then I'll come and pick you up.'

Everyone fell in with his suggestions. The pain was stronger now, more frequent. Joanna wondered if this was as bad as it would get. She could cope with this – just.

James lowered her into the car as if she was ninety and tucked a blanket around her legs. 'Just relax now, darling. Well soon be there.'

She let her head fall back against the seat-rest and closed her eyes. Another pain came, angry, violent. She grabbed the side of the seat and winced.

'Are you all right?' He willed her to tell him that she was, and she knew that he was out of his depth, afraid that he would be called upon to cope with something that he wasn't capable of.

'Get a move on.'

They zoomed into the hospital courtyard and James parked in an emergency bay, leaping out and grabbing her bag, rushing round to help her up. Inside, a nurse at the desk looked up from her figures.

'My wife, Mrs Cameron. Her time's come.'

Joanna just had time to think that it was an unfortunate turn of phrase, then things happened quickly. James was sent away to amuse himself while Joanna was led away to a cubicle. She was helped to undress, put into a gown, shaved, given an enema. The indignity added to her sense of alienation.

'Right now, mother, just lie back here on the bed and try not to tense up.'

'*Mother*'. The title sat awkwardly. No one had called her that before.

Joanna was placed on a narrow couch. It seemed a long way from the ground and she wondered if she might not roll over and fall off. A yellow light was just above her head, another one bearing down on her from the ceiling. The nurse instructed her to bend her knees, let them fall apart. She poked and prodded then gave a sniff. 'A long way to go yet. I'll be back later.'

Joanna would like to have slept but the pains wouldn't allow it. Every minute or two Vesuvius rumbled in her stomach, preparing for a mighty eruption. She tried to relax, to breathe deeply, to think of something other than the pain, but it was all-consuming. An eternity passed before another nurse came in and peered at the crevass in her body from which her child would finally appear. The nurse shook her head and smiled brightly.

'Would you like a cup of tea? Something to read?'

Joanna shook her head. 'It really hurts,' she said hopefully, waiting for some release.

'Far too soon to give you anything. Just try to relax now.'

So it went on, hour after nightmare hour. Joanna felt out of control, unheard. The nurses seemed immune to her agony. Once, a male doctor came and examined her. He was young, falsely jolly. He too, went away.

As the night progressed, Joanna began to despair. She couldn't put up with the pain any longer. She couldn't. She wanted to sleep. She didn't care what happened to her or the baby as long as she could sleep.

'So tired,' she gasped.

At last the nurse reached over and grabbed a mask, holding it against Joanna's mouth. 'Deep breaths now, this will help.'

Joanna grasped for the lifeline but it was snatched away from her.

'Not too much.'

She knew that she was burbling, crying out, becoming hysterical. Things had changed. Instead of the tiger pain there was another one, a great whoosh of agony, mounting pressure waiting for a dam to burst, for the trapped waters to cascade away to freedom.

'Steady on, don't be so impatient.'

At last, long after she had given up any hope of survival, men in white coats came. They seemed detached, matter of fact as if this sort of thing happened every day. One of them gave her an injection and suddenly, miraculously, the pain began to ebb. The second produced an instrument of torture and began to force it inside of her. She couldn't feel anything.

'See, he's got black hair.' He held up a tiny lock of damp curl and Joanna gazed at it with wonder. For the first time her child took on a physical reality.

'Try to relax now.' They gave her orders, inserted the forceps, eased and muttered and then, miraculously, it was over.

She lay back, dizzy, floating, giving herself up to the little piece of heaven that circled around her brain.

'You have a son, Mrs Cameron. A healthy son at –' he looked at the clock, 'Four thirty-four precisely, December 27.'

Thursday's child has far to go.

She said it out loud but they weren't taking any notice. People were busy about their business.

At last they lay him in her arms, a tiny, russet, wrinkled being with hazy blue eyes and a surprised expression.

'Hello, Edward James. I'm your mother. I hope I won't be too much of a disappointment to you.'

She touched him with her finger, not quite believing that he was real. He frowned, his small brow creasing. What must the world seem like at first glance?

Already she was falling asleep and a nurse took the baby, marched purposefully off with him. 'Where is he going?' she managed to call out.

'Just to the nursery. You can have him back tomorrow.'

Joanna slept the sleep of the fulfilled. When she awoke it was daylight. She was in a ward with other mothers. Some had their babies in cribs beside their beds. She felt deprived, suddenly afraid. Supposing. . . ?

As she struggled up, the sister came in. 'Right Mrs Cameron, awake are we? Let's get you a cup of tea and then we'll see about feeding baby.'

As Joanna moved she was aware of the barbed wire between her legs. 'Ouch.' She flinched.

'Nasty stitches,' the sister said by way of explanation. Big boy, your baby.' Was there a grim satisfaction in the remark?

After breakfast, which she promptly vomited back, they brought him to her and instructed her in the art of breast feeding. She had expected it to be wonderful but it hurt. He bit, a savage, primeval grasp for succour.

'Does my husband know?' she managed to ask, easing her bruised nipple from his grip.

'He does. He'll be here at visiting time. Husbands only today.'

She felt like a child, her life organized for her, not having a say in how things should be. Tears threatened and she felt sorry for herself. All of this, this feeding, she would never be able to do it. Supposing he starved to death?

The sister looked at her kindly. 'Nothing to worry about. Lots of mothers find it hard at first.' Joanna wondered what had gone wrong, that women were so out of touch with this primary function.

James arrived with a huge bouquet and a teddy bear. He looked embarrassed, so young, hardly more than a boy himself.

He kissed Joanna on the cheek. She wondered if her breath smelled, if she was repugnant, leaking milk and scarred for life.

'Congratulations, darling. I've just seen him through the window. What a bouncer.'

They talked about the birth, about what everyone outside was saying. Joanna kept to herself her ordeal as a milking machine. Try and make it all seem nice.

Too soon husbands were ordered away and babies brought for the next torture.

'Ouch!' Joanna pulled back from baby Edward who fumbled for the source of comfort that had been so rudely snatched away. His snuffles grew frenzied, about to give way to roars of frustration. Joanna was in equal parts intrigued and appalled at this tiny infant's willpower.

'Here.' The nurse grabbed her breast, lifted the baby higher, changed his position, forced the teat between his avid lips. He reminded Joanna of a piglet. Poor old sow.

'That's better.' The nurse looked pleased. 'You're getting the hang of it now.'

Edward sucked until the effort wore him out then he fell asleep against her breast. The nurse shook him sharply and woke him up, pushing him against Joanna's shoulder, instructing her to rub his back until wind came up. He burped loudly and his head flopped.

Still he wasn't allowed to sleep. There was another side to go and a nappy to be changed. The whole thing seemed to take forever and Joanna felt only relief when the crib was trundled away back to the nursery. She chose not to think of that dreadful day when they would send her home.

Maisie was just combing out Mr Wonderful's mane when she heard the distant sound of an engine coming along the lane. It was unfamiliar, broadcasting its approach with a throaty, rasping quality that she did not recognize. As it drew close, she stopped what she was doing and peered over the stable door. A motorcycle turned into the yard and skidded to a halt. Her heart jolted as she saw Ian dismount and prop the cycle on its stand, then unleash his suitcase from the pillion seat.

As he turned towards the house she drew back, afraid to be seen. His arrival jolted her into another dimension, woke her from the cloistered seclusion that had governed the last two days. The bike brought its own excitement and instantly she imagined herself seated behind him, flying down the lanes like some wind goddess; but the dream was immediately tempered by the knowledge that it would also liberate him from the farm, set him free to go out and meet other people, other friends, other girls. There had been comfort in their isolation.

She realized too late that Ian had seen her for he veered away from the house and came across in her direction.

'Him Maisie. Had a good Christmas?'

She nodded.

'Thanks for the present. It's very nice.'

Again she nodded, aware of the spots of *Californian Poppy* behind her ears. Would he smell them above the pungent scent of the stable? She knew that she too should say thank you. She wanted to. She wanted him to know that she loved the gift, but the words would not come.

Ian poked his head over the door to get a better look at Mr Wonderful.

'How's old Caesar then?'

She nodded once again, asserting that he was well. Mr Wonderful looked up briefly from his bucket and checked to see if Ian had anything for him. When he was sure that he hadn't, he returned to licking up the last vestiges of chaff that stuck to the sides.

'See you in a minute.' Ian excused himself and went back across the yard. Maisie watched the way he walked, the gently rolling gait that hinted that he could hear a secret rhythm inside his head. Now that he was back she was confused by her feelings. All the time he had been away she had missed him, felt the emptiness on the farm, his absence at mealtimes, the silence of the corridor at nights. Now he was back she felt afraid. The strain of trying to behave normally would be too great. Whatever would she do if he guessed her real feelings? How could she possibly hide them for ever?

For the first time she wondered how long 'forever' might be. Her employment was open ended. She might be here this time next year. On the other hand, she might get her notice next month. She dare not think of the consequences. She wanted some certainty and yet in the long run, certainty could only mean one thing – parting from Ian. This year, next year, sometime. . . .

Taking Mr Wonderful's bucket outside, she swilled it out and turned it upside down to dry. As she peered in for one last look at him it dawned on her how familiar he was, how comfortable she felt with their intimacy. She knew every curve of his body, every swirl of hair, the outline of his legs, the untamed strands of his mane, the particular shape of his hooves, they were all important to her. Perhaps a mother felt like this about her child – or a woman about her lover? Involuntarily Maisie's thoughts turned back to Ian, to the shape of his strong, capable hands, his fingernails that always bore the mark of his manual labour. She thought about the curl of his hair, its particular fairness that warned he would probably begin to go bald before he was too much older. She closed her eyes and held on to the sweetness of her feelings for him, for him and the horse. Well, at least I can touch you, she thought, reaching across to give Mr Wonderful a last pat, rubbing him between his ears so that he stretched out his head and curled his top lip with pleasure. She did not pursue her thoughts further.

To her relief, once she was back in the kitchen, things seemed to settle into their old routine. As they ate supper, Mr Draper and Ian talked about the farm and what had happened while Ian had been away. Mrs Draper and Ian talked about Christmas and how all the family had been. She took comfort in the fact that tomorrow would be just another routine sort of day.

In fact the normality continued until New Year's Eve. The advent of a new year had always been ignored in Maisie's family. No staying up until midnight, no wishing each other a Happy New Year. She was therefore surprised when Ian suddenly said to her, 'Are you making any New Year's resolutions?'

She shook her head. They were alone in the kitchen. Mr and Mrs Draper had both gone to bed a few minutes ago and Maisie was about to follow them. Sensing that Ian was in a talkative mood, she began to feel panicky. While she wanted to be with him, the urge to run away and hide grew by the moment.

Hurriedly she went to the larder to get some porridge oats. By mixing them with milk and water and placing them in the bottom oven of the range, she could leave the mixture to cook overnight so that by breakfast time they would have a thick, creamy dish to come down to.

'Why don't you make a resolution to start talking?' Ian sat down in Uncle George's chair. She was trapped.

He added, 'If you don't want to talk to the rest of them, at least you could talk to me.'

She wanted to. How she wanted to, but if she did that then she would have to answer the questions he would ask, have to tell him about the past, about her mother, her father, the gas explosion, *the terrible thing*. . . . She could never do that. Never.

'What are you afraid of?' Ian stretched his legs out in a long V-shape, looking across at her, waiting for an answer. His eyes were clouded, serious, she didn't know how to avoid the compelling power of his question.

'Don't you trust me?' he asked. 'Don't you think I can keep a secret?'

Yes, no. Her mind rebelled.

'There is something, isn't there? Something you're afraid of. You don't have to be, you know. Not with me.'

Panic engulfed her. Like a rabbit mesmerized by a weasel, she froze, staring at him. It took a superhuman effort of will to shake her head again.

Ian gave a sigh, dismissing the subject. 'Oh well, I suppose I'd better get to bed or I'll never get up in the morning. Good night, then. Happy New Year.'

He was gone. Maisie knew that she had failed him, rejected his overture of friendship. After all he had done for her, he must feel hurt that she didn't trust him.

Now that he was gone the significance of the offer hit her anew. What was she, crazy? It was almost as if someone had offered her the crown jewels and she had said 'no thanks'. Upstairs she could hear his footsteps, going along the corridor, the squeak of floorboards in his room overhead. She began to drown in her sense of loss.

On Saturday they were supposed to be taking Mr Wonderful back to the blacksmith. Would Ian bother? If he did, it would be for the horse's sake and not for hers. This in turn brought its own, bittersweet pain. A man who was caring of animals, who put himself out to help them, was the more precious, and greater was the loss.

What must he think of her? Her behaviour was stupid, self-destructive. From now on he would know that in trying to be friendly he was wasting his time. She wasn't worth bothering with. As she turned out the light, her body slouched under the burden of despair. By her foolishness she had just lost the light that illuminated her days. The rest of her life would be lived in perpetual gloom.

As the clock struck midnight, and 1958 dawned, she felt that her dreams, unformed as they were, denied as they might be, were rapidly disintegrating into ashes.

Twenty-Three

JOANNA REMAINED IN hospital for ten days. When they finally discharged her, she arrived home to find her mother already installed and the cottage warm, clean and welcoming. Fresh flowers were on the dining table, a selection of books had been fetched from the library and some magazines that gave helpful hints about babies, and patterns for clothes to knit or sew for them, waited on the hall stand.

In the hospital, the nurses had got Edward into some sort of routine. Joanna tried to be positive, reassuring herself that he would continue to follow the pattern set for him when they got home. As she walked through the door, she reminded herself that every human being walking the earth had at some time been a baby. Hers could not be so different. As long as she kept him washed and fed and loved him, then things would surely work out.

Her mother was sleeping in James's study while for the moment, baby Edward shared their room, his carrycot placed by the side of the bed. That way they would hear him when he cried at night. He cried a lot. The worst thing was not knowing why. Newly fed, freshly changed, each evening they kept him awake and placed him on a rug in front of the fire so that he could kick and get some exercise. Religiously Joanna winded him until there was surely not the faintest breeze left in his tiny stomach, yet he still set up a strident, demanding yowl, twisting his little legs as if he was in agony, frightening Joanna with his intensity.

Her mother spent a lot of time pacing the room with him, propping him over her shoulder and rocking him until exhaustion claimed him. 'He's playing you up,' she pronounced. 'You've got a strong-willed little boy here. You'll have to learn to be firm with him.'

Once his tantrum subsided, Joanna's mother would tuck him up on his side, tiptoeing backwards like some courtier leaving a king's presence. No sooner was he back in his crib than he would start again, first a snuffling sound, then a squawk, then a full-throated bellow.

The crying apart, Joanna could not get used to the fact that from now on, the routine of her life was decided not by her, but by her son. Just as she was falling asleep he would wake up and demand her attention, just when she was thinking of taking a stroll in the garden it would start to rain and her mother would warn against taking him out in this inclement weather. She felt that he was playing a game with her, a complex power struggle that he was sure to win because he was the only one to know the rules.

They called the doctor in to examine him but he declared that there was nothing wrong. The neighbour recommended a teaspoon of whisky in milk fed to him last thing at night, but Joanna was afraid of poisoning him. Warnings not to spoil him only increased her anxiety. At last the district nurse came and announced that, in her opinion, Edward James was hungry.

'You're not making enough milk, my dear. You'll have to supplement it with a bottle.'

She made it sound as if Joanna would be disappointed, but as quickly as she decently could, she gave up feeding him altogether. At last she could reclaim a small part of her freedom. Her mother, James, any visiting relative could take over the burden of feeding him, leaving her free to be herself.

As the days passed, it became clear that sooner or later her mother would have to go home. She had her own life to lead. The weather was bad and she was worried that her water pipes might burst. Besides, James was showing signs of impatience.

In some ways Joanna would be relieved when her mother left

because her presence did feel like an intrusion. Although she made a show of not interfering, deliberately absented herself if ever there was the slightest hint of disagreement between her daughter and son-in-law, in fact, her actions only made things worse. In reality, her mother was always there when they didn't want her, making her views known when Joanna and James held what was meant to be a private conversation, her silences speaking volumes whenever they reached a decision over which she disagreed. The only trouble was, Joanna would then be left to fend for herself. At the moment her mother did all the washing, pressed Edward's little nightgowns, took a pride in the soft, white fluffiness of his nappies that seemed to be everywhere in buckets in the kitchen. Joanna knew that she wanted someone around, someone to do the routine work, someone to give advice when she asked for it, to reassure her when Edward was playing up, to take him off her hands sometimes so that she could just be by herself.

The Thursday before her mother was due to leave, James said, 'Isn't this Maisie's weekend off? What say you that I go and fetch her, have her here for the weekend? We could see how it goes.'

Joanna agreed. She had promised to get in touch with Maisie when the baby was born and guiltily, she realized that she had not done so. She excused herself because there was always too much to do and besides, she was always tired these days.

James rang the farm and spoke to Mrs Draper. When he came back he said, 'I've told the old woman I'll pick her up on Friday evening.' He was thoughtful for a moment before adding, 'If it seems to be working out, she could simply stay. I could always go over and fetch her things. She needn't go back.'

Again Joanna agreed. The thought of Maisie's quiet, biddable presence lightened her mood. She was about to get up to put the kettle on for a cup of tea when she heard the snuffle, the grunt, the querulous prelude to Edward's summons.

Ian took Mr Wonderful to the blacksmith on Saturday but he did not invite Maisie to go with him. When he came over to fetch the horse, he said, 'Aunty Rose said to tell you she wants you to get those blankets out of the cupboard in her bedroom this morning. They're getting damp and she wants to air them.'

Maisie did not look at him. What he was really saying was that he didn't want to be bothered with her any more. Well, she couldn't blame him for that. She tried not to let the knowledge hurt her. Silently she fetched Mr Wonderful's halter and prepared him for the journey, handing him over without meeting Ian's eyes. As soon as the horse was loaded, she held out the thirty shillings that Joanna had given her.

Ian frowned. 'I won't need all that. Anyway, are you sure you've got enough?' She nodded, pushing it at him, indicating that it would go towards what she owed him. With a shrug he took it and slipped it into his pocket.

'OK. Let's call it quits then.' She still owed him five shillings.

She watched him climb into the lorry and start the engine. Soon he and Mr Wonderful were slipping and sliding their way up the muddy track towards the road.

All the time they were away, anxiety niggled at the edge of her mind. Supposing the blacksmith said Mr Wonderful's feet were worse? Supposing he said that there was nothing he could do? Supposing they had an accident, the cattle truck overturned, Mr Wonderful was injured, Ian was killed? By thinking of all the worst scenarios, Maisie hoped to forestall them. Perhaps if she had acted them out in her mind, they wouldn't happen in reality. She scratched around for any disaster she had overlooked, afraid that it might be waiting to catch her out.

As it was, Mr Wonderful was back within the hour and Ian immediately came to tell her that the blacksmith had said there was some improvement. He was to return for his next trim in six weeks. She wondered if, by then, she would be able to save enough money. If not, she would never be able to ask Ian for help. Not any more.

Relief at their safe return had Maisie confused. Now that Ian was back, she made a point of getting on with her work, not encouraging him to hang around. For a while he simply stood and watched her.

'By rights you ought to worm him again. If you like, the next time I'm in Thorley I'll pop into the corn merchants and get some jollop.' The question of money was there again. She had given him all that she had. He seemed to anticipate what she was thinking. 'You can pay me when you get your wages.'

She nodded, her gratitude a humiliation. If it wasn't for Mr Wonderful, she would never ever put herself in this situation.

Another thought returned to torment her. Ian went into Thorley quite often these days, on his bike. So far, although he'd promised to give her a ride, he hadn't done so. This was further proof that he no longer regarded her as a friend. She felt heavy inside, grey, as if a shutter had come down somewhere inside of her and cast out the light.

Turning Mr Wonderful back out into his field she watched him plough his way through the morass around the gate. His hooves made a hollow sound, resisting the suction that held him back. Everywhere was waterlogged. Although she brushed her clothes off each day, it was too wet to dry things properly. Mud clung to her like leeches. She felt unwashed, scruffy, ugly.

Fighting the gloom, she started towards the house to get their dinner ready. As she trudged across the yard, some tiny, rebellious corner of her wondered: shouldn't there be more to life than this – peeling potatoes, washing sheets, wading ankle deep in ooze, cleaning out grates? She explored the possibilities, tried to imagine something better, but as far as she could see, there really wasn't anything else. The things that would make her life marvellous were out of the question. The remaining light that was her spark of hope, turned itself down another notch or two.

There was no one in the kitchen when she went in. From the bangs and thuds from overhead, Rose was still upstairs doing something. When she came down she said, 'Good news, Mr and Mrs Cameron have got a baby boy. Young Mr Cameron rang while you were out. He's coming to pick you up on Friday.'

Maisie's instinctive reaction was to be pleased. It was a knee jerk response. Visiting James and Joanna was something she had always looked forward to, a signal that they had not forgotten her. But even as she experienced it, her thoughts scrolled through a series of contradictory feelings. The news of the baby pleased her, of course. She was happy for Joanna and James, glad that their baby was safely here. At the same time though, it reminded her that she was, after all, only an outsider, an observer of their happy event. Besides, no one had actually asked her if she wanted to go. It was sort of taken for granted, as if her life existed only in relation to other people's. Before she could dwell on the thought however, she realized that going away would mean leaving Mr Wonderful. That was it then. She couldn't go.

As they were finishing their pudding, Mrs Draper said, 'Mr Cameron said he'd be here at five tomorrow. Make sure you don't keep him waiting.'

Ian looked across at her. 'You going away this weekend?'

She shrugged, avoiding his gaze. She tried to form the words to say that she had changed her mind, but before she could do so, he added, 'Want me to look after Caesar for you?'

She tried not to feel grateful, not to succumb to relief. This was Ian's weekend to stay at the farm. If she stayed too then perhaps he might offer to take her for a ride, even take her to the pictures?

I don't want to go. She said the words over and over in her head, judging the lulls in the conversation when she might be able to articulate them, missing her chance, mentally dodging and ducking like a child with a skipping rope, waiting for the moment to jump in, never quite getting it right. Already everyone was getting up from the table, preparing to return to work. As she set about the washing up, she thought, one day, Maisie Morris. One day you'll tell them all what you really want. Not today though. Not today.

James looked pleased with himself. He gave Maisie the full benefit of his smile as he slid into the driving seat and revved up the Cresta.

'Good to see you, then, Maisie. You'll be in for a surprise when you see young Eddie. A great little chap, he is. Joanna thinks he looks like me.' He grinned. 'He should be that lucky.'

Maisie wasn't amused. You were supposed to say 'poor thing', if someone looked like you, and at least pretend that you didn't think you were great looking or anything.

She felt preoccupied. It had rained yet again that afternoon and the wind had swung round to the north, the kind of wind that drives right inside of you. Mr Wonderful had felt cold, really cold. And wet. She had rubbed him down with a wodge of straw like Ian had shown her and left his rug out ready for when he dried out. She was worried about him, though. Could horses catch cold, like humans did? There was a flu epidemic around. Did horses catch flu?

'Bet you'd rather be doing something else than working on a farm in this weather.' James's observation caught her out. She didn't mind the bad weather. In some ways it made her even more indispensable. The livestock depended on her when it was cold or wet, needing to be fed and sheltered.

James chatted away as if she wasn't there, a silent audience to his view of things. She risked a glance at him. Yes, he was handsome. She still thought that, but it didn't engage her any more. In fact the opposite was true. She thought that emotionally he was rather shallow, not the sort of person you could really rely on.

When they reached the cottage, in spite of herself she was struck anew by its quaint appearance that sat so comfortably with the modernizations inside. In contrast to the farm house, the rooms were small, warm and cosy. The fire in the lounge embraced the whole area. The carpet beneath her feet moulded itself to her toes, warming them. It was all there, the telly and the radiogram, the running hot water.

Joanna came to meet them, her baby slung across her hip.

'Maisie! It's lovely to see you again. Come and meet Master Edward.' She exposed the small, unformed face.

The title held Maisie back. It made him sound important, someone to be reckoned with, but he was only a baby. At the back of her mind another film was running, one from a long time ago with a baby boy coming home, everyone having to make space for him.

As soon as Maisie was inside she was sent to make a cup of tea, and when that was done, to heat more water in which to stand baby Edward's bottle to warm.

'I'm not breast feeding any more. Didn't have enough milk.' Joanna sounded proud of the admission, as if it was a compliment to her son who, because of his robust nature, demanded more than a mere mother could offer.

Once the bottle was made up and the temperature adjusted, Joanna insisted that Maisie sit in an armchair and feed the baby. She didn't want to. Nestled into the crook of her arm he felt alien, weightless yet exuding heat, little spasms of movement, tiny electrical pulses of feeling that made Maisie uneasy. As she held him he drew on the bottle as if he would drain it dry with one mighty suck, although conversely she couldn't believe how long it took him to imbibe an inch or two of liquid.

She cooked the tea, rinsed a pail of nappies, ironed some tiny garments that looked fit only for a doll, made up another feed. By the time she sat down, the best television programmes were over. Joanna looked tired. After about fifteen minutes, she said, 'I think I'll turn in. Edward will be waking up again at two. She hesitated, then evidently had second thoughts about what she was going to say. Instead, she turned to James.

'If you hear him in the night, will you get up with him? I really do need a good night's sleep.' James in turn looked at Maisie but he too, hesitated to ask the question that had clearly occurred to him.

Instead, he said, 'OK. Someone else's turn tomorrow though.'

Although she was downstairs and out of earshot of Edward's nightly chorus, Maisie couldn't sleep. She felt out of control. All the while, the film continued to play in her mind. Another house. Another baby. Not Edward. Kenny. Little Kenny. Funny-looking, little, bald, Kenny.

She wanted to turn it off but it wouldn't go away. Kenny in his pram, beginning to sprout insipid, downy hair. Kenny crawling, his nose a permanent plug of snot. Kenny toddling around the furniture in the kitchen, making excited noises. Kenny trailing behind her outside. . . .

She had to turn the image off. Quickly she got up and crossing to the kitchen, made a cup of tea, all the time scrabbling around for something safe to occupy her thoughts, driving out the others. Upstairs she heard Edward start to cry then after a long gap, the creak of a bed. Eventually the caterwauling stopped.

She wanted to go home, back to the farm, but she couldn't ask them to take her. It would look ungrateful, rude, unkind. Wondering how she would endure the hours until Sunday afternoon, she planned to fill them by giving the house a going over, perhaps washing out more nappies, making it easier for Joanna to spend time with her baby. She owed her that much.

Somehow she struggled through the next day, as far as possible keeping herself out of James and Joanna's way. She didn't volunteer to get up with the baby in the night. She knew that they were both watching, hoping, but neither of them quite dared to suggest it. As it was, when she woke again, somewhere in the darkest hours, a maelstrom of images began slipping away from her, frightening, dangerous, threatening to draw her with them. Quickly she got out of bed, seeking once more the safety of the kitchen.

As she walked in, it was to find Joanna sitting at the table with Edward propped up awkwardly on her knee and a cigarette in her free hand. She jumped as Maisie came in.

'Oh, thank goodness it's you.' She looked guiltily at the cigarette, saying, 'I haven't smoked since before I was pregnant, but – it helps to calm my nerves.' Something about her expression begged not to be judged.

They were both silent, then she said, 'I didn't think it would be like this, so – relentless.'

Maisie watched her, glad of having something other than her own devils to distract her. She wasn't prepared for what Joanna said next.

It was clear that she was chewing something over in her mind. With a rush of words, she finally said, 'James and I were wondering if you'd like to come back – you know, to help with the baby. We could pay you.' She opened her mouth several times to say more but nothing came. Eventually, wheedling, holding out incentives, she promised, 'You could have the study.

James is quite willing to clear it out. We thought we could decorate it for you, get you your own telly.'

Maisie began to shake her head more and more emphatically. How could Joanna be so blind? The future she painted yawned like some steep, bottomless chasm. 'I thought you'd want to,' Joanna was saying, making things worse. 'You – you didn't really want to leave before, did you?'

At the back of her mind, Maisie registered the fact that Joanna was admitting to their guilt, their selfishness in driving her out. Anyway, it made not the slightest difference. What had happened before, *the terrible thing*, made it unthinkable. How could they torment her like this?

Still shaking her head she rose from the table. Ignoring Joanna's stark expression, saying nothing, she crossed the lounge and went back to the study.

Somehow they all got through the next morning. Clearly Joanna had told James what had happened and Maisie caught him looking at her with a frown, assessing whether his wife had handled it badly, or simply been misunderstood. After a dreary lunch he prepared to drive her home.

Maisie hugged Joanna goodbye, feeling wave-tossed, reading in her ex-teacher's eyes the disappointment. From habit she castigated herself for not doing as they wanted, but it was no good. She couldn't. Surely they must see that?

As they rode along the High Street, past the Fish Emporium, James said, 'Joanna would like you to come back. You do understand that?'

He glanced at her and she nodded. She understood all right.

'Well then? We'd pay you.'

'No!' She hadn't realized she had shouted with such vehemence. James's mouth dropped and in response he shrugged his shoulders and concentrated again on the road. They passed the rest of the journey in silence. As they reached the farm lane, he made one last-ditch attempt.

'Well, the offer's there. You only have to ring up and say. You'd be doing Joanna a favour, you know that, but of course if you don't want to. . . . It's up to you.'

He pulled in just inside the yard, not bothering to drive her to the door. As she got out, he handed out her case and inclined his head. 'Goodbye, then, Maisie Morris. Good luck.'

Joanna didn't hear James arrive back because for the past half an hour, Edward had been indulging in his afternoon protest. She had tried everything: cuddling him, singing to him, taking him for a walk around the cottage and pointing out items of interest to a three-week-old. In the end she resorted to shaking him but as his screams degenerated into hysterical sobs, she was dragged down by remorse. It was at this point that James walked in.

She looked at him defiantly, daring him to disapprove. Baby Edward was soaking wet, his hair a damp cap clinging to his skull, his face puce, his tiny fists clenching and unclenching in his turmoil.

'What's the matter with him?' James came closer and looked down at them both, like a detective looking for the murder weapon.

'I don't know, do I? If I knew I'd do something about it.' She knew that she was near the edge, in danger of losing her hold on that fragile state they called sanity.

James took Edward from her. He held him awkwardly which did little to comfort the child. 'What is it then, old chap?' He marched him over to the window and directed his gaze towards the garden.

'I've tried that. Nothing seems to work.'

Edward had subsided into grunts and groans, contorting himself in his father's arms.

'You're holding him too tight.'

James responded by placing him on the carpet where he could writhe all he liked. Bending down, he pushed the knuckle of his little finger between his son's lips. Edward sucked on it for a moment then thrashed his head aside.

'Perhaps his gums are sore. Perhaps he's teething.' James spoke with authority. He had seen something about it in one of the magazines Joanna had left scattered about the place. Apparently some babies were even born with teeth.

Joanna shrugged as if she had little interest in the source of Edward's misery. Sensing a storm brewing, James said, 'I tried to talk Maisie round but she was adamant. I don't understand it. I thought she would have liked to come back.' He shrugged off the vagaries of young, working class girls.

'It's no good,' said Joanna. 'He doesn't like me. He plays me up all the time. I know he does.'

She saw the disbelief on James's face and her frustration boiled over. 'Well if you think you can do any better, you do it!'

James let out an appeasing sigh. He stared at her for a long, hard moment as if trying to read something in her mind. If he succeeded she guessed he would see only worry, anger, despair. Eventually he abandoned the baby and made for his study. When he returned he was clutching a sheaf of papers. He thrust them out at her like a child offering his bad school report.

'I don't know what you'll think of this.'

Frowning, Joanna took them aware that her hands trembled. As she began to read she glanced up at him, asking what he was trying to say. The papers were application forms for the job she had seen advertised in James's *Water* magazine. It was for the post of a senior engineer, based in Salisbury, Rhodesia. The salary was huge.

Joanna closed down all her receptors, preparing herself not to feel the pain of abandonment. 'Are you planning on going, then?'

'I haven't applied yet.'

She tried to be calm, to distance herself. She managed to say, 'If that's what you want.'

'I was more interested in what *you* want. We always talked about working abroad. Nothing's changed, has it? How would you feel about going there?'

'With—?' She glanced at Edward who, now that he was deprived of his parents' attention, contented himself with allowing his gaze to roam dreamily across the ceiling.

'Of course *with* – I wouldn't suggest leaving him behind, would I?'

He seated himself on the arm of the sofa, his enthusiasm

getting the better of him. 'It's what we always talked about, isn't it? Just because we have a baby doesn't mean we're trapped here forever. Besides, we'd be earning loads of dosh, and everyone over there has servants. . . .'

Joanna remembered distant evenings when they had talked of working in the Colonies. Then they had both agreed that having black servants wasn't ethical. Now, she tried not to think about leaving her widowed mother behind. She tried to sidestep the issue of having someone to do her work for her. Instead she imagined a rounded, black woman, someone raised with babies always around her, instilled in the natural processes of motherhood, someone calm and trustworthy and reliable who wasn't likely to criticize her – not like an English nanny might do.

A tremor of excitement at the possibilities made her turn towards James.

'Is this what you want to do?'

He nodded. 'But only if you're happy with the idea.'

She didn't say yes, but she didn't say no, either. The possibilities began to germinate in her mind, tropical sun, adventure, liberation from this new life she hated.

In the end she simply smiled at him, lifting her shoulders to show that anything might be possible. 'Well, I don't suppose there's any harm in sending off an application – is there?'

Leaning down, he gave her a spontaneous hug. 'No, I don't suppose there is.'

Twenty-Four

IT WAS STILL daylight as Maisie stood in the farmyard listening to James drive away, her heart pounding at the aggressive thrust of his engine. She felt terrible. Joanna had asked her to stay, almost pleaded with her and she'd let her down. Even James had tried to persuade her and still she had held out. She didn't know herself. The Maisie she had lived with all her life was used to doing what other people wanted her to. Refusing was a frightening step into the unknown. Ghosts clambered in her brain. Surely retribution, swift and savage, would strike her down?

When the car's roar had diminished to little more than a disembodied drone, she picked up her case and started across the yard. The burden of her treachery weighed heavy.

Nobody seemed to be about. She guessed that it must be time for afternoon milking but the milking parlour was silent.

As she reached the garden path she looked towards Mr Wonderful's paddock to see if he was waiting at the gate. With a soothing sense of comfort she realized that she would be in time to bed him down for the night. Herein lay her refuge, escape into the tiny, safe haven that was theirs. The prospect of seeing to him lit up her inner world, cast out the dark shadows, but as she looked out for him, he was nowhere to be seen. She guessed that Ian must have already brought him in.

Ian. The thought of him gave her a rare feeling of confidence. Why shouldn't she say no to the Camerons? Why shouldn't she prefer to stay at the farm where she had Mr Wonderful? It wasn't her fault if James and Joanna had changed their minds. After all, they hadn't cared when she had wanted to stay with them, when she had nightmares about being sent away. The memory of those days still ached like a rotten tooth.

She tried to get it into proportion. Of course she still liked them, but she didn't want to be there any more. This was where she belonged.

Reaching the porch she made up her mind. Dropping her bag outside the front door she veered across the yard in the direction of the stable. As she dodged the puddles, her mother's voice reminded her that she ought to change her clothes, but for once she didn't care. The prospect of seeing Mr Wonderful – of seeing Ian, was too important.

As she drew near, the stable was silent. She reached out to push down the latch on the door of the loose box, a gentle feathering of anticipation somewhere inside of her and in that same moment the door clicked open from the other side and she came face to face with Ian. Warmth began to course through the capillaries in her face but something about his expression halted her delight.

He said, 'It's bad news.'

She had no memory of those next few seconds. Like a break in a film, the next vision she had was of herself trying to see past him into the gloom of the stable.

What was it? Mr Draper? Mrs Draper? Had the tractor overturned? It was something that Mrs Draper was always going on to him about. '*You be careful down in that meadow, George. The ground's proper uneven. That thing could overturn as easy as you like.*'

She looked round for her employers but the yard was empty. Perhaps they had gone to the hospital.

Ian said, 'It's Caesar. He's sick.'

Maisie stared at him. not understanding. She tried to see round him but he blocked the doorway. He added, 'It's the colic. He's got it real bad. I don't think. . . .'

His taut, anguished expression did not change and everything began tumbling away from her. In the darkness of her brain, a voice called out: No. Not this. Anything but this. Somewhere inside her head, she heard the answer: This is your punishment for being selfish, for not doing what they wanted you to.

Ian looked terrible. His face seemed to be clamped into a death mask. He said, 'I found him like it this morning. I've done everything I can but he – he doesn't seem to be getting over it.'

'No!' Maisie's own personal newsreel began to play again, over and over in her head. She let out a wail of agony. 'It's my fault. All my fault!'

Ian shook his head. 'Of course it isn't. You weren't even here. You couldn't have done anything anyway. I'm the one that feels terrible because I should have realized.'

At last he moved aside and what Maisie saw hit her like a whiplash. In the deep recess of the box, the old horse, smothered in blankets, stood with his head bent to the straw. His coat, that deep chestnut that she had grown to love, was stiff and blackened with sweat. Every now and then he twisted his head round, biting at his midriff, or lifted a hind leg to kick ineffectually at his belly.

She swung round to Ian, looking to him to put things right but he shook his head as if he too was in torment. He said, 'It was yesterday afternoon. The hunt were out. They went up over the field next to Caesar's paddock. There was a great pack of dogs with them, all yowling and excited. The riders went galloping up over the path towards the copse, and when old Caesar saw them he got that excited he began to gallop up and down, calling out to them.' Ian sighed. 'When I brought him in he was all lathered up. I rubbed him down with some straw but – well, I was going out so I was in a hurry. . . .' His voice trailed away. 'I should have known what might happen.'

For a brief second Maisie felt a stab of pain at the thought of Ian hurrying into town to meet friends – a girl, then in her mind she saw Mr Wonderful careering around his field, the lightning flash of white down his face, his bent nose, his hairy, clumpy legs, his sweet amber eyes in which she could read all the pain he had endured. Last night he had come in not feeling well. She had let him down, not been there, left him to suffer alone, thinking that she didn't love him any more.

Moving across to him she laid her hand gently against his jaw, wanting to cradle his heavy head. Oh, my poor love, Please get better. Please, please don't die!

Behind her, Ian said, 'I've given him bran, kept him walking but it hasn't worked.'

With an effort Mr Wonderful took a step and began to tuck in his hind quarters as if about to lie down.

'Don't let him do that!' Rushing forward, Ian grabbed his halter, jerking him so that he staggered but kept his feet. To the horse he said, 'Come on, lad. There's a good boy now.' Turning to Maisie, he explained, 'If he gets down and rolls, that's it. He wants to because his belly hurts but like as not he'll twist his gut and then there's nothing anyone can do.' He looked away. 'I'd put a bullet in him rather than let him go like that.'

Maisie closed her eyes to shut out the unthinkable, but it was inside her head. Taking her cue from Ian she began to coax Dooky forward, desperate in her attempt to save him. In response, he took two steps, resisted, then snorting in his distress, began to move again, almost staggering with the effort.

'That's it, good lad.' With one of them on each side of him, they half-dragged him out into the gloom. All the time Maisie talked to him inside her head, her hand against his withers, easing him forward step by step. Come on, my love. Come on, my dearest. Just think of next summer and all those walks we can have. Think of the banks and hedgerows and all your favourite food. Please don't leave me.'

Mr Wonderful stopped. For a moment all his effort was concentrated in his laboured breathing then, splaying his hind legs, he lifted his tail and with a groan that might have come from a bull moose, began to strain.

'Good boy. Good old man,' Ian encouraged him, rubbing his hand vigorously along his neck. 'Come on now, you can do it.'

With a supreme effort, Mr Wonderful clenched his belly muscles and released a series of hard, dry balls of dung. Ian's expression was ecstatic. 'Good man! There, you see, you've been waiting for your mistress, haven't you? You sly old devil!'

Maisie felt mesmerised. For a moment she pondered on this

bizarre scene, wondering at its significance. Looking to Ian she waited for his verdict. 'Does that mean he'll be all right?' She stopped breathing.

The relief on Ian's face was clear, but he was cautious. 'Can't be sure yet. Still, it's a step in the right direction. You walk him on round while I go and make him another mash. Let's try and really get him going.'

Maisie felt as shaky as the horse. Her chest tight with suspense, she led him around to the leeward side of the yard and out of the wind, her arm about his neck, tears staining her face, gently encouraging him forward. Every thought was concentrated on him, willing him to get well. When Ian arrived, they returned him to the box and watched as he snuffled in the bucket, at first disinterested, then eating gingerly, then polishing off the warm mixture.

'Right.' Ian picked up the bucket. 'There's nothing else we can do for the moment. Best to leave him for half an hour so that he can get some peace.'

Maisie wanted to object, but Ian was firm. 'Look at you. You'll catch your death dressed like that, then I'll have two of you to worry about.'

Maisie looked down at her posh clothes, now stained with hair and mud. Ian's words, his kindness, the horror of the last hour welled up in her throat and the dam that had been her defence for so long threatened to break. She tried not to but as he propelled her towards the house, she began to sob, great choking bursts of anguish that left her fighting for breath. Ian squeezed her arm, not saying anything. She struggled to stop but she couldn't keep it back any longer, all the pain, all the terrible secrets she had nursed all these years. Anything, anything was better than the burden of guilt that was crushing the life out of her.

'He'll die. I know he will,' she gasped between paroxysms.

Ian put his arm around her. He cuddled her into his shoulder and his hand stroked her hair.

'No he won't. If it hadn't been for you he'd have died weeks ago. You gave him a second chance. He's a tough old horse.'

Going into the empty kitchen without bothering to remove his boots, he sank into Mr Draper's chair and pulled her down on to his knee. Leaning close, his voice low and flat, he said, 'Come on, girl. Let's have it all out.'

His words opened the floodgates as Maisie remembered Mr Wonderful's arrival, his gaunt expression, his legs so weak that he could barely stand. She'd fought so hard, given so much. Surely she couldn't lose him now? Even God couldn't be that vindictive. As her sobs eased a fraction, Ian gave her his hanky and she wiped her eyes, her nose. 'It *is* my fault,' she said again. 'Everyone who comes into contact with me dies. I must be cursed.'

As Ian went to deny it, she knew that she had to tell him everything. It wasn't fair otherwise. If he wasn't careful, he too might be afflicted by her curse. She said, 'If it wasn't for me, my Mum and Grandad and Aunty Rene would be alive. It was because of me that my Dad died of a broken heart. And it was me – it was me that killed our Kenny.'

'What do you mean?' Ian sat back. She was only half aware of the frown on his face. 'Who was Kenny?'

'My brother.'

'How did you kill him?'

The thought of it all was too much and the news about Mr Wonderful hit her anew. Once again she couldn't hold back the great gasping moans of hurt. For several minutes Ian cuddled her to him, reassuring, keeping her contained. At last she managed to say, 'I didn't mean to.'

'What didn't you mean to?'

'To kill our Kenny.'

'What happened?'

She shook her head, trying to run away from the memory but Ian held her fast. 'Come on, our Maisie, you must tell me. Tell me what happened.'

'I can't.'

'You can. You must. I – I won't tell the police or anything, if that's what you're afraid of.'

She frowned, not understanding what he meant. Neutrally, Ian asked, 'Did you murder your brother?'

Murder? She felt confused. Of course she hadn't murdered him – at least, not deliberately, although when she thought about it, she supposed that she had. Saying that you didn't mean to, or that you didn't know that was what would happen, was no excuse.

Ian said again, 'Come on, you must tell me. You'll feel better when you've – done it.' She knew that he had been about to say 'confessed' but thought better of it.

She said, 'The police know all about it. Everyone knows that it was me.'

George Draper chose that moment to come into the kitchen. He opened his mouth to chide Ian for being late, but seeing Maisie's distress, and guessing the reason, he said instead, 'I'll see to the livestock. You take care of the young maid here.' To Maisie, he said, 'I'm sorry lass. I knew you'd be upset, but the poor old horse has had a hard time. You've done your best for him and that's a fact. It's up to nature now.'

When he had gone, Ian slid out from under her and went to put the kettle on. When it was boiling he made them both a cup of tea and came to sit opposite. 'Now, you're going to tell me what this is all about. No good going on blaming yourself. No good not talking. You've got to put things behind you, get on with your life.'

It was clear that she had no choice. For ages she pondered on where to start. Should she tell him about Aunty Rene? About how she had got proper dopey and how Maisie hadn't told her mother, not warned her, so that Aunty Rene blew them all up? Should she tell him about Dad, how he'd cried at Kenny's funeral, how he'd stopped talking to Mum and to her. How Mum had said he was suffering from a broken heart and then, suddenly he got ill and lost the will to live?

'Tell me about Kenny.' Ian's tone was firm. She glanced at him and saw the compassion in his eyes. She had to look away quickly before the emotion overwhelmed her again.

For a moment she scrabbled round for the right words, then she said, 'It was hot. Really hot. Mum told me to look after him. I wanted to go out so I took him to the river.'

'He drowned?'

She shook her head. 'It's only a stream really. But he didn't want to go. It's a long way and he kept dragging behind, saying he was tired. I wanted to go. I wanted to paddle. I made him come.'

She looked at Ian again to assess his response. He nodded encouragingly.

'The stream wasn't very deep, just up to my shins, but Kenny could sit down in it. He liked it. He kept laughing and splashing himself.'

She stopped, seeing them in the hollow where the brook meandered around tree roots, where everything seemed so perfect.

'Go on.'

Prodded by Ian she said, 'When we got home, Kenny said he didn't feel very well. He was hot. I thought it was the sun because it was a long way back and he kept saying he was tired.'

'And it wasn't?'

She shook her head. 'The doctor came. He said Kenny must go into hospital. They suspected – infantile paralysis.'

'Is that what he had?'

Maisie nodded.

'What happened next?'

She found it hard to find the words. Ian encouraged her to take a sip of tea and after a while she said, 'They had to put Kenny in an iron lung. He couldn't breathe. They said it was touch and go, then. . . .'

Ian reached out and patted her arm. 'How could it be your fault?'

She shrugged. 'Doctor Patterson came round to see Mum. He told her about the illness, about the things that make you catch it. He said people who take a lot of exercise are more likely to catch it. People who bathe in infected water are in danger of picking it up.' She turned to Ian. 'It was me. I made Kenny walk all that way when he didn't want to. I took him to the stream and let him play in the water for ages.'

Ian was shaking his head. 'That doesn't mean he caught it from the stream. And just because he walked a long way doesn't mean anything either.'

'But—' Maisie interrupted him. He didn't understand. She said, 'When Mum asked why I hadn't caught it, Doctor Patterson said it was probably because I was a carrier. He said some people didn't catch the disease themselves but they could pass it on to others. That's what I did. I gave it to Kenny.'

'You didn't. Just because you didn't catch it doesn't mean you were a carrier. And even if you were, it wasn't your fault. Honestly, May, it doesn't follow.'

May. No one had ever called her that before. It made her sound like another person.

To Ian, she said, 'Dad thought it was my fault. He didn't talk to me after that.'

'Did he say so?' She shrugged. Ian added, 'He must have been grieving. Did he talk to anyone?'

She shook her head and he said, 'There you are then. He wasn't blaming you, he was just sad. These things happen.'

Little by little, Ian chipped away at her arguments, brushed aside her guilt. She remembered how, on Christmas Day, she had wondered if Mr and Mrs Draper blamed themselves for letting their son go to war. She had seen the answer then, clearly. One wasn't always responsible for what happened. Whatever you did, you had to make a choice in life, turn left, turn right, stay at home, go out. Whatever you did, something would follow. She might have taken Kenny to the shops instead and he might have been run over.

Ian gave her an encouraging smile. 'Come on,' he said. 'You get tea ready and then afterwards, we'll go and see how Caesar is. If he's all right, we could go out on the bike. There's a new coffee bar in Thorley. We could go there and have a drink and you can tell me the rest.'

Maisie felt drained. Somehow the plug had been pulled on her life and let out all the feelings she had been carrying around with her. She thought again of Mr Wonderful and a sob caught in her throat. Ian said, 'You've been kind to that old horse. If he doesn't make it it won't be for lack of trying.'

She went to give Ian back his hanky, but it was wet and scrunched up so she pushed it up her sleeve and stood up.

'Good. Come on then.'

As she swallowed back the last of her tears, she said, 'I don't know how long I'll be here for.'

Ian frowned. 'Are you planning on leaving then?'

She gave him a 'who knows' look. 'Mrs Cameron asked me to go back and work for her but. . . .'

'Do you want to? Do you want to leave here?'

'No.'

To her amazement, Ian looked relieved. He reached out and pulled her close to him, a big brother, showing his affection, giving her a hug, but as he held her away again, looking into her eyes, there was something else. She looked back hardly daring to think what he might say.

He let his hands fall to his sides but as she went to fetch the cutlery to lay the table, he said, 'What a girl you are, Maisie Morris. I've never known anyone like you. And let's not have any more nonsense about going away.'

As she placed the knives and forks and spoons along three sides of a square, she felt lifted from the quagmire that had held her fast all these years. Mr Wonderful was going to be all right. Suddenly she knew that he was. The best and the worst things had happened all within one afternoon.

Tonight she would ride on Ian's motorbike and sit in a coffee bar, drinking cappuccino. Tomorrow she would work with him around the farm. 'You'd make a good farmer's wife,' – that's what Mr Draper had said. She wasn't thinking that far ahead, but for the first time in her life, such a future didn't seem an impossibility.

Just as she was thinking along those lines, the door opened and Mrs Draper came in. She looked flushed and too late Maisie realized that she had been helping her husband with the chickens and the cows.

'A mite cold out there,' she commented, hanging her coat on the hook behind the kitchen door. 'You're back earlier than we expected.'

Maisie nodded. For a moment she hesitated, then she said, 'Mr Cameron brought me back early.'

If Rose was surprised to hear the girl speak again, she didn't show it. Instead, she said, 'We've just been over to look at the horse. He seems a deal better.'

Thank God! Maisie felt the curse lifting. Was it really all at an end?

Lighting the oil lamp, her back to Maisie, Mrs Draper said, 'I had a feeling you might not come back. With a baby to look after I thought they might decide they wanted you to stay there after all. I can't imagine a young woman like that managing on her own.'

As Maisie struggled for an explanation, Rose added, 'Anyway, I'm glad they didn't. We'd all miss you round here – especially Ian.'

Was this true? Maisie glanced at the older woman and saw the smile crinkling her eyes. 'A good boy, our Ian.' As Maisie's heart lifted, Rose straightened up, casting aside this unfamiliar sentimentality. Taking in Maisie's tear-stained face, she said, 'Now then, no more fussing over that horse. Right as rain he'll be by morning. Just get that kettle on, will you? My old legs are proper killing me.'